FINDING SPRING

BRIDGET E. BAKER

Copyright © 2019 by Bridget E. Baker

All rights reserved.

No part of this book may be reproduced in any form or by any electronic or mechanical means, including information storage and retrieval systems, without written permission from the author, except for the use of brief quotations in a book review.

❀ Created with Vellum

For Emma

*You're the best little sister a girl could have.
I'm glad you found your happily ever after.*

1

TRUDY

I barely survived the burning pile of garbage that was my first marriage. I marvel every single day that I emerged from that nightmare with something as beautiful as my son Troy. Sometimes I catch myself staring at him: the curve of his chubby baby face, the delicate bones in his arms, and the curlicues in his hair.

I'm staring at him and thinking about how quickly he's growing, when he knocks his cereal bowl onto the floor. Milk sprays in directions my high school physics teacher wouldn't have even believed possible.

My sense of wonder evaporates in the heat of frustration.

"Troy, sweetie!"

He turns wide, shining eyes toward me, eyes that could have inspired an anime character. "I'm sorry Mommy."

I sigh and grab two hand towels. I dampen one of them and hand the other to Troy. "Clean up the mess, and I'll wipe it all down for you after you're done."

I'm a firm believer that kids need to try to clean up their own messes, but Troy isn't very effective yet. My knees ache by the time I finish wiping the bottom of the cabinets on the far side of the kitchen. That's when I notice Troy's curly head bobbing up and down toward the front door. He's dragging the tin watering can behind him, sloshing water over the side onto the tile.

I sigh dramatically. "I'm just finishing cleaning up the last mess. What are you doing?"

"I forgot yesterday, Mom."

I shake my head. "We're supposed to be getting ready for your party. Besides, we've talked about this. It's pointless."

He sets his jaw and huffs. "It needs water."

Troy turns four today. His dad won't be at his party, which is both a relief and a sorrow. I'm the one who took out the restraining order, so I can't really fault Chris for not coming. Troy and I are stronger without him, but the absence of his dad has made Troy a little obsessive. His latest hang-up centers on a dead plant in a pot on the front porch.

"I looked it up honey, remember? Gerbera daisies are annuals here in Atlanta. That means they die when the weather gets cold and they don't come back. Once spring comes, we can buy some more, but this little plant is completely dead. Watering it won't help."

Troy opens the door and doggedly hoists the watering can a few inches off the ground to pour water over the blackened stems and leaves of the former daisy. "Plants need water and sun and dirt."

I wait for him to finish and usher him back inside, taking the much lighter watering can from his hands. In Troy's mind, everything can be fixed. Broken toy? Mom can glue it. Hole in his jacket? Mom will sew it up. One day he'll learn that some things can't be saved, but for now, I don't put up more than a token protest.

I'm totally the mom I swore I'd never become, the kind who secretly flushes a dead goldfish and replaces it before my son wakes up. Not that we have a fish, thankfully. I'm at capacity on the total number of living things I can preserve right now with just Troy and myself.

Guests should be arriving any minute. I only invited a handful of people, but Troy won't know it's a pathetically small party. I survey the family room, breakfast room and kitchen. My homemade Lightning McQueen cake sags in the middle and the frosting has slid down in a few places, forming bunchy piles. But the price was right—$4.75 for all the ingredients combined.

Red and gold balloons are taped to the back of each chair, and streamers dangle from the ceiling. His gift from me rests in the center of the table. I stayed up way too late last night making car shaped sugar cookies for party favors, which now sit in clear plastic baggies, all piled in a bowl. I've got a stack of crustless peanut butter and jelly sandwiches in the fridge, along with a bowl of apple slices.

Sadly, this pitiful party still cost more than I should've spent. I need a job so bad.

I cross the room to the built-in desk between the laundry room and the kitchen to check my email before the party starts. Maybe someone has replied to a job application and there's an email inviting me for an interview. It could happen, right? Except it doesn't.

My inbox is as empty as my bank account.

A bright red piece of paper on the fridge catches my eye and I snatch it down and stuff it in my pocket, grateful I remembered to hide it before Mary shows up.

She would not understand the importance of my list. Not that I really need the list taped to my fridge. I know the three things on it by heart.

Trudy Will Not Date Anyone Until:

1. She graduates.
2. She finds a dream job.
3. She repays Troy's medical expenses.

I've been officially divorced for barely more than a month, and Mary's already raring to set me up. Clearly her newfound happiness in love has nowhere to go and is spilling over on her family and friends.

In Mary's defense, lots of women in my place might be dating already. Chris did leave me more than six months ago, even if I didn't want to admit it was real for a while. But I did things wrong the first time around, and I'm not going to screw up again. No dating or even flirting until my three tasks are complete. Graduation hovers right around the corner, but finding a dream job seems like a long and possibly unrealistic trip I won't ever be able to take. And repaying the enormous sum Mary paid for me feels like a distant island only imagined in fairy tales.

Mary loaned me a huge pile of money to cover medical bills when Troy was diagnosed with Type 1 diabetes, and I will pay her back if it kills me. Unless I die of old age first, which seems like a possibility. Right now I can't even come up with any money to pay rent for this house, which means my debt is increasing, not decreasing.

The doorbell rings and Troy races to answer it. He nearly trips over his own feet. "Honey, wait for me. You're too young to be answering—"

Troy doesn't even pause, but he swings the door wide enough that I can see Mary's smiling face. Her grin always lifts my spirits. Her fiancé Luke follows her through the door, and Amy and Chase dart past the adults. Chase and Troy immediately shoot around the corner headed for Troy's room. I almost call them back to interact with the rest of us, but I stop myself. If Troy and Chase want to play boy stuff on Troy's birthday, I should let them. Besides, only three other kids are coming. I'll call them back to greet the other guests when they arrive.

"Trudy, everything looks great," Mary says. "I can't believe you made that cake."

I lift one eyebrow. "You can't?"

Luke shakes his head. "I can't either. It looks amazing, seriously. If you weren't about to graduate in computer stuff, I'd say go find a job at a bakery."

This is exactly why I can't trust a word they say. "I really am looking for jobs. I'll pay you rent as soon as I can."

Mary flinches. "That's not what Luke meant." She crosses the room and pulls me against her for a hug. "You don't need to rush. Troy needs you. You're welcome to stay here for as long as you want."

Tears threaten and I inhale deeply to head them off. The income I earn each month selling handmade home decor on Etsy barely covers the cost of groceries. I moved in with Mary around Christmas, but when she got engaged, Luke bought a new house for her. Mary's been kind enough to keep paying the utility bills on this place so that I have somewhere to live with Troy. She's never once complained, but I feel guilty about it every day.

"I know you're not pushing, and I appreciate it. I swear to you though, I will be able to pay rent soon."

"Aunt Trudy," Amy says.

I glance down at her. She's got one hand on her hip, and the other around a box. "Where should we put Troy's presents?"

She's only holding one, but I don't point that out. "The kitchen table is great. Thanks for being so polite about asking."

Amy glances at our four-person table and raises one eyebrow skeptically. "They definitely won't fit there."

I crouch down and hold out my hands. She's clearly not

accustomed to parties with only a handful of guests. "I think we'll be okay. Here, if you give it to me, I'll make room for it."

Amy shakes her head. "No, this is just the one Chase picked. The rest of the presents are in Dad's truck."

I frown. Surely Mary and Luke wouldn't have brought something huge. I told Mary I bought Troy a remote control Mickey car, and my sister would never upstage my gift. Right?

Amy reaches out with her free hand and pushes on the corners of my mouth. "Don't frown. Dad said you might have forgotten how you couldn't fit the surprise for Troy in your car, but we brought it for you." She leans close and whispers. "*Did* you forget? Because sometimes old people forget things, and Dad says that's really normal. It's the train table Troy loves to play with when he comes to Mom's house, like Chase's."

This time I can't blink back my tears, so I stand up and wipe at my face. "I did forget. Thanks for reminding me, Amy. And you're right, it didn't fit in my car."

Amy claps her hands. "I helped wrap all the trains. I thought Troy would like to open each one." Her eyes sparkle. "I'll go help Dad bring them inside if that's okay."

I point. "Maybe put them over there by the window."

Amy races back toward the door with Luke on her heels. He glances back at me, his eyebrows drawn together quizzically. "I hope you don't mind."

How could I mind that I have such generous family? It's exactly the kind of thing Mary would have done herself before she met Luke. Of course, she and I would have stayed up late the night before putting it together, one dumb piece at a time.

I smile at him. "Of course not. Thanks."

He bobs his head and steps out.

"He's a really, really good guy," I say.

Mary beams. "I know he is. And your guy is out there too, I can feel it."

I roll my eyes. "If you mention Paul's name one more time, I may duct tape your mouth shut."

Mary puts her arm around me. "I didn't say it this time. And you can't be too cranky about it. You haven't even met him yet."

"I've been divorced for one month," I say.

"But you've been entirely alone for five. Most women would be looking around by now."

"You're just in the engagement haze. I'm not in a rush. I'll meet Paul at your wedding, and I don't need you guys to make things unbearably awkward before then. I wouldn't even want to go on a date with Bradley Cooper if he knocked on my door. I'm not ready to date."

"I said something similar not too long ago." Mary drags me into the kitchen and lets go of my hand to sink onto a chair. "Then I met Luke and realized I'd been lying to myself. Everyone wants to fall head over heels. They just need to meet a guy they trust to catch them."

"My heart's deader than those daisies Troy keeps watering. Dating anyone would be grotesque, trust me. Let's all agree to spare poor Paul that miserable experience."

Mary lifts her eyebrows. "I'll do no such thing."

My door bangs open and I'm glad I didn't bother sitting myself.

Paisley flies through the door in front of Luke, sliding along my tile in an unnatural way. "What's up party people!?" She pulls up short and barely avoids toppling right into me. Meanwhile, Luke singlehandedly hefts a huge table through my doorway sideways.

I maneuver around Paisley and rush over to help guide

Luke. Amy follows after her dad with an armful of small packages.

"Thanks guys," I say.

Amy and Luke head back down to grab the rest of the trains and track, all wrapped up individually. Troy unwraps presents slower than an arthritic snail, so this is going to be painful. Before I can follow them out and offer to help, Paisley zooms over to the family room with two more boxes under her arm.

"What in the world is wrong with you?" I squint at her feet. No wonder she practically knocked me over when she came inside. "Please tell me you don't have wheels on your shoes."

Paisley plops both boxes onto the top of the train table. "My rolly footwear is literally the coolest thing ever invented. I can't believe I never tried them before."

"I'm pretty sure they hadn't made them in big people sizes." Mary drops her voice to a whisper. "Not much demand."

"Very funny." Paisley leans close to me, her eyes twinkling. "Don't worry, Trudy. I got you and Troy matching pairs. You're going to *love* these, I swear."

I groan. "You better be kidding. I need a broken wrist about as much as Troy needs a double shot of caffeine."

"What you need is more excitement in your life," Paisley says. "You can't find it unless you look, and maybe I should clarify. You need to look somewhere outside of this house."

"Speaking of excitement, how did you get up the porch stairs?" I ask. "Without breaking your neck, I mean?"

Paisley's grin splits her face and she lifts one foot up. "That's the beauty of these. They're shoes on the front. I walked up."

Mary and I share a glance, but before we come up with

anything witty enough to say about the oddity of Paisley's brain, a boy from Troy's Sunday school class shows up. The other boy and the girl arrive moments after. The next hour and a half is full of squeals, games, and far too many juice box spills for only six kids.

Amy takes it upon herself to enforce all house rules. She follows the four-year-olds around and orders them not to write on anything but paper. She makes them wash their hands before leaving the kitchen area to play. And when one of the little boys dashes over to the table to snatch a handful of grapes, she stops him with a firmly outstretched palm.

"Graham," she says imperiously, "you're welcome to eat those, but in this house, food stays in the kitchen."

Mary and Luke watch it all with identical indulgent half-smiles on their faces. If they weren't so cute, it might be a little alarming. My sister's been replaced. Now she's half of a couple that communicates silently in smirks and loaded looks.

"Amy has turned into quite the little lieutenant, hasn't she?" I ask Mary.

"We're spending more and more time at Mary's place," Luke says. "So that it won't be such a big transition when we move in after the wedding. Amy's happy not to be outnumbered anymore, and she may be taking her job as Mommy's helper a little too seriously."

Mary shrugs. "I think it's harmless. For now."

Luke rolls his eyes. "You would think that. She didn't order you to take your shoes off and leave them by the front door yesterday."

"You were tracking mud inside," Mary says.

Amy approaches, arms folded across her chest. "Aunt Trudy, I think the kids are getting a little bored with the beanbag game. I keep having to stop them from opening Troy's presents. It might be time for cake."

Mary shoots me a sheepish look.

"Why little miss, I think you're right. Why don't you call everyone over?"

Amy herds the kids toward the table like a well-intentioned border collie. Chase bristles a little at his sister's officious commands, but Troy and his friends don't seem to mind. After one look at the cake, even Chase happily stands near the table with his small hands folded in front of him.

"Thank you all for coming," I say to the kids and their parents. "We are so happy that Troy's four years old!"

Troy hugs my leg. "I'm big big big!"

My heart contracts and I crouch down in front of him. "All I asked for this Christmas was for you to stay little."

Troy raises his chin. "But I gave you something different. A stuffed teddy bear. Which means I can be big now."

I pick Troy up. He may be bigger, but he still fits on my hip. "Now everyone wants to sing to you, okay? And then we can cut this cake."

Troy claps, and Paisley lights the candles.

I choke back tears during the song, not ready to acknowledge that my baby's a little boy. But he blows out all four candles without help, and I have to admit it. He's growing up.

We open presents next, and he loves the train table. Even so, a tiny part of my heart soars when he proclaims that the Mickey remote controlled car is his favorite toy. One day I'll be able to afford fancy gifts, but for now I'm glad my boy likes simple things.

After the other three guests have left, Mary calls for Chase and Amy. "Time to go, kids."

"You can stay as long as you want," I say. "No big rush on our end."

"I've got fifty million emails to wade through." Mary sighs.

"And I have to sign off on all the launch plan details." Luke shakes his head. "I know you're actively searching, but jobs are overrated."

"You might have a different opinion if you were in my shoes," I say. "I've filled out eighty-six applications and not gotten one interview."

Mary's eyebrows draw together. "I wish you'd come work for me. I don't understand why you won't."

Mary has always been a genius, and laser focused on top of it. She put herself through college and took care of me at the same time. She found her own job right out of school and worked her way to the top by the age of thirty. She never had a leg up from anyone, so she doesn't get why I won't accept one when she's offering it.

"I need to find a place myself," I say.

"Just apply for a position at LitUp Applied Science," Luke says. "I won't even tell anyone to pick you, I swear."

I roll my eyes. "*Sure* you wouldn't. You guys are amazing, but I'm graduating in two months and I need to do this on my own." Plus, there's no way I want to work at Luke's office, where he will awkwardly try to shove me at his little brother daily. Blech.

"If you change your mind, just say the word," Mary says. "Being the boss should have some perks, right?"

A terrible thought occurs to me. What if they're offering me jobs because they're sick of me not contributing? Mary's too nice to complain, but the idea of her grumbling to Luke about how I'm such a freeloader when I could be earning something to pay them makes me dizzy.

I bite my lip. "If I still can't find anything in the next

two weeks, I'll apply for a job at both of your companies. I know I'm sponging off you right now so I shouldn't be too picky, but I'd really like to try and do this myself."

Mary puts her hand on my arm. Her voice is soft when she says, "Trudy, you are not sponging. You're caring for my beautiful nephew. You watch Chase and Amy all the time, and you're finishing up your degree. I don't even know how you'll find time to work between now and graduation."

"I watched my friend Pam's son Benson for free for two years while she was getting her beautician's license. She's too nauseated by the smell of hair products during her second pregnancy to work. Plus her husband got a promotion, and told her to take some time off. Troy and her son are the same age and they play beautifully, so she's going to watch Troy for free while things level off around here."

"What about school?" Luke asks. "You only had four classes between you and graduation, but that's still a full load."

"Yeah, I was so close. I was such an idiot not to finish. Luckily, the university has a new program that lets me take the computer classes mostly online, which means I could go at whatever pace I wanted. The reason I started looking for jobs is that I'm essentially done."

"How's that even possible?" Paisley has been wiping down the counters, and I almost forgot she was still here.

"I've been working on them every single time Troy takes a nap, and after he goes to bed. I'm finished, other than taking my finals, which I can't do until the first week of May."

Paisley whistles. "Well folks, Mary and Trudy may not look an awful lot alike, but it turns out, Trudy's just as big of a nerd. Good luck living with a Wiggin girl, Luke, that's all I have to say."

"I can't wait." Luke kisses Mary's forehead.

Mary beans Paisley in the head with a grape.

"Nice shot," I say. "See? We're not too nerdy. We can still lob a grape well enough to leave a welt."

Luke's phone buzzes and he checks it. "That's Paul. He needs my feedback in the next hour on the supply chain revisions." He slides his phone into his pocket. "Sorry we can't stay longer."

"If you guys are super busy, leave the kiddos," I say. "They can spend the night."

Luke's head whips toward Mary's so fast, I worry about whiplash. "That's not a bad idea."

Mary shakes her head. "We can't, not tonight. They have dentist appointments in the morning, remember?"

Luke grunts. "Fine, fine. Thanks for the offer, Trudy."

Once they've gathered all their things and extricated both kids, they head out the door. Luke turns back toward me before he heads down the steps. "I'm going to hold you to your promise," Luke says. "Not because we care whether you're paying rent. We couldn't care less, I swear. But you're too great an asset to be wandering around undiscovered. You can keep sending resumes into slush piles for two more weeks, and if no-one bites, then you're going to come work for me."

He hugs me, and I close the door behind him.

Paisley's sweeping now. I cross the room and take the broom from her. "I didn't invite you over to be my maid."

"There were only six kids, right? How come it looks like a tornado went through the house?" she asks.

"It looks almost this bad before I put Troy to bed every night." He's watching Mickey Mouse on TV right now, but I glance at the clock. "Which I have to do in an hour or so, anyway."

"Maybe I'll stick around for a movie, then. Do you have time?" she asks.

"You don't have other plans?" I'm giddy about having some girl time, but I feel bad keeping her here on a Sunday night. I'm sure she has more exciting options. "It's a weekend and you're single and flirty and fun."

Paisley laughs. "It's cute that you think I might have exciting plans. I had a horrible date on Friday. It was so bad I deleted the dating app from my phone."

"Whoa! No more internet dating for you?" I ask.

She giggles. "Let's not get too carried away. I have about ten other apps, but that particular one's toast."

"I don't even want to think about all that," I say.

"You never used apps before you married Chris?" Paisley asks.

"I mean, they existed, but I met him through a friend. After that. . ."

Paisley nods. "Yeah, Mary told me. He kind of took over your life."

I shrug. It's been so strange making decisions on my own, now that he's finally been eliminated from my life. Strange, but also liberating. "Anyhow, I have a while before I need to worry about it."

She narrows her eyes at me. "Do you now?" She snatches my phone and starts poking at buttons.

"Hey," I say. "Give that back."

"I'm bringing you into the twenty-first century."

I snatch my phone back. "I'm not dating at all."

Paisley's jaw drops. "Why not?"

I pull the crumpled list out of my pocket. "Last time I started dating someone and got excited, I got married and pregnant and didn't finish my last semester of college."

"Not everyone is Chris," Paisley says. "In fact, most people aren't anywhere near that narcissistic."

"Thank goodness for that," I say, "but I need to worry about getting my ducks in a row. Besides, right now I don't even want to date." I plop down onto one of the kitchen chairs. "I think my heart died."

"I didn't realize you were so upset over the divorce." Paisley collapses next to me. "I'm sorry. I'm a lousy friend."

I shake my head. "It's not the divorce, or even Chris. My overwhelming feeling about that was just relief."

Paisley leans toward me. "Then what's with the vampire situation?"

"Huh?" I ask.

"Your undead heart?"

Paisley's such a goober. "I don't know. I haven't wanted to watch rom coms, or any kind of love stories. I don't ever catch myself checking out hot guys. If my heart isn't dead, it's broken beyond repair. I don't even think about all that stuff."

"When would you go see a movie if you wanted to? Do you ever leave the house anymore?"

I whap her on the arm. "I leave the house."

"I'm not actually kidding. Other than shipping your Etsy signs and like, grocery shopping, when do you go anywhere?"

My cheeks heat up. "I don't have enough money to pay for a gym membership—I only have one because Mary added me to her account for a Christmas present." My voice drops to a whisper. "I really do need a job."

Paisley's face crumples. "Oh Trudy, I'm sorry. I didn't even think about that. Look, the last year has been a rough one."

"Try the last five."

She slides her chair close and puts her arm around me. "This year is going to be your best yet, then."

A tear slides down my cheek. "Why would you think that? I haven't got a single lead for a job. Not one."

"That's how it works. When life gets horrible enough,

we make changes. It takes time to course correct, but once we do, that's when things improve. I've been watching. You're headed the right way again, so things will come around for you."

I hope she's right.

"Hey what jobs are you applying for, anyway?" she asks.

"What do you mean?"

"You're graduating in computer science, right?"

I nod. "I'm applying for IT jobs, if that's what you're asking. But they all require experience. I don't know how I'm supposed to get any, since none of them will take me without it."

She taps her lip and stands up. "You should search for jobs where the company is looking for an assistant *and* an IT person."

I tilt my head. "Why, exactly?"

"First of all, you have experience as an assistant and you have a reference, too. You've helped with Sub-for-Santa several times. You list that and then you put me down as a reference. I'll give you a glowing recommendation."

"But I don't want to be an assistant," I say. "No offense." I still have no idea what Paisley likes about being Mary's go-fer.

She rolls her eyes. "You might like it once you try it, but even if you don't, it would get your foot in the door, Trudy. Once they meet you and see how smart you are, you'll be a shoo-in for their IT position."

Sly like a fox. My kind of plan.

With Paisley's help, I add to my resume. When she wants me to change Trudy to 'Gertrude,' I balk. "It makes me sound a hundred years old."

"You're applying for assistant jobs. The older, the more competent, right?"

I suppose she would know. We work on applications

until Troy gets sick of Mickey, which is about eleven applications in. Frankly, I was surprised to even find that many places looking for both assistants, and IT personnel.

"An assistant spy," I say. "I like it."

She grins and helps me put Troy to bed. Afterward, she insists on watching *Kate and Leopold*. I almost enjoy it.

The next day, I check my email after my morning walk with Troy. I definitely enjoy seeing not one, not two, but three emails from companies interested in interviewing me. Maybe Paisley's right and things are turning around for me. I'm smiling when I call them one-by-one and set up interviews.

2

PAUL

My door is always open at work, but a knock on my doorframe alerts me to someone's presence. I look up and into the face of my older brother.

Luke smiles at me. "Got a second?"

"Sure," I say. "Come on in."

He sets a large box on my desk. "I brought the packaging sample."

"It's here sooner than I expected." I reach for it, but Luke leans against the desk, blocking my hand. He clearly has an agenda this morning.

"Did you have a good weekend?" Luke asks, a little too casually.

"If working all day Saturday and all day Sunday and still not catching up on everything qualifies as good, then sure. It was fantastic. You?"

"Mine was okay. I didn't catch up either." He smirks. "So what are you doing this weekend? Hopefully it won't be as pathetic."

"I know what I'm not doing," I say.

"What's that?"

"Meeting you and Mary for a double date."

Luke opens his mouth and then closes it, his teeth clicking together.

"I've said this before, but it didn't seem to take," I say. "I don't want to be set up with Mary's loser little sister."

Luke scowls. "She's not a loser, and since you've never even seen her, I'm surprised to hear you say that. You're usually not so boorish. And I thought you liked Mary."

I really stepped into that one. "I do. Mary's great." Maybe too great. "That's not the point. Look, the more someone tries to sell me on how great beachfront property is, the more I suspect it's not even near the water."

"I'm overselling her."

"Yes. And also, I don't need your help finding someone to date."

"I know you don't," Luke says. "You're smart, and funny and kind, and you do great with the ladies. Which is exactly why I want to introduce you to Trudy. She doesn't need our help either, and she's pushing back as hard as you are."

I frown at him. "Wait, she doesn't want to meet me?"

He takes that as encouragement, apparently. "It would be low key, I swear."

"Right, I can see it now. You and Mary would meet us at the restaurant. Your fiancé would walk in arm-in-arm with her mini-me, and you'd be dragging me by the scruff of my neck. We'd get appetizers and chat politics. We'd swap old family stories during the main course, and by the time dessert arrives, Mary and her sister would be clipping pages out of bridal magazines together."

"Oh please," Luke says. "We don't even—"

I cut him off. "Thanks, but no thanks. I know you've found an amazing wife not once, but twice now. I know you're more than qualified to judge whether a woman is quality, and I've proven that I can't always tell. Even so, I don't need you to set me up at all. With anyone, ever."

"Fine, I get it this time. You're serious." Luke points at the mock up for the packaging. "Feel like yelling about this now? Or are you done?"

I chuckle as I turn the box over in my hands. Our four point six pound car battery's biggest selling point is that it's lightweight. Which means we need the packaging for the battery to be light as air and showcase its size, while still protecting it in transit and attracting attention. "No, this actually looks great. Did we get price quotes?"

Luke shakes his head. "We can't shop for quotes until we have an approved sample. If you think this is alright, I'll move ahead on the bids."

"Yeah, I think we're ready for that."

Luke mock bows. "Yes, boss."

The irony of him calling me that, even in jest, stings a little. "I only own forty-nine percent, as you well know. I should be calling you boss."

"As far as I'm concerned, we're even partners. We only did what the lawyer suggested, and it was only to eliminate conflict if we ever disagreed. You insisted that I be assigned the fifty-one percent instead of the forty-nine because I ponied up the start-up capital."

True enough. Luke's a benevolent overlord and always has been. It still irritates me. I stand up and grab my bag. "Get out of my office so I can, too."

Luke lifts his eyebrows. "You working from home every afternoon now?"

I drop my bag on the desk. "I'm sorry. Do I need to check in with you on where I work? Because you were the one who completely abandoned the company for years to drive around in an RV with your kids, playing at being a simple project electrician."

Luke stiffens, and I immediately regret saying anything. Luke's wife died delivering their second child, leaving him to deal with the grief of losing her and the care a toddler and a newborn at the same time. I'd probably have gone insane and spent the next three years talking to a football I named Myrtle.

"I didn't mean—"

Luke cuts me off. "I *am* a project electrician, and I get all my best ideas from work in the field."

Most of our innovations came from things Luke realized the industry needed while working an actual gig. Whenever we ran dry on ideas, I'd send him back out. But I didn't send him out after Beth, and he kept at those jobs for years, unable to come home and face that Beth wasn't coming back. I don't even begrudge him his sabbatical. He worked from where he was and sent a dozen ideas my direction.

"I know you do, and I'm sorry I said anything." I really am sorry I brought it up, but it still annoys me that he's giving me a hard time for leaving the office. "During your working sabbatical, I discovered that I'm more productive during the afternoon at home, where there aren't a hundred and fifty people dropping in to ask me questions."

"Fair enough," Luke says.

I start to walk past him, but he grabs my shoulder and forces me to meet his eyes. "Are we okay Paul? You seem off lately, and I can't pinpoint how. I don't want to badger you, but I need to make sure we're okay."

Luke's the best brother in the history of the world. Seriously. People joke all the time about us being the better Manning brothers, since Peyton and Eli Manning are so famous, but honestly. Luke dropped his life and immigrated to the States with me when I got into Harvard. He worked to pay for my school expenses. I didn't realize the extent of what he'd sacrificed for me by going straight into a job after secondary school until he told me he was enrolling too.

Up until the day I found out Luke got into Harvard, it had never occurred to me that he might be smart. My family always talked about how Luke had common sense, and I was the smart one. I never even considered that he might be smart enough for a US college, much less an Ivy League one. He never hogged the limelight, but he was smarter than me all along. And better looking, and harder working.

I didn't want to let his frat boy, trust-baby friend bankroll out first venture, but Luke insisted and it paid off. Then he met the most amazing girl ever, married her and had two gorgeous kids. It sucked when she died, I mean, I really do feel awful about that. But now he's found someone even more spectacular.

I kind of hate him for it.

Not really. I mean, I'm happy for him and of course I love him, but I'm jealous too. I want a perfect wife. I want to be the one with the ideas, instead of the grunt who hunches over a microscope figuring out how to make the brilliant concepts work. I want to sacrifice for him for once so he can pursue his dreams. I thought I was doing it while he traveled around the world with his kids in an RV, but he came up with the idea that made this dumb battery possible on that hiatus, so again.

I lose.

To someone I adore. To someone I idolize. To someone I respect. To someone I'd jump in front of a bullet to save.

Losing over and over and over still chafes.

But seriously, I really would do anything for Luke. Does

it make me awful that I also want to do something without Luke?

Probably.

I shake my head. "I love you, Luke. You know I do, and of course we're fine. I'm just stressed and tired, that's all. I'll get the rest of the publicity proposals reviewed later today and send them to you and Rob."

Luke releases my arm. "I know you will, and I was only teasing. I don't care where you work. I really appreciate what you've done the past few weeks while I've been planning a wedding. I can't ever thank you enough for the time you devoted and stress you endured the past few years while I was barely hanging on."

"Okay, enough sentimentality. Go get your crap done so you can get home in time to have dinner with Mary."

He grins. "Sage advice."

I sling my bag over my shoulder and head out of the office, but I don't drive home. I head for my other office, my secret office, and the place where I leave behind all the expectations that follow Paul Manning. I reach my tiny office space in Smyrna and park in one of the reserved spots. It's not fancy, but it's in between my house and LitUp's office, which makes it convenient.

Jack Campbell, I remind myself. When I walk through that door, everyone inside knows me as Jack Campbell. Everyone except my office manager Nancy, but she calls me Jack, too. It's not hard to remember, since Jack's my middle name, and Campbell was my mother's maiden name. Nancy didn't understand why I'd start a company with a made up name at first, but once I explained that I needed to keep it a secret until it either took off or failed, she got it.

A very pregnant Nancy meets me at the front door, wringing her hands. "We need to talk."

"Well hello to you too, Nancy. It is a nice day outside, especially for March in Atlanta."

She looks heavenward as if asking God for help in dealing with me. "Alan is waiting in your office."

That's never good. "We haven't had a breach." It comes out as a statement, but she knows it's really a question.

She shakes her head. "No, but he doesn't have good news."

I jog down the short hallway to my office, and Alan stands when I walk through the doorway. His enormous mop of hair looks even more unkempt than usual. Grooming standards differ for IT guys, in my experience. At least he's not entirely covered in colorful tattoos or bizarre piercings.

I set my bag on my desk. "Alan, what's wrong?"

He hands me a white sheet of paper. "I'm offering you my resignation."

My eyebrows rise. I promised a share of our profits to all of the employees who have been with me more than six months when we either sell our tech or go public. "You're leaving now? Why?" We've got a functioning prototype. We had one tiny glitch to work out before we could move to beta testing. I fixed the glitch last night, although I haven't told anyone yet. We're so close I can smell it. "I fixed the glitch. It works."

"That's wonderful news, but I've been working on a side project at night," he says. "A software program for law offices. Last week I found a backer, a partner really. He's a big lawyer and if he comes on, I'll get a lot of business. He doesn't want to wait any more. Your offer of an ownership interest was nice, but it's theoretical. This is real and immediate."

I close my eyes. I can't believe Alan's leaving now. We're

at our most vulnerable. "How long can you stick around? A month? Two maybe? Part time is okay."

He makes the annoying popping sound he always makes with his lips when he's agitated.

"What's wrong?" I ask.

He shakes his head. "I don't have time to do both jobs, not now that my LawFile program will be live. My contract doesn't require two weeks notice. It says immediate termination at will, by either party."

I remember including that because I needed to be able to fire someone immediately. Alan asked for reciprocity. I want to smack myself in the head now for agreeing.

"Fine," I say. "Well, good luck to you."

He makes the stupid popping sound again and skulks out of my office.

"This may not be a great time to remind you that I'm due to have this baby in three weeks," Nancy says. "Which means it's full term now and could come any day. Every candidate we interviewed to fill in for me last month was disappointing, but at this point we have to choose someone. Anyone would be better than nothing. I told you I could keep working some from home, but you really need an assistant to handle everything I can't do remotely. Even borderline incompetent is better than nothing."

I want to scream, but I pinch the bridge of my nose instead. "Fine, that's fine. You can hire whoever you want, like I said before."

She nods. "I sorted through a bunch of idiots, but you never showed up for any of the interviews."

"With a glowing recommendation like 'a bunch of idiots,' I can't believe I blew you off."

She glares.

I throw my hands up in the air. "Hire the best option. I really couldn't care less."

She huffs. "You will be working with this person closely until I'm back from my leave. The person we choose matters. You need to choose my replacement yourself."

"Fine," I say. "Set it up, and do it soon. I really don't have the patience to post job listings or sort through all the junk applicants."

She smiles then. "Helpless as my husband with a cold, which is why you need a competent assistant. I'll line some options up for tomorrow afternoon. Promise me you'll be here."

"Yes, yes, I promise I'll meet with whoever you deem decent enough to be a real candidate, and because I like you, I won't tell your husband what you said."

Nancy rolls her eyes. "Gee, thanks." She drops her voice. "So is it true? Did you really fix the glitch?"

I nod. "I set up calls with 3M and Siemens for tomorrow. I'll need that file we discussed with the specs and the price points Andy worked up."

"On your desk."

I have no idea what I'm going to do without Nancy, who I still can't believe is leaving me for nearly two months. I'm surrounded by happily married people and their growing families. I think maybe all their unadulterated joy is making me crabby.

3
TRUDY

I apply for a dozen more assistant jobs on Monday morning at places that are also looking for IT specialists. Until I have an offer, I should keep looking.

Both of the interviews I set up for Monday afternoon are a bust. The boss at the law firm disgusts me. I can't imagine seeing him every day. The second, an ENT clinic, says I don't have enough experience. Apparently I need several years practice to be competent to make copies, line up appointments, and pick up coffee. I pin all my hopes on the third place, when I head in for the interview on Tuesday. It's a great fit and they love me. Unfortunately, when they make me an offer, the pay is so low I'd practically lose money on the gas to and from work. It hurts me to turn them down, but I don't have much choice.

My phone bings and hope blossoms in my chest. Which is stupid, because no jobs are going to text me with interest.

TROY IS DOING AWESOME, Pam texts. HOW'D THE INTERVIEW GO?

My feet drag as I walk toward the car. I can't quite bring

myself to text her back and tell her I bombed out. Somehow being offered a job and still having nothing to show for it makes me feel worse, not better.

Why is having hope and losing it harder than no hope at all?

I check my email one last time before I turn the key in the ignition, and it's a good thing I do. A company called SITB would love to interview me, and they're in a big hurry. I dial the number immediately.

"It's a great day at SITB," a man's voice says. "How may I direct your call?"

"Uh, I received an email from Nancy Jones wanting to set up an interview. She mentioned you were on a tight timetable. I just walked out of another interview, but I could come by on my way out of Atlanta, if she has time to see me today."

"What's your name?"

"Tr—Uh, Gertrude Jenkins."

"Hold please."

Beep. Beep. Beep. "This is Nancy."

"Hi Nancy. My name is Gertrude Jenkins. I saw your email a few moments ago. I just left another interview and your office is on my way home. I thought I'd check whether you happened to have time to meet with me today."

"You're fast," she says. "I love it. Yes, why don't you come by now. How soon can you get here?"

I glance at the address. "Twenty minutes, give or take?"

"See you then."

The office isn't much to look at. A simple storefront with a modest sign that reads, "SITB." Below the large lettering on the acronym, much smaller letters read: A Tech Startup. I wonder what SITB means.

The pudgy receptionist greets me with a genuine smile.

"Hello," he says, "and welcome to SITB. How can I help you today?"

"My name is Gertrude Jenkins. I called a few moments ago. I'm here to meet with Nancy Jones for an interview as an assistant."

He nods. "My name is Ishmael, but everyone calls me Ish. I'll just need to see your driver's license to verify who you are. And if you can look over this and sign it, I'll let Nancy know you're here." He hands me a document.

I look down and read the heading. 'Confidentiality and Non-Disclosure.' I lift one eyebrow at him. "Is this really necessary? I'm only here for an interview."

He shrugs sheepishly. "The boss is pretty particular, I guess."

Great. Another lunatic. Why is every interview I manage to get at a place run by oddballs? I guess there's a reason these offices are hiring. I try to read the document, but my eyes blur. Finally I give up and sign it at the bottom of the third page next to the x. I hope I didn't just trade Troy for this interview.

Nancy's belly rounds the corner before she does. I remember being that pregnant. I could barely eat, and I couldn't see my toes at all.

"Gertrude." She looks me over head to toe, and her eyebrows rise. "You're a lot younger than I anticipated."

"You're a little more pregnant than I expected." I grin.

She chokes back a laugh. "Understatement of the day. Well, never mind. Come on back."

Ish hands my license back to me, and I give Nancy the Non-Disclosure as he passes her the copy of my driver's license. It takes quite the paperwork shuffle to clear me for an interview. I wonder whether this is a CIA front. I've clearly been watching too many old reruns of Alias.

I follow her around the corner. Nancy waves her hand

at the large space that opens up in front of us. It's segmented into eight or so cubicles, and more than a dozen doors branch off of the central area.

"We're a pretty small office for now," she says. "Twenty-four employees, including me. You'd make twenty-five. Administrative support, as you can see, occupies the cubicles that compose the heart of the office. The programming and testing units are on the far left." She points. "And the business related employees are on the right." She points toward the far corner. "If you're a good fit, you'll be taking my office until my return."

"So this position is temporary?" I try to keep the disappointment from my tone, but I'm not sure whether I succeed.

"Sort of," she says. "It will be an employee position, but we'd be looking at an initial term of three months. I've been pulling double duty as both the boss' assistant and the office manager for eight months, but I recently convinced Jack to hire someone as an assistant until my return. For now, I'll just say we don't let good people go without a fight. There's more than enough work to go around, even after I come back full time. I wouldn't worry too much about the 'interim' in the title."

Weird. "Good to know."

As we approach the corner, she indicates the doorway on the left. "Jack works there. My office is on the right. It's smaller, but it's also way neater if that helps."

She's not lying. Her small, polished wooden desk has one organizational unit where several papers and a file folder are stacked. Notepads sit on top of one another on the opposite corner. There's one framed photo in the center of the desk of a freckled man, Nancy and a young toddler at the beach. Nancy's belly is flat, and they're all beaming at the photographer.

"Let's check out Jack's office," she says.

I follow Nancy through her doorway and take one step into the office that's kitty-corner to us.

A quick glance tells me the guy lives in a state of barely restrained chaos. Piles of files cover the desk, an upright cabinet, and the windowsill. Notepads rest on top of piles, and are shoved in between stacks of paper. Incomprehensible notes and numbers appear to be scrawled across all of it. Post-its are stuck to the desk, notepads, and even the walls. Mary would have a heart attack, and although I'm much less compulsive than she is, my fingers itch to tidy it up. Immediately.

"Would cleaning this up be part of my job?" I ask.

Nancy's laugh starts in her belly and fills the room. "You might never make it out alive. No, Jack doesn't like his stuff touched. At all. In fact, he's pretty insistent no one mess with anything in here. Your job is organizing everything else. Meetings, appointments, phone calls, and presentations. How good are you with Microsoft Outlook and Word?"

I bob my head. "Decent. They're simple programs."

"True. I saw you've had a few years of college. Your major is computer science?"

I nod. "That's right."

She narrows her eyes. "Why apply for an assistant job?"

Paisley and I prepared for this exact question. I'm supposed to tell her that I love to interact with people. I chose my major wrong, which is why I never graduated. I'm excited for this job, and ready to make this into a career.

Except that's a lie, and now that I'm staring her in the eyes, I can't bring myself to say it.

"I'm recently divorced and I need money," I say. "I graduate in May and every single IT position I've found requires two years experience, so I don't qualify. The few that don't require two years of experience are unpaid, and I need income."

Nancy bobs her head. "The good news is, we only *need* you for the next few months. So as long as you can commit to staying for that long, if your dream job falls into your lap after I'm back from my maternity leave, well, I'll be sure to sing your praises. It's hard to find a competent candidate who isn't aspiring to something else, so I get it. And I appreciate your honesty."

I sigh. "That's a relief. My friend thought I should make up a story, but I didn't feel good about it."

"I think we should start the formal interview now, Gertrude. Does that sound alright with you?"

I nod, and she ducks back into her office.

"Do you ever use a nickname?" Nancy asks. "Because my favorite aunt is named Gertrude, oddly enough, and she goes by Gerty. I don't think I've ever met another Gertrude in my life, so I thought it would be funny if you did, too."

No one has ever called me Gerty, not one single time, so of course I say, "I totally do. What a small world."

The words pop out of my mouth unchecked, unapproved, unconsidered. I want to yank them back, but I'd look crazy. Why would I tell the truth about my reasons for applying to be an assistant, and lie about something as stupid as a nickname? A horrible nickname.

I must want Nancy to like me. Which is kind of pathetic, but if a connection to her dear old aunt gets me this job, I'll take it. We chat for another twenty minutes, running through more typical interview questions. My past experience, my skills, my work availability.

"Do you have any questions for me?" she asks.

"If I get the job, what does it pay?" Please be more than eight dollars an hour. Please.

"Since you'd be working full time, we'd offer you a full

employee package. Starting salary would be thirty-five thousand a year, with two weeks of paid vacation and eight holidays per year. I know that sounds low, but with benefits it comes to almost thirty dollars an hour."

I hadn't even dreamed of finding a job with medical insurance. I cannot break down sobbing in the office in front of this woman who barely knows me. I dig my nails into my palms until it hurts and inhale deeply. "When would you expect to let me know?"

She pops up quickly for someone with such a large belly and peeks around the corner. "Ideally, I'd love to have you meet Jack today so we could tell you tonight or tomorrow. We're in a bit of a hurry." She rests her hands on her stomach.

"I'd imagine you can't sleep more than about an hour at a time right now," I say. "Is he or she a nighttime kicker?"

"You have a child." She sounds surprised.

I nod. "A four-year-old son."

"This one's a girl, but I have a nearly three-year-old son at home already."

I mentally stomp on the spike of jealousy that shoots through me. I want another child and I'd love a girl, but I can barely manage Troy. Besides, it's not like I've got any plans of finding someone to father another child anytime soon. "Congratulations. What wonderful news! You're a brave woman to have them so close together."

She sighs heavily. "Well, that wasn't bravery so much as fate."

"Some of the best things in life happen in ways we don't plan."

Nancy perks up at the sound of a deep voice coming from down the hall. "Finally. That's Jack."

My hands shake a little. I need this job. I deserve this job. Paisley said this would be my best year yet, which requires me to find a job that pays a decent wage with benefits.

I need to knock Jack's slobby, disorganized socks off.

I stand up and smooth my shirt and pants, picking at invisible lint while I wait for him to reach the office where I'm waiting. I try to imagine what this mystery boss with the deep, rolling voice might look like. He arrives at the office at three in the afternoon, and his workspace looks like a scene out of *A Beautiful Mind*. Clearly he's a little more creative than business minded, which is probably an occupational hazard when you're developing tech. I realize I have no idea what this company even manufactures. Watches? Phones? Apps? Pedometers?

Not that it really matters to me as long as the checks clear.

"I'm here as promised." Jack walks around the corner with a smile on his bearded face. It's not a shaggy beard, but it's more than scruff. He's got such a pretty face that the facial hair keeps him from looking effeminate. His teeth are straight and white and his hair isn't long and it isn't short. He's a study in perfect symmetry and balance.

"And you've got a candidate, as you promised." He holds out his hand. "I'm Jack Campbell."

I meet his eyes and extend my hand. He clasps it firmly, and his arm flexes noticeably underneath his dress shirt. I should extricate my hand from his, but his eyes distract me. I can't decide whether they're more green or brown.

Nancy clears her throat. "Can you talk to her in your office?"

He drops my hand and cocks his head. "If we hire her, that means I can't ask her on a date, right?"

He must be kidding, but my eyelashes flutter anyway. My heart races and my breathing hitches, because slobby Jack is *the* hottest guy I've seen in, well, in years maybe.

But I need this job, so I hope it was a stupid, poorly considered joke. "I don't need a date, sir," I say. "But I really, really need employment."

"My assessment so far is that Gerty is competent, resourceful and clear," Nancy interjects. "I've interviewed twelve people for this position in the past two weeks. None rose to her level of interpersonal competency or inspired as much confidence." She turns toward me and lowers her voice. "I'm very sorry. He's never been unprofessional like this before."

He waves toward his office. "I'm sorry for the inappropriate joke. I've been working pretty long hours lately, and I think I may need a good night's sleep."

I immediately imagine where he might sleep, and an enormous king-sized four poster bed comes to mind. I think about sinking onto it myself. What is wrong with me? I close my eyes and clear my throat. "No problem."

He motions toward the doorway. "No more flirting, I promise."

I follow him out of Nancy's office and into his. He glances from one black leather armchair to the other, clearly at a loss. Both are so covered with notepads that there's no clear place to sit. Nancy said not to touch anything, but this is unworkable. I carefully gather up the pile of notes resting on one chair and set them on the corner of his desk.

"Not afraid to take action," he says. "I like it. Just make sure you never trash anything, even if it looks useless to you."

He's talking like I've already got the job. Clearly he values Nancy's opinion. "Got it. Never throw anything away, including stained napkins covered in incomprehensible equations. Probably contains the cure to cancer, and I'd doom the entire world."

He barks a laugh. "Exactly."

"Is that what SITB does?" I ask. "Medical research?"

He sits in his desk chair and drops his arms down on the messy surface, undermining my belief in the precious nature of his notes. "Something like that."

"Wait, seriously? You do cancer research?" That was a lucky guess.

"Not cancer, no." He smiles and I'm glad I'm sitting down so my knees don't wobble. "We're working on a prototype for a portable EKG. It'll allow docs to do an EKG from anywhere, including the privacy of a patient's own home. If we succeed, it'll save half a billion dollars on medical bills annually, and allow efficient monitoring for patients who would otherwise be cut loose. Plus it'll minimize equipment waste."

Wow, I really shouldn't toss his old napkins. "That sounds amazing."

He nods. "I certainly hope so."

"What questions do you have for me?" I ask.

"Let's say I have a meeting on the books and clients arrive as planned, but I'm not here. What would you do?"

Is this a trick question? Where else would he be? I lean toward him. "Is your real name Bruce Wayne?"

Blood drains from his face for some reason. "I'm not a hero, that's for sure."

"Is this a real scenario?" I ask. "Do you regularly miss important meetings you've scheduled?"

He sighs. "I have a lot of things going on in my life other than this startup. I'm not Batman, but that's a reality for me. I need someone who can run interference if things don't run smoothly."

I lick my lips. "I suppose I'd let them know you were delayed by circumstances outside your control and make sure to offer them amazing snacks while they wait. There's a great bakery around the corner. I'd order muffins and cookies to be brought in for any days when important meetings are scheduled. Then I'd try and message you to find out whether you're merely delayed, or not coming at all. If you're on your way, I'd do my best to keep them happy until you arrived. If you're not coming, I'd make up a plausible lie, if the truth is off limits, and try to reschedule."

The corner of his mouth turns up in something that approximates a smile.

"It would help if you had someone else prepped to take over for you when you're not around. A second-in-command, so to speak, who could do the presentations without you."

He shakes his head. "Not possible. Only I have all the puzzle pieces of this particular piece of tech. Some of them are up here." He taps his head.

"Can I ask why?"

"You can ask," he says, "and maybe one day I'll even answer, but today is not that day."

"You're the boss."

"That I am. Did Nancy already talk to you about numbers?"

I nod.

"And you're okay with them?"

I nod again.

He stands up and offers me his hand. "Then I guess you're hired."

"Just like that?"

This time he's the one who nods. "Nancy will expect you to be in the office daily by nine a.m. It's short notice, but we'd love it if you could start tomorrow. Nancy doesn't have much time left to train you."

He holds out his hand, and I reach to take it again. It's a

mistake. The second our fingers touch, my heart goes haywire, and my face flushes.

His hazel eyes sparkle at me, as if he knows exactly how I'm feeling. I'm sure every girl he meets goes gaga around him. I snatch my hand away. The joke's on him, because his face might rival a young Brad Pitt. His voice probably causes most women to swoon. None of that makes a difference to me.

I'm as dead inside as Troy's beloved daisy.

I fill out the new hire paperwork before I head out to my car. My excitement one hundred percent stems from the fact that I've found a job with decent pay and medical. It has nothing to do with the mesmerizing eyes of my new boss.

Nothing whatsoever.

4

TRUDY

Nancy spends the first hour teaching me the safety protocols at SITB. We enter my biometric data for the after hours scanner, and I'm issued badges and passwords. I've been here sixty-four minutes and already my head feels stuffed full of pointless information. Basically, it's like being in high school again.

Eventually, when my head feels so full of new stuff it might burst, Nancy starts showing me how to set up appointments in their system and telling me what the various codes and acronyms mean.

"That reminds me. What does SITB stand for?" I ask.

Nancy shrugs. "Jack won't say, so it's turned into a bit of an office joke. We're working on portable medical testing equipment, so most of our ideas have something to do with that. Best idea at the end of every week gets whatever's in the change jar in the break room. We all dump out our pocket change as we come and go each day. We vote on the idea on Friday at three."

"Seriously?" I ask. "Jack knows about this weekly contest?"

Nancy grins. "It was his idea. He says it's good for office morale. I think the lion's share of the change comes from him, actually."

I think about the letters and can't come up with any ideas off the top of my head. Maybe Paisley will be better at it. I probably need to come up with a decent submission for my first week. I don't want to be the office loser.

About halfway through the day, Nancy leaves for lunch. I'm working on a spreadsheet when I realize I never ate anything myself. I pull my peanut butter and jelly sandwich out of my purse, but it looks even worse than I remember them looking in grade school. I decide to try my luck with the vending machine.

Two dollars later, the dumb machine still hasn't spit out a single bag of chips. I kick it.

"Hey now, assault is illegal in Georgia."

I jump at the sound of the man's voice and turn around to face him. A tall guy I saw working in one of the big side offices stands behind me, smiling. I didn't even hear him approach. His hair is perfectly mussed and his shoes are perfectly shined, but a few freckles on the bridge of his nose add a little character to his face.

I laugh. "I'm not even intimidating enough to scare a vending machine, apparently."

"It's more about leverage. You've got to press your numbers and then hit enter. Twice." He points.

I try it again and this time, it works. Two bags of Cheetos drop, so apparently the machine registered my multiple requests at some level. I offer one to my new friend.

"Cheetos?" His eyes and tone judge me. "Really?"

"My son loves these," I say. "Maybe I miss him more than I thought I would."

"I have three boys myself," he says. "Nine, six and one.

I've liked Cheetos since I was a kid. I just didn't peg you for a cheese-powder girl."

"Troy just turned four. They grow too fast."

"Some nights I think they don't grow fast enough." He rubs at his eyes.

"Not getting enough sleep is the worst for sure." I laugh. "My feelings on Troy growing up change by the hour."

"I completely agree." He holds out his hand for a shake. "I'm Greg. Welcome to SITB, an office run by a guy with a Stick in the Butt."

I wouldn't ever describe Jack that way, but it's a funny acronym. "That must have been a weekly winner."

He grins. "Yep, the first month I was here. It's getting harder to come up with something original, but that one kind of stuck. You'll get it once you've spent a little more time with Jack."

"Is he a hard boss?" I ask. "I've only been in the same room with him for five minutes, and that was an interview."

Greg grunts. "He's a maniac. Nothing we do is ever good enough, which is rich coming from a guy who can't be bothered to show up before two in the afternoon. When he's being especially awful, I try to remind myself that he's probably got a lot riding on this. That must be scary for someone who never learned to have any kind of work ethic. It must suck for a trust baby when their parents insist that they finally do something."

"Is he really a trust baby?" I scrunch my nose. "He didn't seem like it to me." But then, I've never met one.

"Oh please, he must be. He's got several cars, breezes in and out like this is a hobby to him, and orders people around like he's Prince Charles."

Jack did say I should plan on him missing important meetings.

"I don't envy you being his assistant," Greg says. "It's hard enough meeting his expectations from the business side. Being his assistant sounds like a job no one could ever win."

"Gee thanks," I say.

"If you ever need anything at all, let me know. I'm happy to help and I've been with SITB since it opened. I can't believe it's coming up on a year."

Greg seems nice enough, but I really hope he's wrong. Even if I don't want to finish my career as an assistant here at SITB, I have to survive at least a few months. Nancy and I work dutifully all afternoon, but in the end, my enigmatic boss doesn't even show up on my first day. Even so, I do the math and realize that I earned $135 today. I'd have to sell sixteen signs on Etsy to make that much money.

It feels good. Really good.

The next day, I know immediately when Jack shows up. The reverb from his shouts echoes from all the way down the hall. Nancy stands up to see what's happening and I follow her to sneak a look around the doorframe.

Jack's face is red, and his arms gesture wildly. "You have thirty-seconds to grab your stuff and get out. I'll leave whatever you can't carry at the front desk tomorrow. Give me your security clearance now, because you're done here."

When Greg walks out of his office, his face is pale enough to pass for a sparkly vampire. My heart sinks. I had one friend and my horrible new boss just fired him. But for what?

"Conference room in five minutes. Staff wide meeting," Jack says to Nancy as he storms into his office.

Nancy crosses her arms under her chest, resting them on the top of her belly. I wish I knew what she was thinking, because I'm a little freaked out.

"Let's finish this up," she tells me. "We should be able to wrap it up before the meeting."

My hands shake as I type the updated press release and drop the document into the email we prepared.

"Send it," she says, "and let's go. We need to make sure Jack has what he needs before he faces everyone. Greg was well liked."

She picks up the phone and calls building security to let them know about Greg's departure.

"How'd you know to do that?" I ask as we walk to the conference room.

She glances my way. "Part of your new job is doing whatever needs to be done so that by the time Jack thinks about it, it's already taken care of."

How am I supposed to know what he's going to think of?

Jack strides up and falls into step next to us. "We need to call security and let them know Greg Killean's clearance is revoked."

Nancy shoots me a sideways glance. "It's been done already, sir."

Jack smiles and takes a seat at the head of the table. Nancy sits next to him, a notepad in hand. Why didn't I think to bring something to write on?

"Why are we here today?" Jack asks.

No one offers any ideas.

"You heard me fire Greg, obviously. I was too upset to be circumspect."

Heads bob silently.

"We've long had a clear company policy that private activities aren't allowed in the office during the day. You're being paid for your time, and most of you clock out at five p.m. daily. That means that when you're here, I expect you to be working and not wasting time and effort on personal websites. Not to mention, your access of such websites exposes us to all sorts of security risks I won't waste time enumerating."

He fired Greg for what? Checking his email? My heart goes out to his wife and three kids. Jack fired him for wasting a little time? I kind of hate Mr. Campbell, even if he does have a beautiful face. That should have prepared me for this, actually. Chris had a pretty enough face and look where that got me.

Jack talks on and on about the importance of following the protocols and rules and then dismisses everyone abruptly.

"I may run to the bathroom," I say to Nancy. "If that's okay?" I wonder whether Jack considers trips to the restroom a waste of valuable company time. Maybe he should ration them.

She bobs her head. "Of course."

On my way back, I notice several people whispering in the break room. A woman I haven't met, Ish from the front desk, and a guy whose office was next door to the dearly departed Greg.

"I can't believe he did that," the neighbor guy says.

I pause, and they notice.

"What?" The woman lifts one eyebrow at me, like I'm an informant. I can't have them thinking I agree with Jack. What he did to Greg was terrible. I should have spoken up during the meeting. Someone should have defended Greg, but it's only my second day. I always assumed I'd have stood up to the regime in Germany before World War II, but now I'm not so sure. Maybe we're all cowards at a baseline, more inclined to duck our heads than risk our necks.

At least the other employees should know where I stand. "I agree with you guys. Jack's a complete jerk. He never should have fired poor Greg. I mean, who doesn't check their email once or twice a day, right? Where are we working? Nazi occupied Germany?"

Ish clears his throat, and I turn around slowly.

Jack breathes in and out slowly and the three people behind me scatter like cockroaches when the light's flipped on. They're the real cowards. I stand my ground, even if my knees shake and my fingers feel rubbery, like microwaved hotdogs.

"I prefer to think of myself as Napoleonic, but I suppose you're entitled to your opinion. Maybe I should shave off my beard and leave a little mustache. What do you think?"

He's making a joke about me mocking him fifteen minutes after he fired someone? Greg will struggle to feed his kids next month, and Jack's smirking about it. Which is infinitely better than fuming at me for my horribly disproportionate and unflattering comparison of him to the most famous tyrant of all time.

"I'm so sorry, sir. I don't know what I was thinking."

He grabs a soda from the fridge behind me. "You were thinking you'd sure like to fit in at your new job, and my other employees were grumbling."

Oh, no, no, I can't let him throw them under the bus. They'll never talk to me again. I shake my head emphatically. "No, sir, they weren't complaining. It was only me."

"Uh huh. Well, a helpful bit of advice. If I were you, I might wait until my second day before likening my boss to Hitler, who was undeniably way, way shorter than me FYI. But it's your life, so it's your call to make."

"Actually, today *is* my second day." I put my hands on my hips. "You didn't bother to show up at all on my first." I could kick myself for being such a brat. I'm so fired.

But Jack just grins at me. "Nancy hired a live one, didn't she? Let's hope you can organize as well as you can mouth off." He spins on his heel and walks down the hall without a backward glance.

My hands shake as I slink back to my office, but Jack doesn't say a word to Nancy. He marches back into his office purposefully and slams the door behind him. Okay, then.

I'm looking over the next two months on the calendar with Nancy when I notice Greg wasn't kidding. There aren't any meetings set up before two p.m.

"Where is Jack every morning?" I ask.

"Does it matter?" she asks.

I shake my head. "I guess not, but he's sort of like Willy Wonka, isn't he? Why not tell everyone why he's always late? And what SITB stands for?"

"We do our jobs and we don't pry into Jack's life. It's none of our business." Nancy hands me a list. "We've got meetings set up with possible buyers for SITB's tech in two weeks. These are the details we need to complete before then. You can see how much time Jack has to deal with them." She points at the calendar. There are about six hours that aren't already blocked off in the next two weeks.

"We don't have enough time to schedule all of this stuff," I say. "Unless he comes in earlier. Can't we ask him to clear some room? Maybe he can come in at nine a.m. two days a week?"

Her lips compress and she stares at me for moment. "Jack Campbell bankrolled this entire company with his private savings. So whether he's golfing, or out late partying, or sleeping in with a hangover, or basket weaving while listening to Reggae music, it doesn't affect our jobs. This is the time he's given us, and our job is to work within it."

I shake my head. "Fine."

I focus on the time blocks again, seeing patterns

emerge that remind me of a puzzle, like an old game Mary loved when we were kids. Tetris, I think it was called.

I point at the details for next Wednesday. "This meeting is across town so we blocked off drive time. That's sort of wasted dead space. Maybe we could do this review." I point at the list. "During that drive." I glance up at her. "Is that kind of what you mean?"

She nods. "This is exactly why I hired you. Do as much as you possibly can to condense this, paying careful attention to the order in which these steps need to take place. Once you've come up with a smaller list of things we can't possibly compress, that's when we go to Jack and ask for his help. Got it?"

"It's our job to inconvenience him as little as possible."

Nancy beams at me. "Yes, precisely."

I hunch over and get to work, calling people on the list to shift things when necessary. I'm about halfway through when Nancy stands up and heads for the door.

"I've got to leave early for an appointment with my OB. They're twice a week now, which is killing me."

"I'll see you tomorrow, then?" I ask.

She nods. "Absolutely. Do the best you can with that, and we'll review your solutions in the morning. Once you're finished there, I need the power point I created reviewed for typos, and two dozen of the portfolios copied and assembled. Think you can do that?"

"Sure." I might be a little late, but I'll text Pam and warn her.

"Great. See you tomorrow."

Jack's door is still shut when Nancy leaves. The red light that represents his phone line is lit up, which means he's still talking to someone. Maybe he's almost forgotten about how I sort of called him Hitler. When my cell phone rings, I'm so startled that I almost drop it. I silence it immediately, Jack's feelings about employees doing personal things during work fresh in my mind, but in the process I notice the caller. It's Pam.

What if Troy's in trouble?

My heart sinks at the thought of answering a private call at work, but Jack's on the phone behind a closed door, and Troy's only been with Pam for four days, today included.

I swipe to answer the call. "Pam?"

"Trudy, Troy won't wake up from his nap. I shook him like you said, but he won't open his eyes."

My heart stops. It's the worst nightmare of every parent with a diabetic child. "Call 911. Tell them to take him to Piedmont. I'll meet them there."

I grab my bag and rush from the office. I barely stop at the front desk long enough to tell Ish I'm leaving.

"Family emergency. If Jack notices I'm gone, tell him I'll be back later tonight to finish the power point and copy the portfolios."

Ish nods. "Best of luck to you, miss. I hope everyone's okay."

Me too.

The whole way to the hospital, I obsess. I wanted this, I wanted a job. I needed to go out into the world, leaving Troy with a stranger. And now he's unconscious, probably suffering a hypoglycemic event. That means I traded a hundred and thirty-five dollars for my child's safety.

I always knew Mary was smarter, and she's undeniably harder working. She made better decisions in love. She took care of me and everyone around her when I could barely care for myself. Mary gives more time to charity, more time to friends, and more time to everyone. But I never doubted one thing: I'm a good mom.

If I don't even have that, if I've failed my son, then who am I?

I race into the partitioned section of the ER where Pam's waiting with Troy. He's sitting up, sucking noisily from a juice box straw. I sprint across the room and yank him into my arms. "My baby."

"Hi Mom. Sorry you had to come to the doctor's."

I rub the back of his curly head. "It's okay baby, it's just fine."

"But you had to leave work. And Miss Pam's real sad."

Pam still hasn't met my eye. When she finally does, she looks away immediately. I'd put my money on her feeling more guilty than sad.

"What happened?" I ask.

The doctor breezes into the room, his white coat unbuttoned over hugely baggy blue scrubs. "You must be Mrs. Jenkins?"

I nod. "It looks like my baby's okay?"

"He's just fine. He suffered a minor hypoglycemic episode, Mrs. Jenkins. Do you know what that means?"

"Yes sir. It means his sugars went too low."

"It can cause sweating, confusion, or even hallucinations, but when young children are napping, you wouldn't see any of that."

"But you can't wake them up." I've feared this exact thing for more than three months.

"We gave him a shot of Glucagon, and he perked right up. Based on what Pam told me, it seems she gave him the proper amount of insulin for the food she prepared, but he failed to finish his lunch."

I close my eyes. How could she not have noticed?

"I'm so sorry," Pam says. "I didn't realize he hid the animal crackers under the sofa, and I'm pretty sure he fed part of his hotdog to Camilla."

Camilla, their stupid, bouncy sheepdog who I now need to shoot.

I told Pam to make sure he ate everything, but this is my fault for assuming she could handle it. I never should've taken this dumb job. I never should've trusted anyone else with Troy. But what choice do I have? I can't sponge off of Mary forever. I want to curl myself around Troy and never move again.

The doc monitors his vitals for another half hour, but his sugars remain stable. "You guys can leave whenever you're ready," he says. "Troy's fine."

I gather him up in my arms, but he shoves against me. "I can walk, Mom. Put me down."

My heart lurches. He's too small to be so big. I slide him down my body slowly until his tiny sneakers touch the ground.

"I really am so sorry," Pam says. "I swear I'll watch what he eats like a hawk from now on. I didn't realize how serious it could be."

One look at Pam's stricken face and I know she means it. We've been friends since before Troy was even born. She taught me how to change a diaper when neither Mary nor I had any idea what we were doing.

"I know," I say. "It's not your fault. It's complicated."

Pam touches my arm. "Please give me another chance. Don't give up your job, Trudy. I know you're planning to from that look in your eye."

I grit my teeth. "It's not that I blame you. It's my fault, not yours."

She looks at the ceiling. "You watched Benson for so long and you never let me pay you a dime. I made one tiny mistake, and I promise it won't happen again. I promise."

"Mom, I like playing with Benson. Please don't blame Miss Pam. I won't hide food anymore."

I crouch down. "You can't ever hide food, sweetie. I know sometimes you don't want to eat every single thing, but you're special, remember? You have to follow different rules. Harder rules."

His lip trembles. "I want to be normal. Like Benson."

I shake my head slowly. "You can't change how God made you. No one in the world is more amazing than you are, but that means you have to pay a little more attention than other four year olds."

"I will do it, Mommy. I will."

I know he will. And at the end of the day, the only way I'll have health insurance for visits exactly like this is if I keep my job. Which means I need to get back to the office and finish what I said I'd do.

I call Paisley. "Hey gal. How do you feel about babysitting for a few hours tonight?"

I fill her in on what's going on during the drive home, and Paisley meets me at my house just in time to take over after Troy's bath.

"Aunt Paisley's going to read you a story or two, okay sweetie? Mom has a little work she needs to catch up on since she left early today to check on you at the doctor's. Okay?"

Troy nods and I kiss him on the forehead. The hardest part about being a parent isn't being willing to do anything and everything for your kid. It's figuring out what to do when the things your kid needs, like direct care and a roof over his head, pull you in two different directions. And now, after hiding his food and feeding it to a dog, does Troy need a hug, or a stern talking to? I opt for a little of each.

When I grab my purse to leave, Troy's small voice calls out. "Mom?"

"Yes, baby?"

"Can you please water my plant on your way out?"

That dumb dead daisy. I roll my eyes.

"Please?"

I dump another cup of water over the top of the rotting Gerbera daisy, because it's easier than trying to crush Troy's treasured delusion. Then I head back to the empty office. I'm going to finish that spreadsheet, typo check the power point, and make those portfolio copies if they kill me.

5
PAUL

My patent attorney is the best in Atlanta, but he's hard to pin down. "So you think we'll have the FAOM this time next week?" I ask.

"Of course I can't speak for the patent examiner, but yes, the hope is that the first office action on the merits will be complete early next week. Todd indicated as much to me."

I close my eyes. I need this wrapped up, or I'm going to get an ulcer. "Fine. Let me know as soon as you hear."

"Of course," Mr. Brighton says.

I hang up. I never make small talk with anyone when those pleasantries cost me six hundred dollars an hour. I learned that the hard way. No matter how close you think you are to your lawyer, the clock is ticking every time you're on the phone with them.

My Outlook calendar indicates the mock presentation is scheduled for tomorrow at three p.m. I leave my office to grab a copy of the portfolio Nancy was preparing so I can run through it tonight. Except Nancy's not in her office.

Gertrude isn't either. I walk to the front of the office. "Ish, what time is it?"

"Hello, sir. It's five minutes until five p.m."

I frown. We're up against a deadline, and both my assistants leave early? On the same day I fired Greg's untrustworthy self? "Did either Nancy or the new girl mention why they left?"

Ish bobs his head up and down awkwardly. "Uh, yes sir, thank you."

Thank you? I swear, if reliable receptionists weren't so hard to find, this odd guy would not still be here. But he's unfailingly polite, and he's never called in sick. Not once in almost a year. I prompt him. "What did they say?"

"Oh, yes, of course, sir. Miss Nancy has a doctor's appointment, and she will see us in the morning."

"Okay, and the new hire?"

"Miss Gerty ran out the door just before four. She looked quite distressed and mentioned she had a family emergency."

I swallow hard, inexplicably worried about someone I barely know. What kind of emergency? Is she married? Why should I care about that? "Did she say anything else?"

Ish shakes his head. "I'm sorry sir."

I stomp back to my office, annoyed that I'll be stuck here prepping for a presentation tomorrow without the proper materials. Why did I hire someone new if she's not even going to put in a full day? I've barely reached my office when my phone rings.

I snatch the handset and hold it to my ear. "Hello."

"Paul, it's me again."

Mr. Brighton. There's no good reason he should be calling me back. "Is everything okay?"

"I wanted to tell you that a nearly identical patent to yours was filed at the patent office two days after us."

I clench my free hand into a fist, but I don't throw anything through the window. Yet. "Two days *after* us this time?"

"That's correct. It looks like your leak was delayed for some reason."

"But we can't sue for infringement until our patent is granted," I say.

"You're absolutely right. If you learn any more about this process, you won't need me anymore."

I wish. "How nervous should I be right now?"

"That depends entirely on whether you can document the date of your discoveries. Last time, your competitor had a working prototype before you did."

My competitor. I roll my eyes. Some shell company we couldn't track down. And now, even though SITB doesn't share a single employee with my last startup, they've managed to infiltrate me again. "What should I be doing, other than preparing records and a timeline?"

"It would help if you could identify this competitor and the leak."

"You'll look into the shell company?" I ask.

Mr. Brighton's frown conveys in his tone. "Of course, but I'm limited in ways you aren't."

He needs to follow all the rules to keep his law license. Any risk taking will have to come from my end. As it should, since it's my leak, not his. "I'll pursue every angle. You can be sure of that."

Mr. Brighton clears his throat. "And I'll lean on my friend at the patent office and let you know if we can expedite anything. I'll also call the court and push for a hearing date. Soon."

I hang up and release a string of expletives. I pore over all my internal email correspondence and memos to prepare a timeline, which takes nearly two hours. I wish we had an IT person to help me ensure our firewalls and data are secure. I don't know enough about computer tech to be confident there. Nancy really needs to find someone new soon. I click send on the email with my timeline to Mr. Brighton and I lean back and stretch.

A run. I need to take a nice long run, and I'll feel better. I stand up to leave for the night, but I'm startled by a noise. Someone else is here. After hours. While I'm already suspicious about a leak.

I poke my head around the corner, expecting Nancy. I do not expect our new hire, Gerty whatever her name is. Nancy's desk is covered with papers, and she's stuffing things into folders.

"What are you doing here?" I narrow my eyes at her.

She jumps and looks up at me with huge, wide, sky blue eyes. "Oh, Mr. Campbell. I didn't realize anyone else was here." Her sweater hangs on the back of Nancy's chair, leaving her in a silky camisole top. Her high heels are piled in the corner of the room, and she's standing in bare feet.

"Clearly."

"I had to leave for, well, to deal with something, but I promised Nancy I'd have these ready for the mock presentation tomorrow. I came back to finish them up, and to do some work on, well. I'm sure you don't care what, but another project Nancy asked me to do today. I'm sorry if I'm disturbing you."

She is, but not in the way she means. Although. The timing is strange. She shows up for an interview on the very day the thief files a rival patent? I do the math in my head.

Even if she had stolen the information, they couldn't have gotten it transmitted and a file prepared on the same day. But that doesn't mean she's not a new leak, either. What if Alan or Greg were the leak and now they're gone, so she's the replacement? Again, the timeline. Alan, maybe, but he left voluntarily so that's unlikely. And Greg left *after* she appeared.

"Since you're here," she asks, "is there any chance you know what this means?" She holds up a note that says, "Diagram G, electrical components."

I nod. "I've got that on my laptop. The specs for the critical components aren't kept on the main server. I told Nancy I'd print a copy of that. Follow me."

Gerty pulls her sweater on and slides into her heels before following me into my office. I hide my smile. She wouldn't have bothered covering up if she didn't find me at least a little bit attractive. Not that I'd actually date my assistant. Especially a mouthy, accusatory one. Who, for all I know, left without notice because she had to help her husband out of a pinch.

I check out her left hand while I'm pulling the file up. She's standing awkwardly by the door, resting it against the doorframe so it's easy to see. Her ring finger is bare, but that doesn't mean she's single. Maybe her boyfriend has commitment issues.

Not that it matters.

"How many copies do you need?" I ask.

"I guess that's your call. I'm preparing ten folders, but I think the idea is that if they make sense to the staff tomorrow, we can use the same ones for the presentation in two weeks. Do you want them all to have one?" she asks. "Or maybe just one for yours if the material is sensitive?"

"Good idea. I'll just print a single one here."

The printer sits on the edge of my desk, right next to my desktop. It clicks and growls, preparing to print. I walk toward it at the same time as Gerty, our hands reaching out simultaneously for the diagram. She pulls back, as do I, and then we both reach for the paper again. This time she steps back, bumping into a potted plant.

She steps forward in alarm, her hand knocking against a pile of files, which tumble behind my desk.

"I am so sorry." Her eyes widen like she's terrified I'll fire her for being clumsy.

"It's fine," I say. "Hard to sneeze without knocking something over in here. I should be embarrassed I suppose, but I haven't had a single extra second for tidying lately, and chaos has always worked for me."

She leans over the desk to where the files fell between the desk and the wall. She's not very tall, so when she leans forward like that, I get a good view of her very nicely shaped backside. Which I should not be ogling. I turn away and force myself to grab the diagram off the printer.

"Uh, Mr. Campbell?"

I turn back toward her, not my fault this time, but she's still bent over the desk. Come on, Gerty, think this through. I'm trying to act like a boss should.

I clear my voice. "If you step back, I'm sure I can reach the files."

She rummages around a little more and my computer shuts off abruptly.

"Hey, what are you doing?" I step toward her, looking toward the wall where she's poking at things.

She finally rights herself, and turns around to face me, brandishing a tiny black cylinder the size of a tube of lipstick.

"Uh, did you just destroy my computer?" I ask.

She shakes her head. "I fixed it."

I raise one eyebrow and point at the screen. "My computer begs to differ. It's most definitely not working anymore."

"Do you know what this is?" She waves the cylinder at me.

"Uh, part of a power cord? Or maybe part of the keyboard controls?"

"Yep." She nods vigorously. "It's supposed to look like that, anyway."

"Are you ever going to tell me what you think it is? Because I'm beginning to wonder whether you're a maniac." An adorable maniac, but a maniac nonetheless.

"This is a key logger."

I've heard of that, but I can't quite recall what it does.

"It logs your keystrokes. One of my professors collects them and plays with the code that interprets what they collect. It's like a puzzle, but they're almost always used for something illegal. Any idea why someone might put one on your computer?"

I curse. Then I curse again. "Tell me how they work, exactly."

"Well, I guess anyone with access to your office could have put this on the back of the desktop keyboard. All the data coming from your keyboard passes through this, one stroke at a time, and this tiny device saves all of it. Until someone uploads the data from it."

"How would they retrieve it?"

"This one looks like it's hooked up to transmit wirelessly," she says. "Maybe a Bluetooth device?"

"So someone in the office is collecting the info every day?"

She taps her lip. "Maybe, but it wouldn't have to be done that often. Especially since you aren't here all day most days so the data set would be smaller."

"How are they doing it? Do they have to come in my office?"

She shakes her head. "Not necessarily. They'd need to come within transmission range, but I'm not quite sure what that would be on this."

"But it's probably an employee?" I ask.

"I would guess whoever placed it was an employee, or someone who could access your computer to add it. But the retrieval could be done by someone from outside the office who visits pretty regularly. I suppose that could be a lot of people. Supply companies, regular contractors, janitors, maintenance staff. It probably could be collected as infrequently as once a week or even every ten days."

"Gerty," I say. Did she cringe for some reason? "That's your name, right?"

She swallows reflexively. "Yes sir, that's right."

"I suspected you at first, if I'm honest."

"Me?" Her eyes widen. "Why?"

"You're new. You've got this innocent look about you, as though you'd adopt a dozen orphans from Africa if only you could."

She frowns. "What's wrong with adoption?"

I sigh. "Nothing, but you show up one day before I get word that—"

"That what?"

"Nothing." She doesn't need to know exactly what's going on. "But the timing is suspicious."

"Why would I hand you my own key logger?" she asks. "Besides, this had to be placed and then checked regularly. You think I had someone else do that for me? And then I showed up and instead of checking it, I what? Hand it over to convince you I'm trustworthy?"

It seems a little convoluted.

"What's going on, anyway?"

I peer at her. Is it an act of some kind? She's prying now, but probably only because this whole situation has crossed beyond bizarre and into absurd, bad spy movie territory. Unless she brought the key logger and pretended to find it to win me over. Then again, she didn't have anything in her hand, and she doesn't have pockets in her pants, so where would she have been hiding it?

I might be going crazy.

"Based on timing and proximity, I don't think you could be complicit, even if you are a new hire." I gulp. "I'm going to share something with you. As of right now, you may be the only person on earth who will know enough about what's going on to help me."

She frowns and backs one step toward the door. "Uh, okay. Are you a CIA agent or something? I thought all that extra security was weird." She glances around her like she's expecting someone to jump out from behind the curtains. Or maybe like she thinks I'm nuts.

"Nothing like that. But I began with another startup and another invention before this one, something in a similar field. It was worth a lot of money, but before I even filed a patent application, someone else stole my idea. They filed first. Game Over."

"That stinks."

"You have no idea. But it's worse than just stealing my idea, really. They stole everything. The tech, the prototypes, all of it. They filed the patent application before me, and I had no way to prove that I owned it. So this time I hired a completely different team. None of the same researchers, none of the same staff. I picked an office in an obscure office park, and it worked. I filed first, but only by two days according to my lawyer. Apparently another shell company just filed and they're going to claim that this new invention belongs to them, exactly like last time."

"Wait, who is it?"

"You need to put that key logger back on my computer," I say. "Because that's exactly what you and I need to figure out."

"Are you serious?" she asks.

"Deadly serious."

"Uh, okay. So you're going to, what? Type in things that will throw them off?"

I think about it. "I think we go about business as usual, especially since this time we have the upper hand."

"Okay," she says. "But then what do you want me to do? Because I can't really do anything dangerous. I've got commitments."

Commitments? What does that mean? I can't think of a way to ask that isn't creepy, so I stay focused. "This is corporate espionage, not a murder investigation. Other than stealing my ideas, I have no reason to believe the thief is dangerous in any way. Even so, if you help me, you'll never go anywhere without me along. And if we see any indication things could turn violent, I'll call the police immediately."

She breathes in deeply and looks up at me with the most trusting, beautiful eyes I've ever seen. "Okay, boss. Whatever you say."

Boss. I'm her boss. I needed the reminder that I shouldn't be thinking about her remarkable eyes. Or how full her lips are. Or how much I want to pull her against me and tug that sweater off her shoulders.

"We'll get started tomorrow," I say.

"You should also make sure IT checks out the firewalls. If anything is down, the person who installed this may not even need to use it. Do you trust your IT guy?"

I close my eyes. "I don't even *have* an IT guy to trust anymore."

She frowns. "Who's making sure your FTP server packet filters are working?"

"No one."

"You're worried about a leak, and you don't have an IT person at all?"

"Sounds like you know a little something about it."

She crosses her arms and leans against the desk. "I should confess something. I applied for the job as your assistant because I saw you had an IT position open. I was hoping if I got my foot in the door as an assistant, I might have a chance to do a little IT work. I graduate in two months with a degree in computer programming and I can't find a job because I don't have enough experience for anyone who's hiring in my field."

"You were playing me, then." I smile. "Just not in the way I thought."

She grins back at me. "I sort of was, but not to steal anything. I almost didn't mention it, but I figure with your current situation, complete honesty's probably the best policy."

"Would you mind taking a look at our firewalls before you head home?"

She bobs her head. "Sure, I'd be happy to do that, and I can lend a hand until you fill the position."

"You may be mouthy, but I guess we're lucky you showed up."

It's like she's my guardian angel. She follows me into the server room and I log her into the system. I hover for fifteen minutes or so, but her fingers fly over the keys expertly. She doesn't seem to be doing anything nefarious, not that I'd know necessarily.

"What are you doing exactly?"

"How much do you know about how firewalls work?" she asks.

I shake my head, but realize she can't see me. "Not that much. I know the Internet is comprised of a bunch of servers in various places that provide information in response to GET commands."

She leans back in her chair. "Not bad, actually. Better

than most people. So a firewall is a set of protocols that control what things can pass through your company's T1 line to access information on your computers. If there's one tiny hole, then people can poke their way through. And you have a hole here." Her fingers keep typing, and I try to watch but can't puzzle out quite what's happening.

"The hole came from Greg Killean," she says. "Wait, is that—"

I sigh. "I fired him because of that today."

Her fingers click away. "For using porn on a company network." She whistles. "A lot of porn. Really gross, illegal porn." Her mouth twists up. "Blech."

"Yep. I didn't figure I needed to disclose the gory details to the entire office, but yes. I only found out because another employee walked in on him, well. It was reported to me. It's not a comfortable spot to be put in, but I dealt with it. I didn't think much about the possible consequences to the network."

"That one is cleaned up now, but why didn't your last IT guy see that?"

I lean against the doorframe. "No idea. He had plenty of experience too, so maybe that isn't all it's cracked up to be. He was working on another project and maybe he'd already checked out, mentally." Or maybe not. "Could he have placed the key logger?"

She shakes her head. "Doubtful. He wouldn't have needed to. He'd have access to your desktop from here. If he had a key logger, it would have been part of some kind of shell and pea game. A distraction, a red herring." Her mouth drops. "So if I were a bad guy, full disclosure, I could have placed that phony key logger to gain your trust so you'd get me access to this."

I bob my head. "I'd already thought of that."

She cocks her head, her lips slightly parted. "You aren't worried?"

"Not really. I trust you for some strange reason. Or maybe I'm just a dupe."

"In my defense, your people did run a background check and pulled all my IDs back to like, grade school."

I chuckle. "There is that. But that's true of anyone. I'd assume someone truly nefarious would have gotten good fakes."

"I wish I had some fake credit cards," she says. "But all I know how to do is tighten up network security and help fix glitches."

"Which is exactly what we need you to do until we can hire a replacement for our last guy. I think until we hire someone new, you may be pulling double duty."

"I'm okay with it," she says. "As long as you'll give me a recommendation for an IT position once Nancy returns."

I doubt I'll be interested in letting her go when Nancy returns, but I don't mention that. "Sure, but our top priority right now is catching whoever installed that key logger. I think we should get started first thing tomorrow morning."

Her jaw drops. "I might have misheard you just now. Does that mean you're coming into the office before noon tomorrow?"

"That's so surprising?"

She shrugs. "Kind of, yeah."

"I don't usually come in until later, but I'll make an exception for this."

"So you aren't in a coffin, or like howling at the moon every day before two p.m.?" Her eyes twinkle at me and my head dips a few inches toward hers before I remember I absolutely, positively cannot kiss her, no matter how funny she is, or how good she smells.

No matter how dark her eyelashes look against her cheeks, I can't touch her face. No matter how soft her hair looks, I can't stroke it.

"I didn't say that," I joke. "But I'll delay my coffin nap tomorrow in pursuit of a bigger villain. Are you with me?"

She nods. "Absolutely."

Before we leave for the night, she follows me back to my office and bends over the desk to plug the key logger back in. I try to look away, but I don't quite succeed. I hope we find the leak soon, because unless she does have a husband or boyfriend I haven't heard about yet, I don't know how long I can spend around Gerty without really infuriating Nancy.

❧ 6 ☙
TRUDY

I spend far, far too long in front of the mirror in the morning. I start with a black sheath dress Mary gave me last month when I told her I'd be interviewing, but it screams 'I'm trying too hard.' I put on a low-cut cotton top and a fitted skirt next, but that's too 'come hither.' Finally I change into a sky-blue button down blouse and black slacks. Mary once told me the shirt exactly matches my eyes.

It's stupid that I'm spending so long thinking about how I look.

Because there's no way Jack Campbell cares how his mousy little assistant dresses. I doubt he could pick me out of a line up. He bankrolled the entire company himself, which means he's someone with means. It makes sense, with his assured nature, and his clear, if somewhat disorganized, genius. Actually, he reminds me a little bit of a younger, more aggressive version of Luke. Better looking, too.

Which makes me think about Mary's repeated efforts

to set me up with Luke's brother Paul. I saw a photo of him, months and months ago. He looked like a dorkier version of Luke. Chunky, black-framed glasses and a sweater vest. I absolutely love nerds, so why do I keep refusing that offer? Unlike my boss, Paul is someone I could actually date, and he's exactly my type judging from that photo. Mary warned me years ago that Chris was a train wreck and I should dump him.

I ignored her, and here I am. Divorced, penniless, in debt up to my eyeballs, to my perfect sister, no less, and raising my darling son alone.

Even so, if I agreed to let her set me up with this Paul, it would be doomed from the start. There would be so many expectations weighing the entire thing down that it would certainly implode. But if I brought an absurdly handsome entrepreneur to my sister's wedding who I met on my own?

That would feel good.

I'd have a job I got on my own, and a quality guy I met myself. Could I ask him to be my date for Mary's wedding? Maybe as a favor to an employee, and after a little light flirting. . .

Great idea Trudy. Flirt with the boss and lose your job. And then where will I be? Back to square one, with nothing crossed off my list.

When I spend a little too long doing my makeup, I stare at the mirror and make a promise out loud.

"I will not smile at my boss. I will not flirt with my boss. I will not, under any circumstance, kiss my boss. I will remember my list and why it matters. I found a job working for a man who's slightly unpredictable and way too good-looking. Which probably means he's a ladies man. I've made progress on turning this temporary placement into an

IT position, so I will not even think about kissing him. I need to save my money and repay Mary. Only then will I start looking for people to date. And I'll only date people who can't ruin my chances at keeping my job."

"Mom?" Troy clutches his teddy bear and blanket to his chest. "Who are you talking to?"

I spin around and cross the room. He holds his arms out, and I pick him up.

"No one baby. Mom was just talking to herself."

He snuggles into my shoulder. "I do that too." I know he does. I hear him every day during naptime.

Or, I used to, back when I was around for his naps.

I miss hearing my baby babble to himself quietly. I miss watching Mickey Mouse with him in the mornings. I miss making eggs and toast or pancakes. But if I want to take charge of my own life and provide for our future, if I want to grow as a person into someone he'd be proud of, if I want to stop wishing and hoping and start doing, then sacrificing a little of this precious time is the price.

It still stings to pay it.

I kiss him on the forehead and shamelessly offer him a bribe. "Life cereal?"

Troy beams. He loves cold cereal, and it's so expensive that we almost never have any. Life is the lowest sugar option that doesn't taste like cardboard.

When I pull into the office parking lot five minutes before nine, I park my ten-year-old Honda next to a shiny blue Tesla. I bet it belongs to Jack. My heart isn't racing because he's already here. It's just because I don't want to be late. I do my best to look casual when I walk inside, waving at Ish, putting one foot in front of the other purposefully, but I'm breathing a little too fast and my cheeks feel warm.

I do not have a crush on my boss. I don't even like my boss. Which means I certainly do not have a crush on him.

"Gerty," Nancy says.

I spin toward her voice, which came from the direction of the conference room. She's standing in the doorway.

"Morning, Nancy."

"Jack's here early today, so change of plans. We're doing the presentation first thing."

I duck into the conference room, where about half the chairs are already full. Jack smiles at me, and my heart throws a few cartwheels. I press against my chest with my hand, hoping it's just a minor heart attack and not some kind of involuntary reaction to Jack's grin. Because that might mean that I do have a crush on him.

He gestures at the chair next to him.

I look behind me to make sure he's not looking at someone else. But no, he's calling me to sit next to him.

My hand shakes when I pull the chair out and sit down. "Morning."

"Good morning, Gerty," he says. "I hope you slept well."

I nod. "I did, thanks."

He leans over his notepad, putting his face inches from mine, but covering his mouth so no one else can see he's whispering. "Let's get this over with so we can put together a plan for tracking the key logger."

"Sure," I whisper back. "I've been thinking about it. I think the easiest solution would be for one of us to be near your computer all day, with a phone open, scanning for Bluetooth devices. Anyone who hovers near your office for any amount of time with an active Bluetooth network becomes a suspect. Employees, delivery people, anyone."

He touches my arm. "Don't take this the wrong way then. I need someone to be monitoring my office while I'm in here. I'm going to give you an excuse to leave and hang out in there."

He sits up and says, "Gerty assembled the folders that all of you will be referring to during this practice presentation. While I appreciate her help, that means she's not going to be very effective as a test subject. Why don't you head to my office, Gerty, and see whether you can organize some of my notes. By date."

Organize that mess? I want to groan and cheer at the same time.

I stand up. "Yes, sir."

Jack lowers his voice again. "Don't throw anything away, okay? Sometimes I make notes on strange things, but they may be important later." He drops his voice, which makes it unbelievably low. His whisper ruffles my hair. "In the lawsuit."

My knees are wobbly, but I don't think anyone can tell. "Got it. Clean up, but no trashing anything Jack Campbell has touched, even old snotty Kleenexes."

"You never know what they might be worth on eBay." He winks. "And depending on how this goes, I might need that money."

I set my phone to detect local Bluetooth networks, but since this side of the office is a ghost town, I figure I may as well try to actually clean this mess up a bit. I spend the next hour trying to tidy up Jack's office without actually throwing anything away. I don't find any snotty Kleenexes, but I do find lots of coffee stained napkins covered in notes. And I notice patterns in the notes. Most of them are dated, including almost all of the post-its.

My boss is a little obsessive.

He returns to his office about an hour after I start organizing.

"Where are my Kleenexes?" he asks. "Because I feel a

sneeze coming on, and who knows what inspiration I might have afterward."

I put one hand on my hip. "You're a little OCD for such a slob."

He grins at me. "I'm clearly not OCD, but this isn't my first rodeo. I know timelines matter. That's the real reason I don't throw anything away. Not until the patent comes through at least."

"Your files are all here, organized by date whenever possible, and grouped by subject matter. I taped napkins and Post-it's to clean pieces of paper so they don't simply disappear."

Jack smiles at me, which gives me the confidence to ask, "What else have you invented?"

"You're inquisitive for such a new employee." He walks around the desk and sits in his chair. "Even so, you've done a pretty good job, Nosy Rosy."

"I could do a lot more with a few hanging file folders," I say. "And if we're going to be here for a while..."

He bobs his head. "It certainly looks that way, doesn't it? Any luck on finding networks?"

I hand him my phone so he can see the networks screen. "Nothing yet, but I've been alone down here. One of us needs to have our phone casually out all day, the sleep function disabled. We're looking for any Bluetooth networks, so no matter what else you're doing, you pretty much need to watch this at all times."

"What transmission distance are we talking here?" Jack asks.

"Thirty feet, give or take," I say. "Which means our best bet is to camp out right by your computer. The network would have to show up right here, at ground zero."

"Good thing you cleaned off that chair." Jack points.

I shake my head. "I can't just sit around now that you're

here. Everyone would wonder what's going on. I've got other work to do anyway. Since you're back, you can take over." I hold out my hand for my phone.

He meets my eyes for a moment, and time stops. My mouth drops open and I draw a ragged breath. I've never been so aware of anyone else's gaze.

His voice is rough when he says, "I'd rather you stayed."

My heart skips a few beats. Okay, a few dozen. I should have spent a few more minutes on affirmations in the mirror.

"I think you're a little too accustomed to getting your way," I say. "Turn on your phone and let me know if you need anything else. I'll be next door." I snatch my phone from his hands and walk out the door before I can rethink my flirty refusal. It's hard not to look back at him over my shoulder.

I struggle to focus after I leave, which is idiotic. He's been in the office almost every day I've been here. I wasn't this moony then. What's different? We're working together now, and we share a secret. That must be it. He feels real to me now that I know him better. He's not the obvious egomaniac I thought he was at first, either.

Which reminds me I need to check on the firewalls. I stand up and start across the office.

Nancy stops me halfway there. "Where are you headed?"

"Jack told me to check on the firewalls until you've hired a new IT person."

She bobs her head. "Smart. How did he know you knew tech stuff?"

I have no idea what Nancy knows, so I make up a lie as close to the truth as I can manage. "I stayed late last night to finish those folders and he had a computer glitch I helped him with."

"Nice," she says. "Maybe we should be looking for another assistant instead of an IT person."

Hope surges in my chest, but I don't want to be presumptuous. "I don't think we're there yet."

"Well, I'm impressed." Nancy turns to head back to our shared office, but she stops mid-step and grabs the partition for the closest cubicle as if she needs it to stay upright.

"Are you okay?" I ask.

"Just a contraction," she says. "Pretty common for me during the last few weeks."

I had contractions too, but none that made me clutch something to keep from falling. But I work for her, so I don't argue about it. Even so, I'm not surprised around eleven a.m. when I reach our office again, and she's gripping both arms of her desk chair tightly, her knuckles white.

"Have you called your husband yet?" I ask.

She nods. "I think Annie may be coming a little early."

"Don't worry. We'll handle things here. You enjoy your baby."

Nancy forces a smile. "I hope so."

"Had a rough first delivery, huh?"

She nods.

"This one will go much better," I say.

"What makes you think that?"

I shrug. "A hunch."

"I hope you're right."

I tap on Jack's door. "Nancy's husband is on his way, because it looks like she's having a baby today."

He gulps and stands up, his hands fisted at his side. "Wow, okay. Well, do we need to do anything? I can take her and meet him at the hospital."

I shake my head. "Her contractions are still almost ten minutes apart, and she said Ken is nearly here."

"Okay. Well, maybe you can tidy in here a little more while I check on her."

It's sort of cute that he looks so discomfited. "Sure." I pull my phone out and turn on the network signal search screen. My battery's below fifty percent. I'll need to plug it into a power bank if I'm in here much longer. Leaving it open sucks up a lot of juice.

I'm sitting in Jack's desk chair organizing some emails by date when a sound like a squeak draws my attention. A very tall, waif thin model who could easily grace the cover of Vogue looks down her nose at me from the doorway. I wonder how long it took to make her eyes that dark, dramatic, and smudgy. Or how she keeps that wine colored lipstick off of her luminescent teeth. Her dark leather jacket probably cost more than my entire wardrobe.

"Uh, hello. Can I help you?" I ask.

"Why are you sitting in Jack's chair?"

"Umm, well, I'm his interim assistant and I'm cleaning things up while he's dealing with his actual assistant."

She raises one carefully waxed eyebrow. "Where is Nancy? And why would he need to *deal* with her?"

"You seem to know a lot about the SITB office personnel. Who are you?"

She crosses the room and trails her fingertips across the front of the desk. "I'm Jack's girlfriend, Cynthia."

My eyebrows climb toward my hairline. "Oh, I didn't realize."

"Clearly not." She crosses her arms under her chest, shoving her ladies up even higher than her push up bra already had. I'm a little concerned they might pop right out of her sequined tank top and poke my eyes out.

"What are you doing here?" Jack asks in a raspy voice.

She spins toward where he's standing in the doorway. "I

came to see you." Her lips drop into what looks like a practiced pout.

Jack steps into the office and Cynthia reaches toward his face. He catches her hand before she touches him and pushes it away. "You weren't invited."

Her pout deepens, her mournful eyes downcast, her dark, full eyelashes fluttering. "You love to hurt me, don't you?"

Jack scowls. "Actually, that's your MO, not mine. Why are you even here?"

"I can't believe you're asking me that," she says.

"We broke up, Cynthia, months ago. And yet you keep showing up like you never got the memo."

I snort. "Did you really break up with her via memo?"

The corner of Jack's mouth turns up. "I should have tried that. It might have made an impression."

Cynthia glares at me.

I might be safer if I change the subject. "Did Nancy's husband pick her up?"

Jack nods.

Ish buzzes from the front. "Excuse me sir, but I wanted to let you know that Billy from Jimmy Johns is here with your lunch."

"Yeah, send him back," Jack says. "And keep your eyes peeled for Miss Dalton. She's on her way out."

Cynthia's pout transforms into an imploring, lip biting simper. "Jack Jack, I know you miss me as much as I miss you. And I heard through the grapevine that you still aren't dating anyone else."

Jack leans against the wall. "You shouldn't conflate my disinterest in others with my missing you."

"Inflate?" she asks. "I'm not a balloon."

I shake my head and suppress a smirk. "Jack said conflate, not inflate, and that means combining two ideas."

I've never been more grateful that my nerdy sister uses such big words all the time. She's forced me to know the meanings of them or routinely look like an idiot.

A short guy with a black and red Jimmy John's shirt and a ball cap appears in the doorway at the same time as Cynthia presses one hand to her chest melodramatically. "You're different when other people are around. Colder."

"Excuse me," the sandwich delivery guy steps past Cynthia and places three cylindrical subs on the edge of Jack's desk. "Where's Mrs. Jones?"

"She's finally having that baby." Jack reaches for his wallet and pulls out a ten-dollar bill. "Thanks Billy."

Billy takes the tip with a smile, but before leaving, he looks from Jack to me and then to Cynthia. He's clearly wondering what exactly is going on. Join the club, Billy.

"Should I walk her out?" he finally asks.

This has gotten pretty awkward.

I stand up. "That's okay, I can do it."

"I don't need an escort," Cynthia says. "I just can't believe you're asking me to leave without even hearing what I came to talk to you about."

I roll my eyes and reach down to grab my phone, freezing when my eyes reach my screen. There's an active Bluetooth network named *Delivery*.

I need to check whether the key logger's active. I leap to my feet and pretend to stumble on my high heel when I straighten up. That gives me an excuse to fall backward against Jack's computer stand. "Ouch."

I glance behind the desk as though I'm worried I knocked something over. The tiny white light is blinking.

I stand up straight and try to look natural when I pick up my sandwich and sniff it. "That smells great. I'm new, so I'm not too familiar with the office rhythm yet. Billy, do we order from you often? Because I could get used to this."

He grins. "Well, Mrs. Jones craved subs this pregnancy, so I've been coming out at least once a week during the past few months."

Often enough that Jack, who's rarely here for lunch, knows his name.

"Speaking of Nancy." Jack picks up the third sub that Nancy won't be eating and holds it out to Cynthia. "Don't say I never gave you anything. Here's one last meal on me."

She wrinkles her nose. "I'd never eat cold cuts, as you should remember."

Delivery. It's got to be Billy's network. After all, he's a delivery guy.

I take the sub. "It would be terrible to waste such great food on someone who won't even appreciate it." I offered to walk her out, but now I need to get rid of the dreadful Cynthia and follow Billy out instead.

How can I delay Billy and kick Cynthia to the curb? Think, Trudy, think. I'd love to widen my eyes at Jack or point at my phone so he'd know what's going on, but that's impossible to do without alerting Billy to the fact that we're onto him.

"Hey Billy, actually," I say, "I heard Jim in the far office saying he forgot to bring his lunch. There's no way Jack and I can eat both of these. Would you mind taking this to him? Because I just realized Jack and I have a conference call in three minutes. I need to dial us in right away."

Jim's already gone out to lunch. But it should take a minute or two for Billy to figure that out, hopefully buying us the time we need to follow him.

Cynthia frowns. "You have a conference call starting at twelve-twenty-four?"

What is with this lady? We've got to get rid of her quickly, and neither my suggestions, nor Jack's cold shoulder are working. I'll have to roll up my sleeves and be the bad guy.

"We're logging in five minutes early to go over our strategy with our lawyer. Not that you'd understand any of that. You don't strike me as a corporate heavyweight." I put one hand on my hip and purse my lips in the snottiest way I can manage. "Please let us get back to work."

Her eyes widen.

"Sorry to be rude to your friend, Jack, but you really do have to get on that call. It's my job to make sure you do it." I move toward her and she backs up a few inches. It's enough that I can shut the door in her shocked face. It feels really good.

"If you could do that again while I record the interchange, I'd give you a really big bonus," Jack says. "She's so obnoxious."

I turn my phone around, but the Bluetooth network has unsurprisingly disappeared. I whisper in case anyone's near enough the door to hear me. "We had a download from a network named 'delivery.' I think Billy's your leak. He comes here regularly enough."

Jack straightens and grabs his jacket. "Let's go."

I hold out my hand to stall him. "We need to leave at just the right time so it won't look like we're following either of them out."

He walks up next to me, the side of his body touching mine, and I inhale with surprise. My traitorous body sways toward him involuntarily and I want him closer still. I breathe in and out once, the scent of outdoors mixed with some kind of spice filling my nostrils. I lift my hand to touch his arm.

Until I realize he's only standing right next to me so he can peek through the window in his door. Of course he is.

He's checking on whether the coast is clear. I force myself to step away from him before I do something idiotic.

"Okay." He focuses entirely on the hallway, like he had no idea we were even touching before. "I think we're good to go. Do you have a jacket?"

I nod my head. "Yeah, I'll grab it so we can go."

We exit through the back door and walk toward the employee parking area. Jack beelines for his Tesla without thinking, but that's a terrible idea.

"Not that," I hiss. "It's too obvious."

He pauses. "Duh. Do you mind driving? I assume your car's not as memorable as mine?"

"Nondescript at its best." I point at my little Honda. "And I don't mind driving as long as you're paying for gas."

He laughs like I'm joking. Yeesh. Hopefully we won't need to drive too much. I just filled up, and this tank needs to last me at least ten days until my first paycheck. I unlock my car, and he climbs into the passenger side. I cringe when he has to shove aside two empty granola bar wrappers and a protein shake container before he can sit down.

"Sorry," I say. "I wasn't really planning to give my boss a ride today."

Unfortunately, the back seat's even worse. I left my booster seat for Troy with Pam so she could take him to the park, so there's a ring of snack debris where it used to be. I close my eyes and shudder.

"It's fine," he says. "You're doing me the favor here, and trust me. The last thing I'd judge you for is the cleanliness of your car."

"I bet Cynthia's car is pristine." Why did I say that? Am I comparing my car to his *girlfriend's*? Ugh. I wish I could retract my words. That should be his next invention, a word retractor. I bet it would sell a gazillion copies. One to every single person on earth for starters.

Jack turns toward me slowly, and I keep my eyes on the steering wheel until motion distracts me up ahead. Billy's car pulls out of the lot, and I click my seatbelt into place.

"Cynthia drives the nicest car her daddy could afford to buy her, and it's clean whenever she makes time to take it for a detail. It's a mess the rest of the time, because she doesn't lift a finger to clean it up herself."

"I bet it looked perfect next to your Tesla." That's it. I need to duct tape my mouth shut.

"And... I need to sell my Tesla now." Jack buckles his seatbelt. "You better go, or we'll lose him."

I slide on a pair of sunglasses and pull forward.

"You're going to sell your Tesla and buy what? A Subaru?" I pull out behind Billy with a smile on my face.

We follow Billy right back to Jimmy Johns. He's only inside for a minute before he emerges with his black insulated bag. We follow him to a dozen other delivery stops and back again. Nothing suspicious happens, unless doing his job with a smile qualifies.

Miracle of miracles, I manage not to say Cynthia's name again.

"I'm guessing his shift ends sometime soon," Jack says. "He mentioned at some point that he has a second job he works in the evenings. Maybe he's uploading from my key logger for extra cash. I doubt he's paid much to deliver subs."

I hope Billy does whatever he's going to do soon. I can't keep driving all over forever. At some point I'll need to take Jack back to the office and leave work to pick up my son. Finally, at four fifteen, Billy leaves Jimmy Johns without any bags to deliver.

I inhale sharply. "Oh, maybe he's headed to meet whoever he's downloading the information for."

"Or he could send the data remotely," Jack says.

Which is, of course, more likely. A face-to-face meet would be moronic. Even so, I hope for it.

We follow him to a Chuck-e-Cheese parking lot. Jack looks sideways at me. "Uh, this is odd."

"Did he mention what his second job might be?" I ask.

Jack shakes his head.

"It may be time for us to confront Billy."

Jack hops out of the car before I've even cut the engine. I have to run to catch up to him after I lock up.

"Wait up."

He turns toward me and shakes his head. "You don't need to come along. Just wait in the car. I promised I'd keep you safe."

Billy turns toward us, all five foot three of him, his eyes wide, his mouth hanging open.

"I think I'll take my chances," I say.

Jack grins. "Suit yourself."

Billy snaps his mouth shut before greeting us. "Uh, hey guys. What's up? I didn't figure you two for Chuck-e-Cheese fans."

"We know about your key logger," Jack says.

Billy's eyes shift to me, clearly hoping I'll explain what Jack's saying. "My what?"

"I think Jack meant to ask you what you're doing at Chuck-e-Cheese."

He scratches his head. "I'm Chuck-e."

"What?" Jack asks.

"You know, I'm the mouse. It's my second job. I don't get enough hours at Jimmy Johns to cover the bills."

"You're the mouse," Jack repeats.

"It's actually kind of fun," Billy says. "The kids love me. If it didn't get so hot in that suit, I'd quit the delivery job and do this full time."

Uh huh. So maybe Billy isn't our guy. "Do you know what a key logger is, Billy?" I ask.

He shakes his head. "Are you locked out of the building or something? Because I swear, I didn't touch anything. I couldn't even find that Jim guy. I had to leave the extra sandwich with the front desk guy."

"Look here, Billy. You may not understand what exactly you're doing," Jack says, "or you may just be playing dumb, but either way, we know you're downloading data when you drop off sandwiches. If you're doing it for extra money, I even understand what got you started. Money gets tight and people get creative, but this is theft. I need you to confess everything you know, or I'm going to have to involve the police."

The color drains from Billy's face. He stumbles back a step. "Mr. Campbell, I would never steal anything from anyone. If things got that bad, I'd move back in with my mom. I swear."

When Jack steps toward poor Billy, his eyes flinty, I imagine how Billy must feel. What if he's innocent? Because if he's dissembling, he's very convincing. Jack's a big guy, and it's clear he works out. He towers over Billy, who looks like he's going to wet his pants and roll over to show his belly any second now.

I put one hand on Jack's arm.

"I think you may be intimidating the wrong person," I say.

Jack turns confused eyes toward me.

"I saw the key logger light up," I say, "but Billy wasn't the only person in the room."

Jack shakes his head. "You said the network was called 'delivery.'"

I nod. "I did, but what types of things would you call a Bluetooth network, if you didn't want anyone to pay attention to it? Delivery. UPS. FedEx. Common, generic words. Something unlikely to arouse suspicion. You certainly wouldn't title it with your actual name. I might have jumped to an erroneous conclusion." I drop my voice to a whisper. "Billy doesn't seem like much of an operative, but someone else does. Someone in the room when I saw that network makes at least as much sense as Billy."

Jack swallows hard and his shoulders slump.

"Uh, do you guys still have questions for me?" Billy shuffles his feet across the pavement toward the entrance to Chuck-e-Cheese.

I shake my head. "No, Billy. We're sorry if we startled you with our misunderstanding."

He bobs his head enough times that I start to worry about him.

"You can go to work," I say. "I promise we won't bother you anymore."

"Good luck, s- s- sir," Billy stammers. "Finding out whoever is stealing from you."

I take a step back toward my car, hoping Jack will follow. He doesn't. I turn and call over my shoulder. "How long did you date Cynthia?"

He frowns at me, but he finally takes a step toward my car. Progress. "I don't know. A few months."

"Was it when you were inventing your last thing? The first idea that got stolen?"

He nods slowly. "The end of that, yes."

"And you mentioned she still comes around sometimes even though you broke up."

He clenches his jaw.

"How often? Like every week or two?"

He shrugs, his eyes clouded. "Maybe."

"In spite of your repeated refusals?" I lift one eyebrow.

"I might have slipped in my resolve once or twice."

I close my eyes. "So she's been around fairly often."

He groans. "How could I be so stupid?"

"In my experience, men's stupidity is usually inversely related to a woman's beauty."

He climbs back into my car, but his eyes don't meet mine. He clearly needs a minute to process this turn of events, so I put the car in gear and head for the office. Jack doesn't stop me, and he doesn't say another word the entire ride back.

7

PAUL

I'm a complete idiot. I've been wracking my brain for months, subjecting employees to background checks and invasive security measures and all along, I was the problem. The girl I was stupid enough to date and then moronic enough to continue to allow into my life has been stealing my ideas and generally ruining my life.

I knew she wasn't a good person. She annoyed me from the beginning, but like Gerty said, my stupidity was directly correlated to the beauty of her face. The only thing I did right was confining Cynthia to knowing me as Jack. I met her as Jack, at the sushi place closest to SITB's office. I never told her my real name or took her to LitUp, thank goodness. I shudder to think what she could have stolen from me there.

Meanwhile, my older brother's been dying to set me up with his perfect fiancé's sister. The one I was too prideful to meet. If she looks anything like Mary, she's beautiful in a much more natural way than stupid Cynthia. What kept me from meeting her?

Pride. Which is basically another way to say I'm a moron.

After Cynthia, the girl I've been most interested in is sitting next to me. An employee. Dating her would be only marginally less boneheaded than dating a scheming socialite. I whip out my phone and text Luke before I can change my mind.

I'M READY TO MEET MARY'S SISTER. SET SOMETHING UP.

I ought to tell him about the train wreck of my startup and beg for his help, but I can't quite bring myself to do that yet. Maybe I can still salvage it on my own.

GREAT. WHEN? Luke texts back.

I'm up to my eyeballs with the launch of our new car battery, and I barely have time to shower with the patent nightmare at SITB. I should tell him sometime after the wedding. I could ask for her phone number so we can text a little beforehand. Except that's a weak move, texting someone back and forth. No, I need to make some kind of tangible step toward something good, something that might be real. Something with someone who isn't a mistake.

TOMORROW, I finally text back. After all, sleep is overrated, right?

I'LL SEE IF SHE'S FREE, Luke texts back. I'LL LET YOU KNOW.

I put my phone back in my pocket. We're almost back to the office.

"We think it's Cynthia." Gerty's voice sounds wobbly. "But we won't know until we have evidence."

She's right, of course. It could still be Billy. Or neither of them. Maybe someone we couldn't even see was standing outside the door. We need to get proof, especially since I really doubt my socialite ex stole my ideas for herself. If she really was downloading, she's got to be working for someone. Which means she was probably paid to be my girlfriend in the first place. Which Gerty must have figured out already, but she's too polite to mention out loud.

I shudder. I need a hot shower right now, but I know that's a silly compulsion. Water won't clean away the dirty feeling I've got.

"Any ideas on how we can get that evidence?" I ask. "I'd rather do it sooner than later. We have a patent hearing next week to sort this preliminarily."

Tiny furrows appear in Gerty's brow. "If it's her, the evidence would be on her phone right now from the latest download. If I could clone her phone, we could prove she was stealing information. As to the buyer, I'd think you could force her to confess that information in court once the judge hears Cynthia placed a key logger. We might even find the information we want on her device, if she doesn't realize we cloned it."

I nod. Gerty's bright. Brighter than I expected from such a young person, and a brand new hire at that. If she hadn't discovered and surrendered the key logger to me herself, I'd heavily suspect Gerty right now. I hope I'm not being blinded by a pretty face again.

"We need her phone?" I ask.

She nods, her eyes on the road. "I think you need to take her to dinner tonight. I can walk you through how to clone her phone."

The idea of taking Cynthia out and pretending I'm interested, especially now that we know she was probably a plant, causes bile to rise in the back of my throat. But my anger surpasses my disgust. I'm ticked enough to do whatever it takes. I dial her number.

"Jack," she practically purrs when she answers. "I knew you'd want to hear me out, once all those people were gone. We've always been so much better one-on-one."

I grunt. "I thought you might want to grab dinner with me tonight, just the two of us."

"Of course I do," Cynthia says. "I've been craving Drift."

Cynthia only eats fish, so we went to Drift a lot. "Sounds great. Meet you there at seven?"

"Perfect. I'm so glad you called, Jack."

I can't bring myself to lie and say the same. "Uh huh. See you then." I hang up.

Gerty pulls into a space in the parking lot outside SITB's office and turns to face me with an earnest look. "Okay, how much do you know about the cloning process?"

Hold up. "Wait, you aren't coming?"

"On your date?" she asks. "Uh, no. Besides, I'm busy tonight. But I can walk you through what I know about it."

"How am I even supposed to get her phone?" I ask. "It's not like that's a normal thing for me to do. I'm not a snoop."

"I'm sure you'll think of something." Her smirk annoys me.

"That's it? It's nearly five, so you're clocking out and I have to fend for myself?"

She sighs dramatically. "You're a big boy. You got yourself into this mess. . ."

"Maybe I did." My voice sounds a little whiny, which probably isn't helping my case. "But when you get right down to it, we don't know whether it is Cynthia for sure. I could really use a little help from someone who already knows how to do all the tech stuff. Plus, I might need your testimony at the hearing or it'll sound like a lover's spat."

"Blech," she says. "I want nothing to do with you and your girlfriend's drama, frankly."

I grit my teeth. "I dumped her a really long time ago. It's been a rough couple of months though, and she's been persistent, okay? Look, I'm not perfect, but I'm not the villain here. I really need your help to figure out the identity of the real bad guy. Cynthia's way too dumb to mastermind something like this."

"Or maybe she's been playing you and she's actually a Harvard grad."

I lift one eyebrow. "She thought limes turned into lemons. And if you left the lemon for long enough, into a grapefruit."

She snorts.

"She also told me she was so upset that Tom Cruise didn't win when he ran for President."

Gerty's mouth drops, and then her mouth shakes with suppressed laughter. "Ted Cruz, Tom Cruise. Potato, poh-tah-to."

I laugh.

Gerty taps her lip. "She could have made that stuff up to convince you."

"She thought the Eiffel Tower was really called the Awful Tower, and she called the end zone in football the 'in zone.'" I let the last one sink in. "Do I need to go on, or do you believe that she's not the mastermind?"

"I believe you, but I've lost a little more respect for you." Gerty smirks.

"Which means I'm probably not convincing you to cancel your plans and help a desperate guy out?"

She sighs. "I'll see if I can work something out, but even if I can, I'd have to meet you there."

"Fine," I say. "That's fine. It's probably better anyway. I'll reserve two tables, and make sure one is out of the way. Actually, it shouldn't take you too long to clone a phone, right? Maybe you can bring your date along. He'd be a good cover for you."

She frowns, and her eyebrows furrow again. I want to reach up and wipe that frown away, but that would be weird, so I clench my fist instead. "Or not, but if you want to bring him, that's fine. That's all I'm saying."

"You're assuming my plans are a date."

"Aren't they?" I hope they aren't. I don't want her to have a boyfriend, or worse, a husband. Even though I shouldn't care. I clearly fall for all the wrong women. Not that I'm falling for Gerty. At all.

"I'll be there at seven," she says. "Ready to clone Cynthia's phone, and with a date for cover."

I nod. "I really appreciate it. This is really above and beyond. And maybe we better exchange phone numbers, in case we need to check in at the restaurant."

"Good idea." She rattles her number off and I save it. Then I do the same.

She clears her throat.

"Yeah?" I ask.

"Not to be rude, but if I'm going to pull this off, I better start shifting things around."

"Right. Absolutely. Of course." She needs me to get out of the car. I open the door, but I pause because I don't want to leave her. I don't want to eat dinner with Cynthia while Gerty's eating at the edge of the restaurant with her boyfriend. I open my mouth to ask her out for real for tomorrow. Besides, I'd rather know now if she's got a boyfriend. It would be better to know.

Except tomorrow I'm supposed to be going out with Luke's soon-to-be sister-in-law. Maybe.

A set-up I agreed to because I'm a moron and a bad judge of character, which is exactly why I can't ask Gerty out. I force myself to climb out of her car and head for the office. I ought to make sure the whole place didn't burn down without me or Nancy around to hold things together.

I should be looking forward to confronting Cynthia and tracking down my thieving competitor. I should be excited to meet a great girl tomorrow night for dinner.

Except I keep thinking about sky blue eyes and light brown hair. When I reach my office, I sink into the chair and lean back. My phone buzzes.

BAD TIMING. TRUDY'S BUSY. MAYBE IN A FEW WEEKS.

I should be upset, or at the very least I should feel annoyed. I finally want to meet Mary's baby sister and she's too busy for me? Instead, all I feel is relief, because right or wrong, Mary's little sister isn't the woman I want to take to dinner tomorrow night.

8

TRUDY

My phone buzzes in my pocket before I can pull out of the parking lot. I check it before leaving, since I never ever text while driving.

Mary texts, YOU FREE TOMORROW NIGHT? I KNOW YOU SAID NO LAST WEEK, BUT LUKE AND I REALLY WANT TO SET YOU UP WITH PAUL.

Is she kidding? How could I have been clearer?

BUSY. SORRY.

ARE YOU REALLY BUSY? Mary asks. IT DOESN'T HAVE TO BE A DATE, BUT IT WOULD BE NICE IF YOU KNEW EACH OTHER BEFORE THE WEDDING.

I'M SLAMMED. NEED TO STUDY. WORKING. PLUS KID. PLUS JOB.

IT'S A SATURDAY NIGHT. TROY WILL BE ASLEEP. WE CAN COME OVER TO YOUR PLACE.

ONCE HE'S ASLEEP, I'LL BE STUDYING. AND I WANT TO PLAY WITH TROY ALL DAY. I'VE

MISSED HIM EVERY SINGLE DAY WHILE I'VE BEEN AT WORK.

ALRIGHT, FINE. RAINCHECK?

SURE, I text. But she knows it's my way of saying 'no way' politely. I'll have to meet this guy at the wedding, and I'll be very nice when I do, but I'm not going to get shoved into some kind of unbelievably awkward date before then. Besides, what if he is adorable and I fall for him, and he doesn't like me back. Or what if we get super lucky and he likes me and I like him? I've still got way too many things to accomplish before I'm ready for something like that. So, just, no.

I call Paisley through my Bluetooth in the car on my way to pick up Troy. Pick up, pick up. Luckily she does, right before it would have gone to voicemail. "Hello?"

"Oh thank gosh you answered," I say. "I'm calling to ask you for a major favor."

"Why Trudy, it's so nice to hear from you too," Paisley says. "I've had a busy week, but I'd love to hear about your new job."

"Yeah, yeah. I'm sorry I'm skipping over all the niceties. I should call Mary, but I'm sure she'll be stuck at work until like ten p.m. Plus, I'd be too embarrassed to tell her what I need and why."

"Now you've piqued my curiosity," Paisley says. "So I guess I'll forgive your atrocious manners for now. What do you need so badly?"

"First, a confession. I might have a crush on my boss."

Silence.

"I know, I know," I say. "It's idiotic, and I'm aware of that. I'm not doing anything about it, but he needs my help tonight. It's a long story and something I can't really share details on, but let's just say, we knew they needed an IT person, and tonight I have a chance to audition. Sort of.

But to do it, I need someone to watch Troy. Do you have plans?"

"Actually I do," she says. "My brother's visiting."

Paisley has a brother? I always assumed she was an only child. She mentions her parents sometimes, but she's never mentioned anyone else. Actually, I don't even know where she's from. I'm a terrible friend. But now is not the time to rectify that. One thing at a time. "Oh. Crap. Don't worry about it then. I'll see if Pam can help me out."

"My brother loves kids," she says. "So he's sitting next to me saying it's fine."

Inspiration clobbers me over the head. "Actually," I say softly. "What does your brother look like?"

She giggles. "He's kind of a fox. I mean, he looks like a manly version of me. Why do you ask?"

A masculine version of Paisley? I try to imagine all that manic energy, bossy pushiness, and bubbly vivacity shoved into the body of a guy and my brain reboots.

"Why do you ask?" Paisley prompts.

"Uh, I sort of need a cover for my audition. My boss wants me to bring a date if I can. Dinner's included, if that helps, and at a nice place, too. If you wouldn't mind watching Troy, it shouldn't take too long, and your brother will get a free dinner out of the deal."

"Let me ask him and I'll message you back," she says.

"You would be saving me," I say. "Seriously."

"Uh huh," Paisley says. "I'm already practically a saint, you know, with all the stuff I do for you and your sister. And if I agree to this, you better bring back some amazing take out."

"Of course," I promise.

I'm buckling Troy into his seat when Paisley texts me. WE'LL DO IT. HOW NICE SHOULD COLE DRESS?

WE'RE GOING TO DRIFT FISH HOUSE.

She sends back a heart eyes emoji. I've never been there, but I'm gathering it's nice, which stresses me out. Forget Cole. What am *I* supposed to wear?

I rush to feed Troy dinner once we're home. Then I race to my room and put on a grey skirt and pink button down shirt. After all, spring is theoretically around the corner.

I hear a knock at the door, but by the time I get outside, Troy's already opened it, and he's watering that stupid dead daisy.

"Troy," I say, with as gentle a reprimand as I can manage. "Don't answer the door, baby. It could have been anyone." Including your insane father.

"It's Aunt Paiswey," he says. "She told me that through the door. And she has some guy with her."

"It's her brother," I say absently.

I take the dripping watering can from Troy and glance up at Paisley's brother. And up and up. I freeze with my mouth hanging open stupidly. Cole is tall. Like, *tall*, tall. At least six four, maybe six five. And he's got coal black hair, and bright green eyes.

Not gold like Paisley's eyes or hazel like most people who call their eyes green. Not even the bluish green of Mary's, which is plenty uncommon already. Cole's eyes are the green of emeralds, or a super shiny holly leaf. Or a bough of evergreen, or bright green paint, maybe. Once I finally stop gaping at his eyes, I notice that his jaw is chiseled and his nose aquiline.

Oh. My. Word.

If Jack likes me even a little bit, this guy will be perfect.

"I hear I'm your fake date tonight." Cole's voice is deep, like Mufasa in the Lion King. Troy loves that movie, so I've seen it way too many times. "And I'm supposed to make your boss jealous?" Cole grins and my ovaries faint.

"Something like that," I say. "But it's less about making him jealous, and more about acting as my cover so I can get the information he needs. He'll be on a date a few tables over, and I need to see whether the woman he's with stole some valuable information from him."

Cole's eyebrows rise approvingly. "This gets more and more interesting. Plus, I love lobster and it's hard to come by at home."

"At home?" I smile. Maybe he'll tell me where home is, and then I don't have to admit I have no idea where Paisley's really from.

He doesn't take the bait.

"Then you really will love tonight," I finally say, "because we're both getting the lobster. And one to go for your amazing sister."

Paisley picks up Troy and carries him behind me into the kitchen where I'm emptying the watering can into the sink.

"That all sounds great," she says. "But."

I turn around to face her. "But what?"

She points at me.

"What?"

"You aren't wearing that," she says. "How well do I know you?" She raises her eyebrows knowingly at Cole. "What did I say?"

Cole's mouth turns up naturally into a smolder. "She said you'd be wearing a 'kindergarten teacher ensemble.'"

"And I was right, she is!" Paisley purses her lips. "Well, grab it then."

"Wait, grab what?" I ask, but Cole's already ducking out the door.

Paisley just shakes her head when I look at her, and before I can complain, Cole's back with a black garment bag over his arm.

"What exactly is that?" I ask.

"It's the right dress for the job."

I groan and take it from him. When I unzip the bag in my room, I discover a short, low cut black dress with crisscrossing straps all over the back. I'll have no room for breathing, much less eating lobster. "I can't wear this," I yell.

"She said you'd say that, too," Cole says.

"Just try it on," Paisley says. "I'm here doing you this last minute favor. The least you can do is humor me."

I grumble, but I put it on, and then I walk out to show them how awful it looks. I could barely get the zipper to go all the way up. Clearly I'm too fat for this dress.

"See?" I spin in a circle, wishing heartily that Cole wasn't also in the room.

Paisley shakes her head and turns to Cole. "She's wearing that."

His eyes are wide. "Definitely. I've never seen a kindergarten teacher that hot."

This two Paisleys thing is bad for my blood pressure. I hope this gorgeous man hunk will be headed home soon, wherever that is. He may be beautiful, but he's pushier than his sister. "Fine. I'll go to this stupid thing half naked, but we need to leave soon, or we'll be late."

"Mom you're leaving? To go where?"

Troy's tiny voice stops me in my tracks. I crouch down so we're eye level. "I'm sorry baby. Mom has to help her boss out, but it's almost your bedtime. So I'll only miss out on a few minutes with you."

His frown breaks my heart. "Can you read me *I'll Love You Forever* first?"

Jack can wait. My baby can't. I pull Troy close and rub his curls between my fingers. "Yes, baby, I can."

Troy's tiny legs pump as he runs into his bedroom and

finds his favorite book. It always makes me cry, no matter how many times I've read it, so by the time I'm done, my mascara is smudged. Paisley wipes her fingers under my eyes and cups my face in her hands. "You've got this. And I'll take great care of your angel."

My heart swells a little bit and I wonder sometimes if that's how life works. Someone awful comes along and torches your heart just to watch it burn. All that's left is a hard black lump, but over time, kind acts of friends and family restore the blood flow. Bit by bit, my heart's starting to pump again. Mary. Troy. Paisley.

"Thank you Pais. It means a lot."

She grins. "Anything for one of my Wiggin girls."

I grab my purse and my black wool peacoat. "Ready to go, Cole?"

"Absolutely." He opens the door for me and takes my arm in his. "Did your son plant seeds in that pot? It seems a little early in the season for that."

I glance down at the mushy black and brown mess of dead daisies and laugh. "Not seeds, no. He thinks if he waters it, that plant might come back. Obviously that's not going to help, because that thing is dead."

"Kids are funny," Cole says. "But it's good he's so hopeful, especially since you're pretty recently divorced, right?" I realize he has a faint accent, but I can't place it. It's not like Luke's, so Australia's probably out.

Cole insists on opening my car door, too. Once we're in the car, I answer his question.

"Troy's dad left us back in September. I hid for a while, like an ostrich with my head in the sand. I knew he was gone, but I guess I was paralyzed by what that might do to Troy. I finally filed for divorce in December. Of course, it wasn't final until the first of February, and it only went so quick because he literally could not wait to ditch us. I didn't have anything he wanted, and I didn't ask for anything from him. I only recently filed the forms for child support garnishment."

"That sounds rough, but Troy seems okay with all of it, and you do, too. Good for you, getting out and finding a job. And apparently finding an attractive boss as well."

I laugh. "It's not really like that. Actually, I'm doing my boss a big favor. I think he was worried if I showed up alone, his ex-girlfriend would immediately spot me. She met me at the office today and wasn't my biggest fan."

"So I'm here less to make some guy jealous and more to pull off an operation?" He raises one eyebrow.

"Which is exactly what I told Paisley."

"I'll admit, I'm a little disappointed, but you're beautiful enough I don't mind much."

My cheeks heat up, but it's dark enough I'm sure he can't see. "Where are you from, anyway? I've known Paisley forever, but for some reason I thought she was from somewhere around here. You sound exotic though. I'm realizing I'm not a very good friend."

Cole lifts his eyebrow. "Paisley said you and Mary and some woman named Geo are her best friends in the world."

I nod. "I don't disagree. I see her several times a week, and Mary sees her every day, obviously."

"And she hasn't told you where she's from?"

I glance his way. "I didn't know she had a brother until today. I expected you to be really weird, or ugly, or embarrassing. Now that we've met, I have no idea why she never mentioned you."

Cole frowns. "I don't think it's my place to say, not if Paisley hasn't been forthcoming. But I'll warn you about one thing. I'm here because my parents have requested that she return home."

My tiny charred heart stutters. "I need her."

"Our family needs her too. More than you do."

I don't press Cole for any more information, afraid to poke the bear. I can't survive Paisley leaving. I just can't, and it feels like asking him about where he and Paisley are from led to this anvil dropping. Her family wants to summon her home? I don't know where it is, but I don't even want to contemplate her leaving Atlanta. Leaving me.

When we arrive, ten minutes late, our table is waiting just like Jack said it would be. Cole and I follow the hostess toward the corner of the restaurant, and I don't see Jack or Cynthia anywhere. At least, not until we're two steps away from our table. That's when Jack comes into view. His eyes light up when he sees me and I smile. Then his gaze shifts sideways toward Cole and he glowers.

I toss my hands up in the air. He told me to bring a date. I whip out my phone. WHAT'S YOUR DEAL?

YOUR BOYFRIEND'S TALL. FREAKISHLY TALL. I BET HE HAS MARFAN SYNDROME.

I roll my eyes. HE HAS NO SUCH THING. BUT IF HE DID, YOU'D BE PRETTY INSENSITIVE TO SAY THAT.

OKAY FINE, I'M SORRY. Tiny dots appear, and then the words, YOU'RE LATE.

BUT I'M HERE AS PROMISED. NOW GET YOUR GIRLFRIEND'S PHONE ALREADY.

I SHOULD STEAL IT AND THEN JUST LOB IT AT YOU?

That earns him an eye roll emoji. IS HER PHONE LOCKED?

IT NEEDS A PASSWORD, YES.

THEN I NEED HER TO ENTER HER ITUNES PASSWORD IN THE TEN MINUTES BEFORE I ACCESS IT OR I WON'T BE ABLE TO GET IN.

"You text really fast," Cole says. "What did you say your job was? Professional texter?"

I smile. "Not yet. But I'm hoping to go pro by September if everything falls into place."

He grins back at me and now that my hormones are done going haywire, I can totally see Paisley in his features. "You're funny." He glances down at his menu. "Have you been here before?"

I shake my head. "Nope, but seeing as neither of us are paying, I vote for lobster rolls, lobster bisque and lobster tails. How does that sound?"

Cole grins at me. "You had me at lobster."

"Clearly we see eye to eye, or we would if I was about a foot and a half taller."

"You are pretty short."

I gasp. "I'm normal. You're just ridiculously tall."

"Maybe in America."

I really, really want to pry after that bizarre comment. Does that mean Paisley's not American? And if she's not from some small town in the Midwest like I assumed, where is she from?

My phone buzzes. HOW AM I SUPPOSED TO GET HER TO LEAVE WITHOUT HER PHONE?

ASK HER TO SET A NEW PHOTO OF YOU AS HER LOCK SCREEN, THEN SET YOUR HAND ON HER WRIST AND COMPLIMENT HER. SHE'LL DROP IT. MENTION SHE'S GOT LIPSTICK ON HER TEETH AND SHE'LL RUSH OFF TO THE BATHROOM WITHOUT IT.

THAT'S PRETTY GOOD, Jack texts back. WHAT ABOUT THE ITUNES PASSWORD?

CAN'T YOU DO ANYTHING YOURSELF?

He shrugs at me sheepishly and everyone in between us disappears.

TELL HER YOU WANT HER TO DOWNLOAD A NEW RING TONE FOR YOU. ENDLESS LOVE.

NOT FUNNY.

I glance his way and he's still staring at me. If he's not careful, Cynthia's going to look this way and recognize me. FOCUS ON YOUR DATE, IDIOT.

"I assume all that texting is with the guy over there who's been looking at you like you're air and he's asphyxiating?" Cole asks.

I set my phone down. "Yeah, that's my boss."

"Good news. If any part of you wanted to make him jealous, it's working."

"What?" I ask. "Why do you say that?"

"That guy hates me more than the French hate American tourists," Cole says.

The waiter arrives with our lobster rolls and bisque, but as soon as he leaves, Cole grabs my spoon.

"Hey, I'm hungry," I say.

He nods his head. "Of course you are. Now follow my lead." He scoops up a spoonful of my soup and holds it out to me.

"Oh, gross. There's no way I'd be one of those people."

He grins at me. "Come on. You adore me. I fill your heart with sparkling stars and rainbow-pooping unicorns. You'd share spaghetti with me just to kiss me over a noodle."

I snort. "Oh please."

He shakes the spoon at me. "Trust me."

I lean forward and take a bite, grinning like an idiot the whole time.

My phone buzzes. I DID THE RING TONE THING. I COULDN'T THINK OF ANYTHING BETTER. I'LL BRING HER PHONE TO THE COAT CHECK CLOSET IN TWO MINUTES.

I look up at Cole. "It's almost go time."

He nods. "What do you want me to do?"

"Other than bail me out if this bombs and I'm hauled off to jail?"

He laughs. "Yes, other than that."

I shake my head. "Hopefully nothing but eat lots of food and act casual. But if I'm gone more than five minutes, maybe come find me. I'm aiming to get this done quickly in the coat check closet."

"Got it."

I bolt my soup to calm my growling stomach, and also to give my shaking hands something to do.

"You look nervous," Cole says.

"The thing is, I know how to do this in theory," I say. "And I've got my old phone handy to use, so I won't have to involve my actual phone. But I'm still a little nervous. I mean, did you drive a car flawlessly the first time you tried?"

His smile's cocky, so cocky. "I could yeah, but I understand your point. Not everyone can be as amazing as me."

I want to roll my eyes, but judging from his appearance, he may be one of those disgustingly perfect people. Too bad I'm not. "Some of us botch things up on the regular."

"Oh I've made my share of terrible mistakes."

"Let's put a pin in that one for later," I say, "because now I'm intrigued. But—"

Cynthia stands up and rushes toward the restroom. Jack picks up her phone and slides it into his pocket. I meet Cole's eye and leave for the coat check, my purse over my shoulder.

His whisper follows me. "Good luck."

I hope that wish works, because cloning a phone is a crime. I really don't need to add a rap sheet to my existing court records. One divorce is more than enough drama for my lifetime.

Jack must have tipped the coat check attendant big time, because the second I arrive he motions me past him. I duck below the rack of outerwear and slide past scads of coats hanging in rows. Jack's standing in a small alcove in the back.

"Ready to work your magic?" he asks.

I sure hope so.

9

PAUL

When I place the phone into Gerty's small hands, my fingers brush against hers. I close my eyes and remind myself that she works for me. I'd step back a little to give her space, except we're standing in a two by two foot cube. If I back up, a casual passer-by would be able to see me. There isn't really anywhere else to go.

Her fingers fly over the phone. "Did she enter her iTunes password?"

"Yeah, but why does that matter?"

"It's an old trick, and I hope it works. It'll only work once, if it does at all."

"What are you going to do if it doesn't work?" he asks.

"Let's hope it does." She presses the home button and asks, "Siri, what time is it?"

Cynthia's phone displays a clock with the time. Gerty taps on the clock, which brings up the world clock screen. Then she taps on the timer option and selects "when timer ends." She scrolls to the top of the list and selects 'Buy More Ringtones.'

That opens the Apple Store.

Gerty hits the home button and opens the phone, completely unlocked. I swear under my breath. It's pretty disconcerting that with one little backdoor, like the owner entering an iTunes password in the past few minutes, Gerty can loop around the phone's security. "That's amazing."

"Don't distract me," she says. "We don't have much time."

"Do you see anything?" I ask.

Her fingers fly past screens so fast I can't even tell what she's doing. "Yep," she says. "It's here. Look, see the network?" She shows me. Delivery, just like she said. She takes a screenshot of it, forwards several files to another email address, and deletes the file send path.

Then she starts doing something I don't understand.

"What's going on now?" I ask.

"I'm cloning her phone so we can send messages from it and receive hers, too."

She finishes and hands the phone back to me. When her sky blue eyes meet mine, I've never been more impressed by any woman in my life. I know a lot of genius researchers, but some of them can't tie their shoes. This woman is smart and capable, and heart stoppingly lovely. "You did all that in minutes, while remaining completely calm. How many times have you done this before?"

"Never." Her eyes are wide, her mouth parted. Almost invitingly.

"You've never done that?" I ask. "And you did it that fast? Without any issues?"

"It's a good thing it worked," she says. "Because you need to get back with this or Miss America will start to suspect your absence."

I reach for the phone, but she reaches around my hand and slides it into my suit pocket.

"How's dinner going for you?" I can't quite keep myself from prying. "Was he upset you asked to change your plans?"

She turns up to look at me like I knew she would, her lips parted again, and her hair tumbling down over her shoulders in messy curls. I lean down without thinking and press my lips against hers. She curls into me with a tiny sigh and my arms reach around behind her back to pull her closer still. Her lips move softly against mine, and a voracious hunger consumes me. I want more, so much more.

"Excuse me," a deep voice says behind us at coat check. "You haven't seen my date, have you? She's wearing a black dress and silver heels. She thought she left her phone in her jacket and came back to look for it. It's been almost five minutes since she headed this way."

Gerty stiffens next to me and I back away from her, pushing flat against the wall. Her voice wavers when she speaks. "I better go."

I nod. "Call me when you get home so we can go over what we found."

She swallows and tucks her hair behind her ear. I want to reach out and trace the line of her jaw. I want to press my fingers against her lips. I want to drag her toward me and claim her mouth again. But that's moronic. The guy five feet away is probably her boyfriend. The perfect Adonis guy with the exotic accent.

But she trembled against me when I kissed her, and she sighed. Unless I'm misreading everything. After all, I'm her boss, and I just badgered her into coming here to do something illegal. Then I kissed her in a coat check closet like a creeper.

She ducks out, and I follow thirty seconds after. When I head back for my table, Gerty and her date are already eating lobster. Good for her, ordering the most expensive thing on the menu.

Cynthia looks distinctly annoyed about being alone. "Where did you go?"

"I had a call and didn't want to be rude to the restaurant's other guests. It's about my new prototype and I had to take it, so I stepped out. I'm sorry you had to sit alone."

She looks around. "Thanks to your leaving, I think my phone may have been stolen. I left it at the table when I went to the restroom, but now it's gone."

I point at the ground. "Is that it?"

She curves around to look, but I dart ahead of her and pull her phone out of my pocket. "Is this it?"

I hand it to her and she glances at the screen. Locked. She beams at me. "You are so smart. I swear I looked everywhere, but it must have been hiding under the foot of the table."

"I do my best."

The rest of dinner is pure torture, trying to pay attention to what Cynthia's saying when all I really want to do is go introduce myself to Gerty's date and find out who he is to her. His coloring is too different to be her brother, and he called her his date. Still, maybe he's just a friend? Or a cousin perhaps? She chastised me for assuming her plans were a date with a twinkle in her eye. Didn't she mention she was still in school? He could be a professor, maybe?

I'm grasping at straws here, but they aren't wearing rings, so at least I can assume they aren't married. The waiter shows up with both checks in the same folder like I asked.

"Hello?" She snaps at me. Cynthia must have asked something and I tuned it out.

"Oh, sorry. What was that?"

"I said, your place or mine?" She bats her eyes.

I put down enough cash for both checks, including the food Gerty ordered to go.

"I think something I ate didn't agree with me. I feel nauseous." That's true enough, although the cause of my nausea is actually the thought of Cynthia trying to extend this date one second longer than necessary. "I better head home."

"You're sending very mixed signals, Mr. Campbell." She's trying for coquettish, I think, but it comes off both petty and shrill.

"Let me be clear, then. I invited you here tonight for one reason." I consider telling her the bald truth, but that would tip my hand. "I wanted to very kindly, very rationally, inform you that we are entirely done. You aren't welcome at my home or at my office, or anywhere else. You didn't seem to understand me earlier, and I loathe big scenes at my office or elsewhere, but you and I are entirely incompatible. I'll inform my receptionist not to let you back again, and I've changed my gate code so you shouldn't try my house either."

Her mouth drops in a very satisfying way.

"Thanks for meeting me for dinner, and I wish you the very best in the future."

She stands up and grabs my hand before I can walk away. "You don't mean that."

I shrug. "Actually, you're right. I don't."

She sighs in relief. "You have such a weird sense of humor, Jack. I swear, sometimes I don't get you at all."

"Oh, I wasn't making a joke earlier," I say. "All of that was true. I didn't really mean it when I wished you the best in the future. I don't care much what happens to you tomorrow or any day after that. It's just something people say."

I don't wait to see how she takes it, and I don't look

back when she exclaims in outrage. I stride toward the door purposefully and drive home like a madman. Once I'm home, I decide to go for a run instead of just staring at my phone. After all, I have no idea how late it will be before Gerty's date is over and she contacts me.

Four miles later, I shower. Only after I'm clean and dry and dressed do I allow myself to glance at my phone screen.

Gerty texted me twenty minutes ago. I THINK WE HAVE WHAT YOU NEED.

I call her, hoping she can talk.

"Hello?" she whispers.

Is she still with that guy? Worse, is he asleep next to her? I stifle a groan.

"Are you okay?" she asks, not whispering this time.

"I'm fine. Just wondered why you were whispering. I mean, I'm obviously dying to know what you found, but I've completely taken over your life and I feel bad about it."

"I am exhausted," she says, "but I've been distracted decoding the files I found. And there's definitely correspondence between Miss Dalton and a man named Bennett Parker. He's an executive with a company called WelshAllyn. They're a pretty famous medical equipment manufacturer, right?"

I lean back against the headboard of my bed. "They are, yeah. I've got a meeting with them next week, actually. Can you send me what you found?"

"Sure. What email address do you want to use?"

I can't give her my SITB one. Thanks to the key logger, they can probably access that email. But I can't give her my real email address without telling her my real name, which gets sticky. I trust her, but do I trust her that much?

"Actually," I say, "Why don't you give me yours. I'll email you in a minute, and then you can reply with the documents."

"That's fine," she says. "Mine is Jenky Girl 123 at gmail dot com. And yes, I know that's a stupid email address, but I've had it for a while."

I wish I could see her face right now. She's so pretty when she blushes.

Which I should not be thinking about.

There is absolutely no way she can work with me every single day as my assistant. It'll drive me mad, but I can't fire her. That would be utterly unfair. She's been an absolute champ. She basically saved both me and the company in the last twenty-four hours.

"Hey, listen," I say.

"Yeah?" her voice is husky.

I imagine she's lying in bed just like me. I wonder what her pajamas look like. I shake my head to clear it. "You've gone way above and way beyond. I know you didn't want to be my assistant."

"It's been fun, actually."

"Even so," I say. "What you really wanted was an IT spot."

"True," she says tentatively, clearly unsure where I'm going with this.

"Well, consider that my repayment for your help. I'm promoting you to head of Information Technology for SITB. If you need an assistant in there, well, we can hire you one. But as of Monday, you'll be IT manager, not my administrative assistant. You're clearly too talented to be stuck doing scheduling and files."

"That's so generous of you," she says. "Thanks. A lot."

"It comes with a pay raise," I say. "Of course."

Silence.

"Hello?" Is she still there?

"I don't even know what to say," she says.

"Being speechless is fine for now, but I hope you're okay

with testifying next week. Because the second we get off the phone, I'm calling my lawyer. This is such amazing news."

"Well, don't let me keep you." Her voice is small. Is she upset for some reason? Or does she just want to get off the phone with her absurdly inappropriate and possibly way out of line boss? Oh my gosh, is she going to sue me? Was I that off base?

"Thanks again," I say. "I'll send you an email momentarily." As soon as I can set up a new account.

"Goodnight Mr. Campbell."

"Sleep well, Miss Jenkins."

Even though the files she sends me have everything she said and more, I can't sleep, not for hours. I keep thinking about her soft curls, her sky blue eyes, and her long legs in that black dress.

10

TRUDY

I spend all day Saturday doing anything and everything Troy wants, and we stay up late watching a *Cars* marathon on Saturday night. Sunlight streaming down on my face wakes me up on Sunday morning and I stretch luxuriously. Days when a mom can sleep in are good days.

I still can't quite believe that, thanks to my resourcefulness, I'm the new IT manager at a startup. It's my dream job, and one that should have taken me a year or two to achieve. Maybe more. I should be giddy. I should be on cloud nine. I can cross something huge off the list on my nightstand. I pick it up and look at the lofty goals I created for my new life.

I crumple the stupid list in my hand.

Before I have time to try and puzzle out my bizarre lack of excitement regarding my promotion, Troy pads into my room, his 'blue blue' blanket trailing behind him. "Mommy, someone's knocking at the door."

I pick up my phone and look at the clock. Nine-fourteen a.m. Troy needs breakfast soon. I shouldn't have slept in, but who in the world would come over this early on a

Sunday? I swing my feet out of bed and into a pair of slippers. I shiver and pull a jacket on over my pajama t-shirt. "It's okay, baby. I'll come answer it. I'm glad you didn't already open it."

Troy tilts his head and scrunches his nose. "Uh, I never answer the door. You told me a lot and lot of times."

I pat his head on my way past. "I'm glad you were listening."

Could it be Chris? My pulse accelerates and my hands shake at the thought. Per the court order, he's not supposed to come by my house at all. His parents supervise his visits with Troy when he asks for one. The court ordered not more than twice a month, but he's only requested to see him twice since leaving us.

Luckily, my former in-laws seem to understand he isn't responsible enough to take Troy on his own, at least, not until Troy's old enough to manage his diabetes himself. If Chris ever demonstrates enough discipline to learn about managing it, then we can revisit the idea. Seeing as he didn't even want to *have the baby at all* when we found out we were pregnant, I doubt he's about to reverse his level of interest without some other motivating factor.

I did just file for garnishment of his wages. He could be here to yell at me for that. I've been expecting it.

"Please don't be Chris," I whisper softly. "Not today, not here." I force myself to breathe in and out, and then I walk to the door. I wish Mary had a peephole. Since she doesn't, I hold my phone in one hand, ready to dial 911 if necessary. I shift the door open a few inches, slowly.

The old man standing in front of me braces himself on a cane to stand upright. He couldn't possibly look less like my ex-husband. Underneath a puffy jacket, his blue shirt buttons down, but the buttons are skewed by one and his grey pants look two sizes too big. His sky blue eyes light up when he sees me, and I realize inasmuch as he looks nothing like my ex, there are a few similarities between them.

"Hey Daddy," I say. "Long time no see."

"Gertrude!" He lifts one shaky hand toward my face, like he wants to touch me.

I step back from him and his eyes fall to look at his feet. "I was hoping we could talk."

"Who is that, Mommy?" Troy asks.

His head pokes around my leg, and I pull him toward me and close the door until there's only an inch of space through which to see. "Go play with your new train table, baby. Mom's got to talk to this man for a minute."

Troy's curious eyes peer at my pathetic father, looking him up and down. Eventually he shrugs and turns around like I asked.

My dad's eyes fill with tears. It might work on someone else, but I don't appreciate the obvious manipulation. I've endured years and years of his crocodile tears anytime things were bad to inure me to them.

"My grandson," he chokes out. "He's so beautiful."

"He is." My voice is flat. "What do you want, Dad?"

He looks up at the sky as though praying and then turns back toward me. "Can't I come inside for a moment? I need to talk to you. I knew Mary would slam the door in my face."

"Oh please," I say. "Don't act like I'm a monster. I come visit you four times a year. It usually takes me days to track you down first, and you're almost always drunk as a skunk. I haven't shut you out of my life or abandoned you. I'm just keeping a healthy distance between you and my perfectly beautiful baby. I think that's a reasonable boundary, Dad."

He looks so frail this time, like a stiff wind could knock

him off the steps and he'd shatter like a glass vase on the ground below.

It's like he can sense that my resolve is wavering. "I'm sorry about that. I need to apologize to you, but it's so cold out here."

I glance behind me at the junker car parked in my driveway. The passenger door is red. The rest of the car is silver. Except the back fender, which is blue. "Your project car?" I ask.

He nods.

Dad always works on a project car when he's sober enough. Once he sold one for an eight hundred dollar profit and in a fit of generosity, he bought Mary and me both our own pair of rollerblades. It's the only gift I can recall him ever giving me, other than the occasional black eye if I riled him up while he was hammered. "Sit out there while I feed Troy. Once I've got him fed, I'll turn a movie on for him and let you come inside."

He nods and hobbles down the stairs. I really hope this isn't a terrible mistake. Once Troy has swallowed his last bite, I turn on Mickey Mouse for him in my bedroom and wave my dad into my tiny breakfast nook.

"Did you want some coffee?" I ask.

"Do you have any tea?" he asks.

"Since when do you drink tea?"

"I'm avoiding anything with addictive substances of any kind," he says. "Coffee has caffeine and it makes me jittery."

I cross my arms and glare at him. "You're telling me you're actually sober? Like, for more than two days? Or because you can't afford booze? Are you here because you need money?"

He flinches. "I know it's hard to believe, but when I heard Mary was getting married and I wasn't even invited to my own daughter's wedding, it woke me up." His eyes fill with tears again.

Which makes me mad. For him to act like he suddenly cares and Mary and I have shut him out is offensive. "Dad, drop the act and get to the point. What do you want?"

"I want to go to your sister's wedding. I've been sober for seven weeks now." He pulls out a one-month chip and shows it to me. "I'll have my two month chip next Tuesday." His grin showcases several missing teeth. The ones he still has don't look very functional.

I should bundle him out the door and down the steps right now. After all, the wedding isn't about my dad. It's about Mary and her happy day, but Dad's never even tried before. If he's actually trying now, would Mary want to know? I bite my lip. I don't know what to do.

I turn around and busy myself with making mint tea. It gives me time to think. I'm the one who keeps checking on Dad. I'm the one who feels sorry for him. Mary likes to pretend she doesn't even have parents. In a lot of ways, our lives would have been easier if we hadn't had any. I hand Dad a mug of mint tea.

I put my hand on my hip. "I need to think about this."

"I know I wasn't a great father, at least, I wasn't half the father you girls deserved."

I nod and sit down next to him. He's right. He wasn't, not by a long shot.

He sips his drink. "I came to your wedding."

"You only came because Mary forced you." She felt bad for telling me that marrying Chris was a mistake. I was angry with her, and I was so young and so stupid that I told her I didn't want her to fill in for Dad like we had planned. I told her I didn't want to be the girl without a dad to walk her down the aisle. Mary suppressed her own distaste for the entire situation, and probably her hurt feelings, and hunted down our dad. She cleaned him up and dragged him to the wedding for me. That entire wedding was a mistake, and any real dad would have told me to walk away from the whole thing the same way Mary had.

My dad grinned like a loon the entire time.

"I just want the chance to walk her down the aisle like I did for you," my dad says. "And this time I'm clean and sober for it without any arm twisting or bribes or threats or anything."

My voice is soft when I ask him, "Why do you think I never told you I was having a baby?"

"I figured you were too sick," Dad says.

I shake my head. "I had a lovely pregnancy. I just didn't want you to ruin it." The truth is, I struggled that whole pregnancy, wondering whether I'd be like my parents. I was scared I might not really connect with my child, or that I wouldn't love them, just like my parents didn't love us.

He crumples. I don't want to hurt him, but I'm more worried about not hurting Mary. And if I vouch for Dad and he lets her down. . .

"I've missed everything other than your wedding, but I don't fault you for it." He sets his nearly empty mug on the table. "But I did try when you were little. When your mom left, I tried. I did my best."

"Your best sucked, Dad."

He nods. "I know, but I held down my job. You have no idea how many days I didn't think I could do it. I didn't want to move at all. I thought about giving up all the time, about killing myself. But then I thought about you girls, and where you'd be if I was gone."

Probably in a foster home where we had regular meals, at least.

"I stayed alive for you. I went to work for you."

"And then you spent every dime you earned on booze,

Dad. Mary had to steal from you and walk to the corner store to buy food, and then hide it so you didn't spank her for taking your money."

His nostrils flare. "I wasn't that bad."

I stand up. "Get out, Dad. If you can't even face the real truth of what our life was like, then leave now. I won't revise history for you, even if that means you lose your stupid chip."

He stands up slowly. "I'm sorry. Sorrier then I can say. If I was really that negligent, if I was really that awful, I am so —" He chokes up. "I hope one day you can forgive me. And I beg you to ask Mary the same. I wake up every day now and pray that God will soften her heart so I can walk her down the aisle."

"There's no way that's happening," I say coldly. "I'm giving Mary away. We've both always had one person we could rely on. Each other."

My dad's bottom lip trembles. "Can you just talk to her? I'd like to at least be there to see it."

I take my dad's arm so I can hurry his departure. "I'll think about it."

He hands me a folded piece of paper, dirty and smudged. "That's my phone number. If you need to reach me, call it. Anytime, day or night."

"Sure, Dad."

I don't call Mary after he leaves. But when she invites me over for dinner that night, I get Troy ready and go.

Her new house, around the corner from her old house where I live now, is stunning. Luke bought it as a surprise when he proposed, to show her he intended to put down roots. To show her he was committed, that he would give her the dream she always had. She and I rode the bus past it every day on our way to school when we were kids. And now Mary's even remodeling it, one room at a time, so it'll be even more amazing inside.

I carry Troy up onto the porch and knock on the beautiful blue front door. Andromeda immediately begins barking, in case they didn't hear the knock.

Amy opens it, and Andy runs out to lick Troy's face.

"Aunt Trudy's here!" Amy screams, as if her parents didn't already know. But then she cocks her head sideways and leans toward Troy conspiratorially. "Me and Chase are playing the best game. Do you want to play with us?"

I set Troy down so he can respond. He wisely asks for more details before committing. "What is the game?"

"Chase has all the animals' powers. He can command any animal to do anything he wants. Dolphins, killer whales, tigers, horses. Even elephants."

Troy purses his lips. "What could I do?"

"What powers do you want?" Amy counters.

"I want to fly," Troy says.

Amy's eyes light up. "I even have a cape for you. You'll want that, since it'll ripple in the wind."

Troy nods. "Good idea. And I want the powers to be strong enough to pick up this whole house. Or maybe everything in the world."

I roll my eyes and usher Troy past Amy and inside the house.

"What are your powers?" I ask Amy.

She and Troy head for the playroom, but she tosses her answer over her shoulder like a rippling cape of her own. "I have all the powers in the universe, of course."

Obviously. I chuckle as I walk into the kitchen where I hear Mary and Luke talking.

"We can do that when he gets here," Luke says.

"When who gets here?" My hackles rise. If they're

inviting Paul over, even though I refused to meet him last night, I'm going to explode.

"Luke's buddy Trig is coming by with his new fiancé," Mary says. "Calm down. You've met Geode before. She's my wedding planner, so they're completely harmless. Believe me, you were crystal clear. We wouldn't dream of springing Paul on you without your permission, although he is Luke's brother so you're going to be around him eventually."

I sigh. "Right, sorry. It's been a long weekend."

Mary hands me a chocolate chip cookie. "Eat this. Cookies help everything."

Luke makes the best cookies on the planet. "Thanks." I bite into it and the chocolate melts in my mouth.

"Why has it been such a long week?" Luke asks. "Is the new job stressful? Because I am always looking for good IT people at LitUp."

I shake my head. "I like it actually, and I just got promoted."

Mary's mouth drops open. "You've been there four days. You got a promotion to what? Senior assistant?"

"You're looking at the new IT Manager for SITB."

"What the heck does SITB even stand for?" Luke asks.

"It's a strange name," I say. "The owner, Mr. Campbell, won't tell anyone what it means."

Luke frowns. "That's odd. Campbell you say?"

I nod.

"I know a lot of Campbells. Maybe we've met. What's the product?"

"It's a tech company," I say. "Kind of like you and Paul's, except for it focuses on medical technology."

"Huh," Luke says. "Maybe one day I'll meet this guy. I always like to connect with other inventors."

"Maybe I'll bring Jack to your wedding," I say without thinking. I immediately wish I could take the words back.

"What happened to your list?" Luke asks.

At the same time, Mary asks, "Who's Jack?"

"Just a cute guy from work," I hedge. I'm not about to tell them he's my boss. Luke's being nosy enough already, and that conversation would be way too awkward.

"I like the sound of that," Mary says. "So you worked hard this week, met a cute guy, *and* got a promotion? What's the plan for next week? Announce your candidacy for president?"

I roll my eyes. "Hilarious, but no. That's already part of your five year plan. I'd never want to steal your thunder."

The doorbell rings. Mary's supermodel wedding planner arrives with a guy who's nearly as tall as Paisley's brother Cole. "You must be Trig." I hold out my hand. "I'm Trudy, Mary's baby sister."

"Nice to meet you, Trudy. I've heard good things. You're graduating soon, right?"

I nod. "It's about time. And it can't come soon enough. I wish I could take my finals right now, before I've forgotten everything I learned doing my coursework."

"Very exciting," Trig says. "And you have a young son, right?"

I point toward the back of the house. Peals of laughter drift our way, punctuated by periodic shouts. "My son is lost forever now. He's joined the mob in the playroom, roaming free."

Luke and Trig start talking about work stuff that I don't understand, so Geo, Mary and I drift into the kitchen. "How are your wedding plans coming?" Mary asks Geo.

Geo beams, and I check out her finger. A stone the size of a large grape winks at me from her hand. I try not to gape at it, but judging by the rock size, Trig must be even richer than Luke. "We've set the date at least. August first. Now we just need to decide where to have it."

"How did it go with Trig's mom last week?" Mary asks.

Geo sighs and turns toward me. "Trig's mother is a force of nature, like a hurricane, or a tornado, if the tornado could ruin your credit, bankrupt you, and insult you all at once, while wearing four inch Manolo Blahniks and a plastic smile that never droops thanks to excessive Botox."

"She sounds even more delightful than my mother," I say.

"I haven't actually met her yet," Geo says. "That's just what Trig says. She's rescheduled our meeting four times now. I think she's hoping if she never meets me, maybe this whole thing will magically disappear."

"I thought she was supportive of Trig getting married." Mary frowns. "Or you know, at least not opposed, relatively speaking."

"Maybe she was before Trig disclaimed his entire inheritance, but now she blames me for that. Which is probably fair."

When Geo laughs, I marvel at her beauty. Her cheekbones are high, her eyes piercing, her skin flawless. Her black hair shines like a Pantene commercial, and although she's wearing a simple pair of jeans and a sweater, she still looks runway ready. Great career, amazing fiancé, immaculate looks.

Some people have all the luck.

The next few hours fly by, punctuated by a yummy steak dinner, kid squabbles and games, and more wedding talk. I try to be a good sport, but by six-thirty, if I have to hear one more thing about venues or bridesmaid colors, I might puke up my barely digested steak.

I lean close to Mary and whisper. "Can we talk for a second?"

Her eyes immediately meet mine. "Is everything okay?"

I nod. "Mostly, but I need to talk to you about something privately before I take Troy home."

Mary turns toward the other adults. "Trudy and I need to finalize a few details real quick. We'll be right back."

No one bats an eye when we head for Mary's bedroom. She pats the bed, and sits down next to me. "What's up?"

I inhale through my nose and exhale through my mouth. I don't even know how to approach this. She's usually the delicate one and I'm the blunderer. Finally I just blurt it out.

"Dad came by to see me this morning."

Her hands fist in the comforter. "How does he even know where you live?"

I don't actually know. "Not sure. I guess I didn't think about that. I send him money or gift cards sometimes. Maybe I wrote a return address on it the last time."

She scowls. "You send cash to an alcoholic, Trudy? What were you thinking?"

"Not enough to do any damage. Mostly I send McDonald's gift cards, but that's not the point," I say. "He's never come looking for me before, not ever. And he was sober this time, voluntarily."

"What did you want to talk to me about?" Mary's eyes are flinty. "Because you never felt the need to tell me about Dad before now, and I know you check in with him sometimes."

"Why don't you?" I've always wondered. Mary's such a kind person, such a forgiving person. She's forgiven me over and over, never blaming me, even when something's my fault.

"You don't remember enough," Mary says. "But I do."

"He just wants a second chance," I say. "And I think maybe he's really trying this time."

Mary shakes her head. "This wouldn't be a second chance though. It would be a one-thousandth chance. A ten-thousandth. You started making excuses for Chris from the very beginning, and Dad's even worse."

I don't know about Dad being worse. Alcoholism is a disease, and the symptoms suck. Chris made his decisions entirely out of selfishness, but I don't argue with her.

"Besides," Mary says, "It's not only me anymore. If I let him back in my life, I'm putting Amy and Chase at risk. It's not about how much abuse you and I can endure, Trudy. We have a duty to protect our family from this garbage."

I think about Chris, and how I wish he cared enough to even make an effort with Troy. Now I'm stuck protecting Troy from the true extent of his dad's indifference. "Fine, it's your call. I wasn't even sure whether to tell you. I figured you're a big girl, and you might like to know."

Mary stands up and walks toward the door, but when she reaches for the knob, her hand freezes. "Tell Geo Dad can come, but he has to sit on the back row. He can't talk to me or my kids. He can't introduce himself to Luke, or act like a proud father. He's a bystander, nothing more, or he's bounced."

When she turns back toward me, her eyes are haunted.

"It's more than he deserves," I admit.

She shakes herself off, like a dog after a bath. "I'm done thinking about it, okay? My wedding's going to be a happy day. I won't let him ruin it."

I hope I didn't just ruin it for her. But I still think she needed to know Dad was trying. Now that I've done my duty, a wave of exhaustion crashes over me.

"Time to go, sweetheart," I tell Troy. He doesn't want to leave, but he never does after being with his new cousins.

He hugs Chase tightly around the waist. "I can't go. I'm stuck. See?"

"We have to go, baby. We've got to get you to bed, and tomorrow's a work day again."

He whines, but eventually lets go of Chase, puts his shoes and coat on, and trudges alongside me to the car. His tiny voice interrupts my thoughts on the way home when we pass Dee Dee's Donuts. "Mom how come we never get donuts anymore?"

I'm a record stuck on repeat. I can't quite bring myself to say, "Because you're diabetic now sweetie," one more time. "Honey," I say. "The thing is—"

"I know I'm not supposed to have a lot of sweet stuff, but you told Aunt Mary you have a new job. Can't we celerate that with a donut?"

Sometimes we need something to look forward to, even if it's not the healthiest thing for us. "I did get another new job," I say. "And we should celebrate, with a b. So yes, we can get donuts tomorrow."

I sort of hope he'll forget about it overnight, but I have no such luck. As soon as I get his shoes tied on Monday morning, Troy jumps up and down. "We're getting donuts!"

"Get your jacket and we'll pick them up on our way to Miss Pam's."

"I want blue with sprinkles," Troy says, "and donut holes, and chocolate with sprinkles, and a cinnamon one. Or maybe a maple."

I shake my head indulgently. "How many do you get to choose?"

Troy folds his arms and frowns at me. "We're celerating. You said."

"Cele**b**rating," I say, "and we are. But that doesn't mean you should eat your weight in fried, sugar-covered dough."

"Fine. Blue with sprinkles and donut holes."

I pick up Troy and swing him in a circle. "I think I can

do that. Maybe your friend Benson would like one with chocolate sprinkles and a cinnamon twist."

Troy bobs his head up and down eagerly. "And if he doesn't like them, I could eat those too."

I kiss his greedy little face. "Maybe so. Who knows?" Like any pre-school aged kid is going to not want a donut of any variety.

I grab Troy's bag and head for the car.

"Wait, Mom. My flower."

I groan. "It's dead, honey. We don't need to water it every day. I hear zombie flowers only need water once a week, tops."

Troy scowls at me. "It's not a zombie flower."

"Do you even know what a zombie is?" I ask.

Troy holds his hands out in front of him and rolls his eyes back in his head before shuffling toward me. He moans and waves his arms around.

"Um, how exactly do you know that zombies shuffle and make that horrible sound?"

Troy drops his arms and laughs at me. "Benson loves a game called plants versus zombies, Mom. It's so funny. And my flower is not like those at all. It's a plant, not a zombie."

I water the stupid thing so we can go, but I contemplate bumping the pot off the edge of the porch. If it crashed to the ground...oh well! Wouldn't that be a terrible accident? I think about Troy's innocent little face asking me what happened. And I remember how he used to ask me about his dad with the same sad eyes.

I can't do it. If he wants to badger me to death over this dumb plant, then I guess that's okay.

Troy doesn't want me to leave Pam's that morning, so I spend an extra few minutes with him. Between that and the donut run, by the time I reach the office, I'm nearly an hour late.

"Morning Miss Jenkins," Ish says with a smile.

He's a little odd, but he's always happy. I admire that about him. "Morning Ish." I open the pink donut box. "Chocolate donut?"

His eyes light up and he snags one. "Thanks!"

I take the box to the break room on my way to the back of the office. I'm setting it on the main table when a voice startles me. "You brought donuts?"

I spin around to face Jack. "Morning. Sorry I'm a little late."

"I'd say you're entitled to a full day off if you need it." Jack leans against the wall. "You went above and beyond."

"I have two jobs to do right now, unless you've hired someone for the assistant job over the weekend?"

Jack shakes his head. "I'm not sure bringing in anyone new right now is our best call, especially without Nancy around to vet them. If you think you can handle both jobs for a bit, I'll happily pay you double."

The cha-ching sound in my head is practically deafening. "I think I can hold on for a bit."

When Jack smiles, my heart executes a perfect front flip. "I appreciate it." He turns on his heel to head back for his office. The second work day in a row that he's been here early.

I trot after him. "Do you have a hearing set up?"

"Tomorrow morning. My lawyer jumped on those files and the evidence of corporate espionage like a duck on the proverbial June bug."

"Does that mean I need to wear a suit tomorrow?" I ask.

"If you don't mind. SITB's entire defense rests on your testimony to bring in the evidence we found."

No pressure. "I'll be ready."

"We should go over some documents to get ready," Jack says.

Two hours later, we're still reviewing exhibits and files. My eyes are blurring a little about the medical and technical jargon, but I understand the computer parts at least.

"I think you're ready," Jack says.

"I was born ready." I lift my eyebrows suggestively.

Jack, the man who kissed me two days ago, turns back toward his screen so fast I'm worried he might have gotten whiplash. Come to think of it, he hasn't flirted with me a single time all day. What's going on? That's when I finally admit to myself that I do like him. In violation of my list, my plans, and my own better judgment, I really like Jack. I mean, I need to get to know him better, but I want to do that.

"About Friday night," I say softly.

He turns back toward me slowly. When his eyes finally meet mine, I can't read what he's thinking at all.

He grunts. "I owe you a major apology. I don't know what I was thinking. I blame the combination of the late hour, my stress with Cynthia, and my fear over SITB's leak. I swear nothing like that will ever happen again. In fact, I'll do my best to communicate with you after tomorrow via email as much as possible so my presence doesn't make you uncomfortable."

What? My stomach ties in a wicked double knot. That's the opposite of what I want. Is he just being noble? Or does he regret kissing me? Maybe he didn't feel what I felt. When tears threaten, I blink them back. Something about giving birth to Troy broke my hormone regulator or something. Now I cry at everything from Finding Nemo to babies hearing their mom's voice for the first time when they get hearing aids. Doctors prepare new mothers for stretch marks and late nights, but they do not prepare you to be a hot mess for years after having a child.

This is so not the time for me to have a mommy moment.

"I have a confession," I say. "That was a first date. I barely know Cole."

Jack's hands tighten on the edge of his desk until his knuckles turn white. "Even if he was your boyfriend of a year, that would be completely fine. I'd have zero input about that, because I'm your boss, Gerty."

When he finally meets my eyes, his are awash in guilt, so much guilt.

At least that's a feeling I understand. My job is way more important than some flirtation, no matter how great his biceps look in that polo shirt, or how his smile makes my pulse race. "I get it."

I head back to Nancy's office and catch up on my most urgent tasks. Then I spend the next two hours dealing with a backlog of IT issues. Emails that aren't loading right, a power point program that's fighting with the anti-virus software, and a malfunctioning mouse. By four-thirty, my head is pounding. By five o'clock, I need to get home and hug Troy in the worst way. I wrap up a few more things, but by five-thirty, I'm ready to go.

I stop by Jack's office before I leave. "Hey boss. Just checking in before I head out. I prepped the Exhibits you sent and I think we're ready to go tomorrow morning."

I set my old phone on the corner of his desk, the one I cloned Cynthia's phone with. I figure he can monitor the texts and emails she gets as well as I could, maybe better.

Jack hasn't even looked away from his computer, and his fingers are clicking away steadily. Okay, so maybe he's full-on ignoring me at this point.

"Alright, well, I'll see you tomorrow."

"Wait." He spins around in his chair. "If I pause when I'm in the middle of a thought, I lose it. I'm sorry if that was rude. I wanted to tell you that two other employees have come in to tell me what a great job you're doing. I'll text you the address for court tomorrow. The hearing starts at eight a.m. I know that's early, so it's probably best if you meet me there."

"Oh. I'll grab the Exhibits on my way out, then."

"Perfect. Thank you again," Jack says. "You've really gone above and beyond."

I bob my head in acknowledgment, a little embarrassed at the praise, and head to Nancy's office to grab the box with the Exhibits for tomorrow that I printed off earlier.

I'm reviewing our arguments in my head on my walk out to my car, which is why I don't even notice Chris until I reach for the door handle. I nearly drop my box when I hear his voice.

"Well, well, don't you look fancy?" His words practically drip with contempt.

I hate that he looks so good. He's leaning against my little Honda like he owns it, which he doesn't and never did. It was another in a long string of hand-me-down gifts from Mary.

"Is that why you're stealing my money now? So you can buy more high end escort clothes?"

11

PAUL

I go over the plan for tomorrow with Mr. Brighton on the phone once, now that we have the Exhibits all prepped. "I think this is an open and shut case, now that you've got that information. Obviously, we'll need to track this to the end of the line, but from what I did today, it seems to point directly at WelshAllyn. The judge will find that quite compelling."

I lean back and close my eyes.

"You said this Miss Jenkins is responsible for you obtaining the information?"

I grunt.

"You owe her a big thank you."

He's right about that, and mere words aren't enough. I ought to cut her into the venture like I did with Nancy. Another quarter percent won't impact me much, but if this goes as big as I think it will, it could change her life. I think about her cute little old Honda and how embarrassed she was about a granola bar wrapper in the seat.

I hope it doesn't change her too much.

I spin around in my chair to work on some files I brought

over from LitUp. If I don't start spending more time on the car battery launch, Luke's going to fire me himself. I should tell him about SITB, but I really want to wait until I've sold the tech or gone public with it. I can't tell him until it's an actual success, a done deal. There are still too many ways this could fold like a house of cards. Next week or the week after, I should wrap this up one way or another. I'll tell him everything by the time he returns from his honeymoon at the latest.

I can't wait to see his face when he hears about what I did on my own. My idea, my product, my launch. My success start to finish.

I'm digging into an advertising proposal when I notice something odd out of the corner of my eye. Something pink. There's a phone on the edge of my desk, and it's got to be Gerty's. She must have left it by accident. If I hurry, I might still catch her. I rush out the back door with it, but what I see stops me in my tracks.

Gerty's talking to a guy, a tough looking guy with a scowl on his face. I ought to run over, hand her the phone, and then leave. I should give her space. This really isn't any of my business, but something about the guy bothers me. Her date on Friday was too good looking and I hated him on sight, but this guy's different. He looks. . . menacing.

I probably sound as crazy as Trig did when he tried to convince me he was going to Macaroni Grill to protect Geo from her oldest friend in the world, that tough looking Marine. Except when this guy waves a piece of paper in Gerty's face, she flinches. He slams his other hand down on the hood of her car right after, his voice strident and his eyes sparking with anger.

That's about enough of that.

I jog toward the car. "You forgot your phone in the office," I yell, hoping to distract them so Gerty can put some space between herself and that paper brandishing idiot.

She spins around with one hand against her chest, and I'm glad I ran over. Her eyes dart between me and the other guy nervously.

"I didn't realize you were talking to someone," I say casually. "I just wanted to catch you before you left so I could give you this."

Gerty pulls a phone out of her purse. "I left that on purpose. It's not mine, it's Cynthia's." She widens her eyes intentionally, reminding me I'm holding the cloned phone. Duh.

I ought to head back inside. Gerty's a big girl, and she clearly doesn't welcome my interference. But I'm not going anywhere until I know this guy's not a threat. "I'm Jack." I reach my hand out to shake.

The loser looks at me with unbridled disgust.

"I'm her boss."

"Maybe you should pay her a little more," the guy says. "Maybe then she wouldn't be trying to steal from me."

Steal from him? I glance her direction and notice something in the car that wasn't there on Friday afternoon. A booster seat with red fire trucks driving across it. I squint at the paper the guy's holding. Garnishment of Wages is printed in big, bold letters across the top.

"Do you have a kid?" I ask.

Gerty lifts her chin. "I do. A four-year-old son named Troy."

She had plans that night alright, but they probably weren't a first date with that tall guy like I assumed. She missed out on time with her son because of me. Poor thing had to scramble for a sitter, no doubt. Which begs the question, how did she procure Cole so fast? And that makes the guy who's slamming his hand down on her hood and making her flinch in fear... her ex?

"I'm gathering you're the ex-husband?" I raise one eyebrow and spear this guy with my baddest boss glare.

He bristles and puffs his chest like he and I are two apes about to fight over a box of bananas. Which would be fine with me. I can't handle men who intimidate women, no matter the circumstance. But there's a special place in hell for men who won't pay child support, and I'm happy to expedite his check-in.

"I'm Chris, yeah."

"Child support payments aren't stealing," I say. "Paying them is the law. If you're making it hard for her to get money from you to support your own child, it doesn't speak much about you as a man, does it?"

Chris's face turns bright red and his scowl deepens. "None of this is any of your business, man, so go back inside to your little wussy desk and leave us alone."

He's a real winner. "I'll go inside when she tells me to." I glance toward Gerty. "You okay?"

She swallows, her face still unnaturally pale. "He's not supposed to be here."

"Here, as in at your office?" I ask.

She nods. "He's not supposed to be within five hundred feet of me, not ever."

I close my eyes. She has a permanent restraining order against him, which means he has a history of violence. Now I really have no tolerance for his nonsense. "Hey, Chris, I get it. You're pissed off that some of your hard-earned money is being taken, right? I work hard for my money, too, so I understand."

He nods. "Twenty percent, which is way too much. Total BS, man."

"I'm going to talk really slowly, okay?" I point behind us at the SITB office building. "See that camera?"

Chris scowls at me.

"I take security seriously around here. I have a state of the art system. If you mess with it, like throw a rock at it, or try to cut the wires to it, the police will be here in less than two minutes. And your remarkable and quite recognizable face is now recorded in HD on that video feed. Which means one call to my good friend on the Marietta Police Department and you're going to spend the next thirty days in jail for violating your restraining order."

Chris swears. "Are you kidding me right now? I just came to talk to her. If she'd give me her actual address, I wouldn't have to come find her at work."

"How did you find her?" I ask.

"Man, none of this is any of your business, okay? So go back to your own stuff and leave us alone."

I cross my arms. "In the several seconds after I came out that back door, I saw you slam your hand down on her car. I saw you threaten my employee in my parking lot. It's all on film, Chris. And while you don't seem like a very bright person to me, I think you'll understand this part. Twenty percent off your paycheck might suck. But thirty days without a paycheck would suck more. How long do you think your new girlfriend will remain faithful to you while you're in prison for violating a court order keeping you away from your ex?" That last part was a guess, but I doubt he left one branch before having a fist tightly wrapped around another. And Gerty's far too cute for him to leave without someone else in the picture.

"They don't put you in prison for making someone flinch. They just yell at you for not listening," Chris says.

I step toward him purposefully and he stumbles back.

"The only reason I haven't already called the cops," I

say, "is that if you don't go away, my friend here won't even get a lousy, unimpressive twenty percent out of you. But I'm going to make you a promise, and I think now that you've met me, you'll believe that I'm someone who makes good on his promises. If you contact your beautiful ex-wife again, I'll send this tape to the police, press charges against you as the owner of this property, and after all that's over, I'll beat the ever loving crap out of you myself."

I step closer to Chris, and I whisper the last words. "Did I mention that I'm a boxer, Chris? In fact, if my business hadn't done so remarkably well that I never need to work again, I'd have become a prizefighter. I had an offer in Vegas my last year of college. It's been a long time since I beat someone to a pulp, and between you and me, I miss it. Badly. Don't give me a reason to turn your fairly nice face into hamburger meat, because I won't pass on that opportunity."

Chris scowls at me, but he backs off and climbs into a shiny orange mustang. I wish he'd had a little more gumption. I really am jonesing for a fight right now.

When he roars off, I turn around to see how Gerty's doing. Her hands are shaking, and I step toward her and put an arm around her without thinking. When she turns toward me, my arm around her morphs into a side hug.

"He's gone," I whisper into her hair. "And I think I scared him enough that he won't be back anytime soon."

"He hasn't ever hit me hard," she says. "I don't think he would."

Very reassuring. "I'd rather you never find out."

"Me too." She squeezes me around the waist and then pulls back. Her hair has fallen over her left eye.

I reach out and tuck the silky strands behind her ear, and then I follow the path my hand took, bringing my lips down against hers for the second time in three days. Which is not enough, not nearly enough. Her hands reach up and wind around my neck this time, pulling me against her forcefully. I spin her around so her back is against the car and press into the kiss. I see the bright red fire trucks on the booster seat out of the corner of my eye, and I remember who I'm kissing. A single mother whose ex just accosted her.

My employee, my subordinate, in a vulnerable situation.

I break off the kiss. "I am so sorry. Again." I stumble backward, needing some cold air in my lungs so I can think straight. "I don't know what keeps coming over me."

I can barely hear her when she speaks, her words are so breathy and quiet. "I don't want you to stop."

I'm not the creepy boss forcing myself on a young, impressionable employee? My heart lurches in my chest and I close the gap between us. "Are you sure?"

She reaches up and yanks my collar down, pulling my face toward hers until my mouth closes over her lips again. She melts against me and I fist my hand in her hair, tilting her head up toward me. Her eyes stare into mine unafraid, her lips swollen, and I don't think I've ever seen a woman more beautiful in my life.

"Let me take you to dinner," I say. "I don't want to say goodbye, but we can't loiter in the parking lot half the night."

"No, we can't. That's true." She stiffens against me and rests a hand on my chest.

She's changed her mind. She doesn't want me. I swallow hard.

"I would love to go to dinner, but I can't, not right now. I've got to pick up my son. I'm already late, and he's struggling a little with the fact that I'm gone all the time for my new job." She drops her voice as if she's embarrassed. "I used to stay at home with him."

"That's a very impressive sacrifice. My mother stayed home with my brother and me."

Her smile thanks me for understanding. Not everyone comprehends the difficulty and the importance of putting kids first.

"Not that I think it was a bad decision to go to work. You're obviously a valuable member of our team." I force myself to let go of her and step back so she can open her car door.

"Maybe another time," she says. "A weekend or something?"

"Absolutely."

Except when she unlocks her car and starts to get inside, I almost can't bear to let her go. Not yet. I'll see her tomorrow, but in a suit at a hearing. I want more of the wide blue eyes. I want to meet her son. I want to see more of this side of her, the soft side that gave up a career to take care of a baby.

"Or."

She turns toward me. "Or what?"

"We could go to dinner *with* your son."

"He's four," she says.

"What am I missing?" I ask.

"He doesn't do well sitting down quietly in a restaurant," she says. "Especially not when he's been at my friend's house all day."

Right. That makes sense. "Another time then."

"Unless." She grips the steering wheel.

"Unless what?"

"I have chili in the crockpot," she says. "It's nothing fancy. We eat it over Fritos."

"I love Frito pie."

She finally meets my eyes. "You do? Really?"

I beam at her. "It was a special treat when I was in college."

She snorts. "Oh good. One of my go to meals was your college food, like ramen noodles and nachos."

I laugh. "I mean it though. I love chili, with or without Fritos."

"Well, okay. If you want to come to dinner, you're welcome to. Just don't expect a lot."

"No expectations," I say. "Can I pick anything up to bring? A dessert, or a side or something?"

She shakes her head. "We don't eat a lot of dessert at our house. I hope that's okay."

"Fine by me, but I have a little bit of work I need to finish and send. Can I meet you at your place in forty-five minutes or so?"

She exhales deeply, like that's a relief somehow, and slides the key into her car. "That's perfect actually. I've still got to grab Troy, remember?"

"Right. Well, text me your address and I'll see you soon."

"See you soon." She tosses me a half wave and a tiny grin on her way out of the parking lot.

I wait until she's gone to start beaming like a simpleton. This is the first date I've been giddy about in years, our plan is to eat crockpot Frito pie with a four-year-old boy. I definitely did not see this one coming.

12
TRUDY

I didn't particularly think my house was a mess when I left this morning, but when Troy and I walk through the door, it looks like Pigpen was playing in here. With charcoals. The chili is ready, but I spend the next half hour frantically cleaning. Eventually I give up and simply start grabbing everything off the counters, from photos to decor to toys, and dumping it into the master closet. I'll sort through it all later. The counters and surfaces look a little bare, but that's better than cluttered. So what if he doesn't see any photos of me and Mary, or the cute decor I've made to turn the house into a home.

I can impress him with all that later, when I have time to put the Toy Story figurines, Legos, and army men into the toy box one by one. I'm sweeping the kitchen floor when the doorbell rings, and my heart flies into my throat.

"Is that pizza?" Troy asks.

I crouch down. Maybe instead of cleaning, I should have been explaining to my son that a friend was coming over, especially since I've never had any guy in the house other than soon-to-be-Uncle Luke. "Um, no, we're having chili, but I invited a friend to come over and eat with us."

Troy nods. "Does she have kids to play with?"

"No, and it's a he, not a she."

"That even better," he says.

"Why is that better?" I ask.

"Because boys like trains more than girls do." Troy picks his train up again and pushes the button on top that makes the wheels move.

I stand up and brush off my pants before walking to the door. I breathe in and out slowly, and then I open it. Jack's smiling at me from the front porch. I told him not to bring anything, but he's holding a bouquet of Stargazer Lilies.

I love lilies.

"Those smell so good, thanks!" I take them from him. No one has brought me flowers in. . . Ever. Other than Mary, no one has ever brought me flowers. Which is really pathetic, now that I think about it. "Come on in."

Jack walks inside and looks around like he's sweeping the room for terrorist threats. I almost chuckle when I realize he's looking for Troy, who's hunched over the train table.

"Troy, this is my friend Jack. Come and say hello."

My adorable son straightens up and walks over to the entryway. "I'm Troy. I like trains even more than cars and I'm happy you're a boy."

"I'm happy to be a boy, and I like trains, too. Maybe after dinner, we can play with yours. If you don't mind sharing with me," Jack says.

Troy's face lights up. "I got so many for my birthday, and my mom never wants to play with them."

"I play trains with you all the time," I protest.

Troy scrunches his nose. "Yeah, but you don't *want* to

do it. I can tell. You always set up a track and say, 'okay now we're done.'"

"My four year old son can see right through me, apparently," I say.

"Well, you're in luck," Paul says. "I have a real knack for train tracks, and I might even be able to come up with a setup you've never seen before."

Troy beams at him.

I've never seen Troy eat his dinner so fast. He shovels the Frito pie in his mouth in heaping spoonfuls and barely even chews. Once his bowl is empty, he wipes his mouth on his sleeve. I bite my tongue and let it go.

Troy sits up straight and beams. "I'm all done, Mom."

My heart contracts. He misses having a guy around, clearly. Not that Chris ever played with him, but it looks like he still feels the lack.

"It might take me a minute longer than you to finish," Jack says. "But why don't you get started and I'll join you momentarily."

Troy leaps to his feet, but I snag his arm before he can dart away. I lead him to the sink and give him his shot quickly under the guise of cleaning him up. Jack doesn't notice, luckily. Troy gets embarrassed sometimes around people he doesn't know, and the cooler he thinks the person is, the less he wants them to see him getting shots and being told to eat every bite. Troy hurries over to the train table, and I walk back to the kitchen table.

"Sorry." I say. "He's excited to have a visitor. Clearly we don't get out much."

"I don't mind. He's adorable." Jack's hand inches over until our fingers are touching. A little thrill zings up my arm to my heart. "Thanks for letting me invite myself over," he says. "I know it was short notice."

"Kind of a lame dinner. Sorry about that."

Jack puts his hand over mine. "Stop apologizing. I'm having way more fun here, eating chili with you, than I ever did with Cynthia. Even if you sucked every tiny second of fun out of the time we spent and aggregated it all, I'd still have had more fun in this one night."

I find that hard to believe. "Whatever you say."

Jack scoops three bites into his mouth in rapid succession, and still manages to talk around all the food. "I do say." He stands up and crosses the room to sit next to my son, whose whole face lights up.

Troy frowns and whispers, but I can still hear him. "If you didn't wash your hands, my mom's gonna fuss at you."

Jack choke laughs and walks back into the kitchen to wash up, catching my eye and widening his. He shakes his head at me as he walks back. "Your mom sure has a lot of rules, huh?"

Troy sighs as though he's quite put upon. "You don't even know."

Jack winks at me before he turns around to focus on the train track. "This won't do at all." He points at the current configuration. "Whoever built this has no vision."

"That's me," I say. "No vision Mom. STEM isn't really my thing."

Jack starts taking pieces off the table and stacking them on the floor. "Your mom's got quite a lot of vision, but maybe her strength just isn't in the train arena. Did she tell you that she saved my entire company last week?"

Troy shouts, "No way!"

"Indeed she did. Without her, someone bad would have stolen all my hard work and my company would have collapsed."

"That's so cool, Mom. You caught the stealers?"

I stack up the dirty dishes and carry them to the sink. "Something like that."

"Why didn't you tell me?" Troy asks. "That's cooler than being a police person."

"It's kind of a secret, baby." I doubt Jack wants Troy telling the world. Although, who could Troy really tell?

"Your mom's right," Jack says. "Until some things get announced, maybe we keep this between the three of us."

Troy looks unconvinced. "Mom says no secrets."

Jack grins. "She's right, no secrets at all from your mom. But she's in on this one, so I think it's okay."

Troy bobs his head. "Only until the police can arrest the bad guy, right? Then I can tell Benson about it?"

"Sure," I say. "But it could be a bad girl." I'm quick to correct him about this kind of thing. I can't have him thinking only men are bad. And in this case, it was a woman.

"Hey kiddo, I might need to lend your mom a hand real quick." Jack hops up and walks toward me. "I'm sorry. I didn't mean to leave you to clean everything up, especially after you fed me."

I shoo him back. "No, play with Troy. Trust me, that makes my life easier than if you help with the dishes."

Jack heads back to the train table, where he and Troy are building a double decker train track, complete with a directional control flip that sends trains different routes. Jack even manages to integrate the loading arm.

"This is the coolest track ever," Troy says. "Can we leave it like this until Benson comes over to see it?"

Now that he's there every day, Troy talks about Benson nonstop. "I'm sure we can." Heaven knows I never want to change it. Once I finish in the kitchen, I head for the family room to relieve Jack.

"Hey baby, did you want to watch one episode of Mickey in my room?"

"No way. This is way more fun."

"Wait, did you just say something is more fun than Mickey?" I clutch my chest in mock horror. "You can't be serious."

Troy scowls at me.

"Jack was so nice to help you set this up, but I doubt he wants to sit here and watch trains go around and around all night."

"We're racing them, Mom. Look, mine is going to beat his." Except Troy's doesn't beat his. They crash into each other and the red train falls off the track.

"Ah, you killed me," Jack says.

"It does look like fun, but sometimes adults want to talk instead of playing," I say, determined to save poor Jack.

Jack pats the ground next to him. "I'm having fun right here. I knew you had a four-year-old son when I decided to come. Why don't you join us?"

Troy runs off to grab his dinosaurs and army men, and the three of us sit in front of the train table, setting up barricades and reptilian attackers, knocking little battery powered trains off the tracks and laughing. I don't think I've sat down and played with Troy like this since before Chris left me. Normally I'd feel guilty about that thought, but tonight I just enjoy myself.

Until I notice it's nearly eight p.m.

"I've got to get this one to bed," I say. "Troy, go find your toothbrush and meet me in the bathroom."

"I want your friend to brush my teeth."

I sigh. "That's not Jack's job."

"I don't mind," he says. "My nephew likes me to brush his teeth too. In fact, he says I do a better job than his dentist."

Right after Jack brushes Troy's teeth, he gets a phone call. He steps outside to take it. I run through Troy's bedtime routine, and tuck him into bed. By the time I sink down onto the sofa, it's already eight-forty five.

The tap on the front door startles me, but then Jack pokes his head inside. "Am I okay to come back in?"

I wave him inside, and my heart somersaults when he crosses the room to sit right next to me on the sofa. "You're a really cute mom."

"You're a pretty hot boss."

He winces. "And... that's my cue to go."

He starts to stand up, but I grab his hand and he stops. He turns toward me, slowly. Too slowly.

"Don't go yet," I say.

"No?"

I shake my head.

"How likely is Troy to come out here and ask for a glass of water or another story?"

I laugh. "Pretty likely."

"How scarred would he be if he saw me doing this?" Jack lowers his head toward mine and brushes his mouth against my lips. When he pulls back, I follow him for an inch or two before flopping back against the sofa.

My hands shake at my sides. "On a scale of Sponge Bob to Marilyn Manson?"

He grins. "Sure."

"I'd say closer to the Sponge Bob side. He's a pretty sheltered kid, but he pays attention to stuff around him. He knew what a zombie was this morning when I asked."

"So you think he'd survive this." Jack kisses me again, leaning closer to me this time. His hand cups my face and when he stops, it's to trail kisses across my jaw. He whispers in my ear. "This is kind of exciting. Like making out in a dressing room or a movie theater."

"Or the theater catwalk."

His eyebrows rise. "Now I wish I knew you back in high school."

I think about the four shirts and two pairs of pants I owned in high school, and the one pair of shoes. Scruffy, hand-me-down Keds. I doubt Mr. Polished Jack would have liked high school Trudy. I'm frankly shocked he likes present-day me.

But any doubts I had about whether he likes me are kissed away over the next few minutes. I'm lost in a haze of strong arms, bristly kisses and whispered compliments until I hear a very loud ringer.

He pulls back and groans. "I'm sorry, but I've got to call this guy back. So many work things to deal with right now."

"No, go ahead. It's completely fine. I'm just happy you made time to come for dinner."

Jack kisses me on the nose. "Best part of my week so far."

Really?

"In fact, I'd love to see you again tomorrow. Assuming the hearing goes alright, I should be able to carve out a little time after work. Are you free?"

Troy's got a doctor appointment right at 5:30. I shake my head. "Not tomorrow. Maybe Wednesday?"

"I've got a dinner meeting that night. Thursday?"

I laugh. "I'm busy all of this weekend, but I could do Thursday night. What did you have in mind?"

"How does Troy feel about dogs?" Jack asks.

"He loves them," I say. "Why? Do you have a dog?"

Jack nods. "I grew up with just one sibling and always wanted more. Until I have kids of my own, I wanted a furry pal to keep me company. He's a very bouncy, very energetic golden lab. He's going to be mad at me for ignoring him for so long today."

"I'm sure we'd love to meet him."

"And since you cooked tonight, I'll provide food Thursday."

"You're cooking?" I ask.

He shakes his head. "Not unless you want grilled cheese. It's about the only thing I can make passably, but I order some mean take out. I'm getting a little work done at my house right now, but we could meet at the park." He checks his phone. "It's supposed to be perfect weather. Assuming that doesn't change, would you be up for it?"

"It sounds fun," I say.

"Like visiting crazy Uncle Elton fun, or like exciting second date fun?"

"Is it a date when I'm bringing my son with me?" I ask. "Was this a date tonight? Frito pie and train tables?"

Jack pulls me up against him. "If we're judging by how fast my heart is beating and how excited I am to be here, this is definitely a date. The first I've had in a long time." He kisses me until I believe him, and then he leaves.

I fall asleep with a smile on my face.

❧ 13 ❧
PAUL

WelshAllyn sends its scariest lawyers. Three men and one lady, all wearing expensive black suits. I'm actually a little nervous when Mr. Brighton walks in. His suit fits well enough, but he's got quite a girth about him and his breath smells strongly of coffee. Is the best patent lawyer in Atlanta in the same league as WelshAllyn's fancy New York City lawyers? Probably not.

Will it matter? Gosh I hope not.

Gertrude clearly despises being on the stand. She's shifty and nervous and licks her lips in between every question. In spite of all of that, she does a brilliant job at the hearing. Her answers are clear, her mannerisms endearing and honest, and she explains the technical bits in a way that anyone can understand. The judge loves her and calls her 'darling little Miss Jenkins' twice. It's more than a little patronizing, but she never lets her annoyance show. I'm not surprised when he gives his final decision.

"I'm throwing out WelshAllyn's claim. The evidence is clear. Whether or not there was any fraud or wrongdoing is a matter for a civil court, but I'll be surprised if I don't hear that you brought a claim there." The judge looks pointedly at me.

After the hearing, Mr. Brighton asks me what I want to pursue against them. "They're all assembled here, boy. So now's your best chance at negotiating a settlement."

I hate when he calls me boy, but he did a great job today, so I try to focus on what matters. "What do you think we should demand?"

"My fees as a baseline," he says. "Plus a big chunk of change for bad faith. But the real question is whether you want to pursue criminal charges."

"Let's hear what they have to say first, and we can go from there."

We approach WelshAllyn's team together, with Gerty trailing slightly behind us. I want to take her hand, but I settle for gesturing her over to stand next to me.

"Before you move ahead with anything," the flinty-eyed female named Mrs. Stone says, "you should know that WelshAllyn had absolutely nothing to do with any illegal dealings. We purchased the information we submitted in good faith." She hands a folder to Mr. Brighton.

He flips it open, and I look over his shoulder. Gerty peers over his other shoulder. It's a contract.

"It's for nine thousand, nine-hundred and ninety-nine dollars," Gerty says. "Doesn't that seem a little low for this tech?"

Mr. Brighton turns back toward the group of lawyers and clears his throat. "With whom exactly did you make this deal?" He shakes the folder. "This says J.F. Holdings."

"Their lawyer approached us," Mrs. Stone says. "He offered us the deal with a lot of stipulations, the privacy of his client foremost among them."

"You didn't find that offer suspect?" Mr. Brighton lifts one eye accusingly.

"We'd have been moronic not to take it."

"You were negligent not to examine where it came from and why the information was being offered so inexpensively." Mr. Brighton frowns furiously. "Which you clearly know."

"Maybe," she says. "Maybe not. That's a matter of fact for a jury to decide."

Mr. Brighton rolls his eyes. "Common sense may not be plentiful or well regarded in New York, but the jurors in Georgia don't love big corporations who hide behind excuses and willful ignorance. You had received proposals from my client for this same tech and replied with interest. In fact, in light of that, I imagine if we poke into the last deal I handled for SITB, we'll find WelshAllyn behind the shell company that filed for the patent first."

"Not that we admit anything," Mrs. Stone says, "but what are you asking for?"

Mr. Brighton glances my way and I shrug. We haven't suffered any damages on this tech, other than the extra legal fees, but the last venture was worth something. I'm smart enough to know that proving WelshAllyn's involvement or wrongdoing for that snafu will be much tougher, given the timeline. Those employees have scattered, and it's been over a year.

Mr. Brighton clears his throat. "My client might be appeased if you were to pay my fees and a restitution fee of five-hundred thousand, which is an absurdly low, limited time offer, if he even agrees to that."

It's half a million more than I expected this morning, so I nod. "I will agree to it, if you accept or decline here today, and sign a document to that effect by close of business. I want the funds transferred within three business days."

Mrs. Stone's face hardens. One of the men next to her whispers in her ear. She taps into her phone and watches the screen. A moment later, she looks up, her face twisted into a sour expression. "WelshAllyn accepts your demands as long as this agreement includes a provision that protects us from any claims relating to any other, prior, purchase of tech involving your client."

So they did buy the prior tech. Interesting.

Mr. Brighton's face reddens, but before he can argue, I put a hand on his arm. "We'll accept those terms."

"Fine," Mrs. Stone says. "Draw up an agreement and we'll sign."

The second they're gone, Mr. Brighton curses. "We should've asked for more. They agreed too easily, which means we could have linked them to that first patent."

"Maybe we could have, but it's done at this point and I don't want to spend years in litigation." I smile at him. "I've got lots of other ideas I'd rather focus on, and I'm pleased with the outcome." I look around the room at Mr. Brighton's associate and legal secretary, and Lenny from SITB who came to testify about some of the tech research. "You've all done a great job."

I catch Gerty's hand on the way out without thinking about it. Her eyes widen in alarm and I let it go, but I don't want to.

"I've got a favor to ask," I say.

"What?"

I'm distracted for a moment by the sky blue of her eyes. I smile and she returns it.

"The favor," she prompts.

"Right," I say. "Sorry, you're so adorable that sometimes I forget what I was thinking."

She blushes and looks down at her cute black high

heels. A row of dainty black flowers crosses over the toe of each shoe.

"I instructed Mr. Brighton to send me a copy of whatever's inside that folder they provided. I really need to figure out who it was that put Cynthia up to all this, since it clearly wasn't WelshAllyn. I've clearly got an enemy, and I want to know who it is."

"Why do you think you've got an enemy, as opposed to just a thief on your tail?" Before I can answer, she inhales. "Because they sold the information they stole way below market value."

I nod. "Exactly, which is why WelshAllyn was so quick to settle. I'm meeting with several buyers this week to decide whether to manufacture these wireless EKG transmitters myself, or whether to sell them. Ironically, WelshAllyn was one of the possible purchasers."

She frowns. "If you sell, won't we all lose our jobs?"

"Not at all. They'll insist we provide support for a while, usually a year, and after that we'll have new tech to work on." I tap my temple. "I've got lots of ideas. Don't worry."

"I'm happy to dig around to try and find the owner, but I've never done anything like that before."

"You'd never cloned a phone before either," I point out.

The right side of her mouth creeps up into a smile.

"What about running an operation on a corporate spy?"

She shakes her head again, but the smile widens.

"Had you ever been an assistant before?"

Another head shake. "I'd never kissed my boss before either," she whispers.

I drop my voice too. "It seems like you're good at everything new you try. I have faith you can do this, too."

She doesn't whisper, but her voice is small, and her eyes downcast. "I may let you down."

I reach beneath her chin and lift it with two fingers. "You'll never let me down. Even if you can't find this, I won't fault you. Clearly whoever did this knows how to cover his or her tracks."

She bobs her head, but still doesn't meet my eyes. I want to track down her ex and drag him into my office so I have an excuse to thrash him. How badly must he have treated this phenomenal woman to make her doubt herself so badly? She's excelled at everything I've seen her do in the past week and a half. She's one of the best moms I've seen. She's kind, hard working, gorgeous, and feisty.

The more time I spend with her, the more I like her. But when I see the nervousness in her eyes, when she worries she'll disappoint me after doing everything right, I can guess where that came from. I head for LitUp right after the hearing, trying to catch up on the prep work for the upcoming launch. Luke's still steady as a rock a few days before his wedding, but he's handling a lot of last minute details for that. I'm mostly staying away from my own home as much as possible so that Geo and her employees can change everything about it.

Part of me is annoyed I can't just invite Gerty over to my own house. I mean, it's sort of weird to make her meet me in the park, but maybe it's for the best. Her house is adorable, but I could stack ten of her place inside of mine. It might freak her out, especially since she thinks of me like a startup kind of guy. Which is fine, but I don't have the house of a tiny tech startup guy.

On Wednesday, I meet with four possible buyers. 3M, Stryker, Siemens, and Philips. They all make offers by the end of the day. The offers are bigger than I expected. I've got meetings next week with Cardinal, Johnson & Johnson and GE Healthcare. All four today offered a ten percent uplift if I sign before meeting with anyone next week. I've also got some preliminary projections on the market if we push this product out ourselves. I'd make more, and I could still sell later to one of these companies, but how much more of my life would I spend splitting time between two offices?

I want to call Luke and ask him what to do. This was supposed to be my chance to do something without him, something just for me. Except now, I wish he were here. I wish I could talk to him about it, or if not him, anyone I trust to guide me.

I'm going over the numbers again, trying to make sense of the bottom line on the various offers when I hear a tiny tap at my door. Gerty's head pokes around the corner. "Hey. You got a minute?"

I lean back in my chair. "Of course. Come on in."

She sits on the very edge of the chair across from me, a folder on her lap. "I almost came to see you yesterday, but I didn't have the answer yet, not for sure. I think maybe I do now."

I sit up a little straighter. "An answer to what?"

"Did you know most agencies have twenty business days to respond to open records requests?" She wrings her hands. "I might have expensed a mini muffin basket to expedite a few of them." She coughs. "Or six."

I laugh and pull out a stick of gum. If I can convince her to close the door, I don't want my breath to smell like the French dip I ate for lunch. "And?"

"Do you know someone named James Fullton?"

I stop in the middle of unwrapping the piece of Trident.

"I take your absolute stillness as a yes."

I meet her eyes. "I know a James Fullton the fourth. Is that the one you mean?"

She nods. "Parents James Fullton III, and Violet Kennedy Fullton?"

I clench my hands into fists, forgetting momentarily

about the spearmint gum. I drop the squished mess into the trashcan. "J.F. Holdings." I swear under my breath. "I should have thought of that."

"It's hard to take an acronym and figure out what the letters stand for," Gerty says. "Like SITB for example. No one has any idea what it stands for."

I'm barely listening to her. I reach for my phone, ready to call that vindictive, lazy freeloader and tell him what I think. But my hand stops before I pick up the receiver. What good would calling him do? He'd probably be delighted to hear from me. He obviously didn't do this for the money.

This was straight up revenge.

Calling him would tip my hand. For the same reasons that I kept that key logger, I'm better off not letting on that I know what he did. He'll know I made Cynthia, and he'll know I beat him this round, but he may think he covered his tracks well enough that I haven't figured it out yet.

"How hard was it to figure this out?" I ask.

Gerty sighs. "I guess that depends. I didn't obtain the information legally. J.F. Holdings is set up in Switzerland. He clearly spent a lot more creating this company than he earned from the two sales, assuming they were both for under ten thousand."

"How did you get any information from a Swiss company?" I ask.

"My ex has an old friend who... never mind. The point is, it took some real digging and a little bit of pressure. But if I could find it in two days, I'm sure someone else could too. I'm not a private investigator or anything. I just happen to have a few friends in low places. I figured you wanted to know the answer more than you wanted a well-documented paper trail. I hope that was right."

"That's absolutely right. You did a tremendous job. I really appreciate it. I hope you didn't put yourself in danger or call in any favors."

"Nothing that will put me in a bind." She stands up and sets the folder on my desk. "You seem upset. I'm really sorry if I had anything to do with that. I totally understand if you're not able to do the picnic tonight after all."

I close my eyes. I'm an idiot. Gerty did an amazing thing here, and crossed some lines to get what I needed. She worked hard on this, and instead of paying attention to how she's feeling, I got caught up in my own garbage. I jump from my chair and stride over to the doorway, swinging the door closed. I open my arms to her and she rushes toward me. I kiss her until I'm sure my face is covered in her cute pink lipgloss.

"I don't want to reschedule," I say softly. "I was surprised at your discovery, but thinking about our plans has kept me going all week. I'm certainly not going to let James ruin another minute of my life if I can help it."

She ducks her head against my shoulder and I breathe in deeply. I love the smell of her shampoo. It's floral, but not rose or lavender. I don't know what it is exactly, but I know I can't get enough of it.

"If it makes a difference," I say, "weather reports indicate it should be a perfect day. Sixty degrees."

"You looked it up?" The corners of her mouth turn up, but it's not quite a smile. "I'd probably hesitate to cancel even if it was predicting a downpour. I may have stuck a raincoat and galoshes in my trunk just in case." She glances up at me, her eyes sparkling like clear ocean water from beneath thick eyelashes.

"You are breathtaking," I say.

"You're not so bad looking yourself."

I kiss her again, only pulling away when a knock at the

door startles me. Gerty leaps back so far she nearly crashes through my office window. It's only Ish with a pile of messages, but Gerty shoots out the door like a cat whose tail was stepped on.

I sit back down to try and compare the offers. My eyes start to cross, and with the varying structures, I can't quite puzzle out the tax impacts. If Luke knew about this, I'd run it past Mary for sure. I curse under my breath. I want to do this alone, but I didn't really give enough credit for our success to the support team we assembled.

I pick up my phone to call Luke, but then I put it back down. I'm so close to closing this. I want to tell Luke when I can say, "Look what I did. All alone." I don't want to call him on the ten yard line and ask him to help me keep from fumbling the ball.

I dial another number instead. I don't even realize until I hear his voice how much I needed to talk to someone else who knows James.

"What's up Paul?" Trig asks. "You engaged yet? I hear everyone cool is doing it."

Why did I call him? He's such an idiot. But he's a genius with numbers, and he's discreet. "I need some advice."

"I think my reception is failing. It sounded for a second like the great and mighty Paul was asking for my help."

I grit my teeth. "This was a bad idea."

"Oh come on. I've earned the right to give you a hard time."

He probably has. "Fine, you heard me right. I've sort of been keeping a secret." He doesn't interrupt me a single time while I explain what I've been up to with SITB.

"No wonder you didn't have time to act as best man for Luke. You were too busy being Super Man." Trig whistles. "Two launches at the same time? And Luke doesn't even know about one of them?"

"I'm not launching this product yet. I just finished the prototype. The tech is done, but as you know, that's a far cry from ready for market."

"Still," Trig says. "I'm impressed and not much impresses me."

That's true enough. I walk him through my offers and options and he points out several things that hadn't occurred to me.

"I've got one question," he says.

"What?"

"Why didn't you do all this at LitUp? You've already got a team. Why keep it from Luke?"

There's no way Trig will understand this. I've watched him share a toothbrush with Brekka. Gosh, I hope they never shared underwear. But if I don't try and explain this, at least in some small way, he'll never keep his mouth shut until I'm ready to tell Luke myself. "I've always been second place around him."

"You're partners, you and Luke. I remember, I worked on that first deal," Trig says.

"Not fifty-fifty," I say. "Forty-nine, fifty-one."

"But he treats you like you're even," Trig points out.

"He does. But Luke's older and everyone always looks to him. My parents always congratulated him, and then would sort of tack on, 'oh, you too, Paul.'"

"Isn't your mom dead?" Trig's blunt, and I actually appreciate that.

"It's not about my parents," I say. "I'm sick of always following him around."

"Didn't he follow you to Boston?"

I knew he wouldn't understand. "Yeah, I got perfect grades. I was the smart one. That was my thing. Mom and Dad were poor, which I'm sure you know. We grew up in a two-bedroom apartment. I worked hard on school, while

Luke worked part time after school to help put food on the table. Everyone said I'd make it, that I'd be the first college grad. Luke, on the other hand, became an electrician right out of high school."

"Whereas you got a scholarship to Harvard."

"And Oxford. I could have gone anywhere, but it's expensive to live in America, and I'd have graduated with a ton of debt."

"Which you'd have easily repaid," Trig says.

"I was scared to leave Australia. That's what it came down to, until my brother agreed to move here with me."

"I didn't remember that. I thought you came out and he followed."

"That's how he tells it, because Harvard was my thing. Luke paid for our apartment and food and I had my tuition covered by the school, more or less. But after being here six months and meeting some of my professors and classmates, my Chemistry professor had a problem with his home wiring. He had this old house and nothing worked. Luke helped him every day after work for a month and wouldn't let Professor Burrell pay him. My professor was so impressed he convinced Luke to take the SAT. He wrote him a recommendation that got Luke a scholarship. And a year after I started, my older brother enrolled as a freshman."

"I know," Trig says. "We had Chem together. He told me he got in because Harvard was looking for diverse applicants. Made it sound like it was his career as a full time electrician that attracted them, or maybe being from Australia."

"That's Luke for you. Always humble."

Trig sighs. "And suddenly the one thing you had on Luke, poof. It was gone." Maybe he sort of gets what I'm saying.

"It's been like that ever since. Luke casts a wide shadow."

"That he does," Trig says. "Look, if you send me the documents, I swear I'll keep my mouth shut. I'm leaving for Atlanta in thirty minutes. I can go over them on the flight and make my recommendation."

"I know you're leaving soon, but I've got another question for you," I say, my pulse pounding in my ears. "Have you talked to James Fullton much since graduation?"

"First off, he's your age, so you saw him a lot more than I did, but second, graduation?" Trig snorts. "He didn't graduate, remember?"

Of course I do. Of all people, I'm not likely to forget. "What I mean is, since he left Harvard, do you ever talk?"

"James and I never really saw eye to eye."

I find that very hard to believe. "You're two peas in a pod."

Trig makes a choking sound. "I'm going to pretend you didn't just compare me to that spoiled, entitled, playboy wannabe."

"That might be a little harsh." But his critical words somehow cheer me up.

"Why bring him up?" Trig asks. "He missed the bachelor party, but according to Geo, he's coming to the wedding. Are you worried he's going to punch you or something?"

I hadn't even thought about that. "You think he's still that mad at me?" Which of course, he must be. Why else would he hire someone to pretend to be my girlfriend to spy on me and sell my work secrets? For that matter, how did he even know about SITB? No one in my life knows about it, and I never even told Cynthia my real name. I guess that's why Gerty saying James Fullton's name sort of blindsided me. I expected it to be corporate espionage fueled by a competitor of LitUp, but not something linked to my old college days.

"James Fulton the Fourth should have majored in grudges at Harvard," Trig says. "He could have taught the upper level classes. In fact, he might have been able to teach a thing or two to the infamous Count of Monte Christo."

Trig sure has some strong feelings about this. "You said you never even talked to him. Why do you think he's so great with grudges?"

"You and James were a year older than me so we didn't have many classes together, but he left his laptop open that one time. When he fell asleep in the library."

I remember. Trig sent out an email from his account. It was obviously a joke, but it was a little outrageous. A love letter to a particularly awful professor who happened to be male. People weren't so accepting of homosexuality at the time, either. James and the Latin professor both took a lot of heat for it, especially when Professor Snider turned out to actually be gay.

"Is he still mad about that? It was a joke."

"He was irate at the time," Trig says. "But I figured he got over it quickly. I didn't realize he hadn't until he tanked one of my deals three years back, for a product called Hyped. It was an appetite suppressant that made Fen Fen look like Chiclets. We had FDA approval, and everything was in place. Then our funding fell through, and our suppliers backed out, and a million other little things happened all at once. Brekka and I about went crazy trying to stick our fingers into every leak that popped up. I've never had a deal completely fall apart like that. The more we dug into the oddities, like the bank yanking funding at the last minute per some buried clause, the less we could figure out the cause."

"That sucks," I say.

"It was worse than I'm making it sound. It was like death by a thousand cuts. Each individual thing seemed solvable, but then something else, and something else. We didn't sleep for a week, trying to fix the house of cards as it collapsed one level at a time."

"How do you know it was James?"

"I had no idea what was going on at the time, but I got an email a week later," Trig says. "It read, 'Hyped for Snider. We're finally even. JF'."

"He waited more than ten years," I say. "That's messed up."

"And in his mind, it was completely *even* that he tanked a fifty million dollar deal because I wrote an email that was obviously a joke ten years ago."

I swear under my breath.

"He was a lot madder at you," Trig says.

And I still haven't gotten an email. Which probably means that according to James' ledger, we aren't square yet.

"What's going on?" Trig asks. "You worried about your launch?"

"Now I am," I lie.

"Want me to dig into what he's been up to lately?" Trig asks. "I don't have the reach I used to have, but I employ some pretty hard hitting investigators."

"Nah," I say. "I appreciate it, but I'll handle this myself."

"You got him kicked out of Harvard," Trig says.

"He did that to himself. He shouldn't have been cheating."

"He swore he wasn't. He said he only had the answers in case he got nervous."

"Do you believe that?" I ask.

Trig sighs. "I think you were pissed about that stupid girl you thought he stole from you, and you didn't care whether he was cheating or not. You only knew he had it because he offered you a copy of the same cheat sheet. He thought you were friends, whether you did or not, and you threw him to the dogs."

A pang of the old guilt eats at me. "So he cheats his way through school, and I'm the bad guy."

"I didn't say that. In fact, I never understood how you and Luke could stand him."

I never liked James. I hated all the legacies at Harvard, including Trig. When Luke started a year after me, he thought I was close minded. He liked everyone back then, just like he does today. Luke always gives people the benefit of the doubt, and for the most part, people don't let Luke down.

"Has James done something?" Trig asks.

"No." I don't want to get into any details of my first epic failure.

"So why are you asking me about this?" Trig asks.

I sigh. "He might have tried to steal my tech on this startup. Only one really resourceful employee kept that from happening."

Trig's quiet for a moment. "I think your older brother may be James' only real friend in the world. He cheated back in school because he was lazy and he didn't think there would ever be consequences for someone like him. He's a smart SOB, and he doesn't like anyone. Except he liked Luke a lot."

I think Trig may be right. "Which means he never did anything to me before. . . because I was in business with Luke."

"You're lucky you've been working with your brother," Trig says. "Because hurting you hurts Luke, and I can't see James doing that. But watch your back out on your own. In his mind, you're fair game now."

"Alright, well thanks for the advice."

I lean back in my chair and think about what Trig said. I'd met James' attack and defended against it this time, but he tanked my first venture. Why didn't I get an email after that one? Is he going to plague me forever unless I'm hiding behind Luke?

I check my email like an idiot, even rummaging around in the spam, hoping stupidly for something from James that I missed. No luck.

I send the numbers to Trig and head out to grab Winnie for our picnic. He's bouncing up and down like Tigger when I reach home, but he hasn't destroyed any of the piles of wedding junk. He didn't knock over any of the chairs set up in the backyard either. I squat down to eye level and rub him all over. "Good boy, Sir Winston. You're a good boy."

His mouth always pulls back into a big smile and his entire body shakes with his tail when I come home. James may hate me forever, but at least this guy loves me.

When I stand up, Winnie bounds over and grabs the running leash between his teeth. "Not a jog today, boy. We're going to play, though." I snag the bag with his tennis balls and he leaps even higher, incorporating a few spinning circles into his jumps.

I throw a picnic blanket into the back of my car, along with Winnie's ball bag, and he leaps into the passenger side, slobbering on my leather seats. I usually drive my Range Rover when I take Winnie with me, but Gerty's already seen my Tesla, and I don't want her thinking I've got two cars. Not until it's the right time to explain why I have four.

I meet the driver from Dave Poe's BBQ at the edge of my driveway. He's holding the bag for me when I open the gate. "Thanks Steve."

"You're welcome Mr. Manning."

It pays to always use the same people if you tip well, which I always do.

Gerty pulls up in front of the park at the same time I do. She unbuckles Troy, and I clip Winnie into his retractable leash. Winnie bolts toward Troy and I lock the leash before he can bowl him over.

"That's a cool leash," she says.

"It's almost thirty feet long when I want it to be. It lets him run around me fifteen times before going another direction and knocking me over like a bowling pin. I'm guessing Troy will enjoy watching it."

I pulled Winnie up short, but Troy closed the gap between boy and dog immediately. He's currently in danger of having his face licked off. He doesn't seem to mind, but Gerty's expression is priceless.

"I give him heart worm pills every month," I say. "If that helps."

"Boys and dogs. They're a match made in heaven, but also kind of gross." I hand the leash to Troy and let him run around with Winnie for a bit. Even though it's a gorgeous day, there aren't many people in the park. Plus, as much as he whines and whimpers, Winnie always listens to me. The leash is more of a reminder to Winnie, than a safety protocol. Besides, it provides peace of mind for the other people around.

When Troy poops out, Gerty spreads the blanket so he has a place to collapse. I unclip Winnie's leash and throw the ball a few dozen times. Eventually, Winnie settles down on the blanket next to us.

"Troy loves dogs," Gerty says. "But the one he sees the most won't fetch. Like, not at all."

"I'm pretty sure Winnie would rather play fetch than eat filet mignon."

"He's kind of dumb," she says. "I'd always pick the filet."

"Which is why we're the masters, and they're the pets."

Gerty helps me take containers of meat and sides out of the bag, and then she starts pulling measuring cups out of her diaper bag.

"What are those for?" I ask.

Troy's gotten a second wind I suppose, because now he's throwing the ball for Winnie. It only goes five or ten feet, but Winnie doesn't care.

Gerty doesn't whisper, but she definitely speaks quietly. "Troy has type one diabetes. I need to measure his food and make sure he's eating the right amount, or I'll give him too much insulin."

I heard of someone else whose little kid was diabetic, but I can't think who. Someone's friend or something? I wish I'd paid more attention so I would have something intelligent to say. "That must be really hard."

She shrugs. "We're figuring it out. When I left early on my second day—" She chokes up and shakes her head.

"Is everything okay?"

She nods. "It's hard to leave him to go to work, that's all. Not everyone does such a good job monitoring his intake. If you're off by even a little bit."

"That's a little scary. Gosh, are kids diagnosed this young very often?"

"No. It's very rare, thankfully."

"Can his dad handle it?"

"He didn't even know for the first month after Troy was diagnosed, because he couldn't be bothered to check on us. The good news is that he doesn't ever try to take Troy. He can't see him unless he's supervised anyway, but I'd prefer he just stay away, honestly. I know that sounds terrible."

"You just want what's best for your son. It sounds like what's best is not having much to do with his father."

"Yep."

"Do you miss his dad?"

She meets my eyes. "Not even a little bit. I miss having someone else to rely on, a partner, but if I'm being honest, Chris wasn't ever much in the reliability department."

That sucks, but it lines up with what I saw when he came by to scream at her for taking state mandated levels of child support. What a loser.

I watch the gorgeous woman in front of me, her delicate hand measuring her son's food into cups carefully on a picnic. She's been there for me every time I needed it in the last two weeks, and it's been more often than I'd like to admit. She's wearing jeans and a t-shirt and her hair's pulled back into a ponytail. No high heels and impractical sheath dresses, no pretentious airs or complicated makeup. No expensive highlights, and her sunglasses look like they came from a convenience store.

I love all of it.

It's like coming home for the first time. I've been wishing I could find what Luke has, and what Trig has, but maybe I've been looking in all the wrong places. I open my mouth to ask her to come with me to my brother's wedding this weekend, but then I remember she had plans already. Besides, to take her with me, I'd need to tell her about SITB and that my real name is Paul Manning, not Jack Campbell. I'd have to explain that everything she knows about me is pretty much a lie, and that would destroy the entire evening.

An overwhelming desire to tell her grips me. I want someone other than Trig to know, to understand why I'm doing it. My reasons feel stupid and small all of a sudden, but I want her to tell me she gets it, that she understands.

But I have no idea whether she will. Doing something on your own is a preposterous idea. No one does something entirely on his or her own. Even at SITB, I developed the product I did because of my team. This woman takes care of her son, but to put food on the table, she has to rely on someone else to watch him. She didn't tell me about Troy or her ex at first. Maybe she'll understand why I've been lying. I hope she understands.

"Hey, so there's something I was going to talk to you about."

"Yeah?" she asks. "Work something? Or personal?"

"Personal," I say.

"Is this about how you know the James guy?"

"I—" I stop. "Uh, well. No, that's not what I was going to say, but I could tell you that if you want."

"No, I'm sorry," she says. "I was just thinking what a terrible person he'd have to be to do something like that, to lie to everyone about who he was and hide away and steal someone's ideas like that. I've never understood shell companies and fake names. I mean, my ex tried stuff like that. He had this company, but when it didn't do well, he walked away from it and left the creditors holding the bag. He said that's why people have companies, to limit their liability. It just felt like another way to let other people deal with your mistakes instead of cleaning them up yourself. Family is the most important thing to me, and real family requires honesty."

Her big eyes look up at me and I gulp. "Sometimes people set up companies so that they can do something without every single person around them watching them like fish in a bowl."

"You think that's why this guy used a bunch of companies with other names?" She frowns.

"No, not James."

She exhales. "Phew, because all I'm saying is that I support you, no matter what his reasoning was. That guy seems super shady."

Maybe I shouldn't tell her about my fake name and company yet. She may need to get to know me a little better, or she might assume I'm just like her ex.

"I'm sorry I interrupted. What did you want to tell me?"

"Nothing big. I guess it is sort of business related," I say. "I thought you should know that I told all my core employees when I hired them that I'd give them a one-eighth percent share in the company if they were dedicated and worked hard during the start-up phase. I gave Nancy a quarter percent share. After what you did to save us with your quick thinking and observant nature, I cut you in for a quarter percent too."

Her mouth drops open. "I don't know what that means precisely, but I assure you I was just doing my job. Accounting already notified me that I'm being paid for two jobs this quarter. That's more than generous. You don't need to cut me into anything."

It's already done, but I drop it for the time being. Tonight is not going like I expected. "Uh, right. Well, we can talk about the details on that later I suppose."

Troy bumps into me then, and Winnie comes flying over next, upending the container of pulled pork.

"Winnie, no. Sit." He hops over and sits where I point, his head pointing down shamefully.

Gerty helps me clean up the mess.

"Can I get a photo with your dog?" Troy asks, just as we finish.

I snap a few shots of Troy and Winnie, and text them to Gerty.

"I can take one if you want." Troy holds out his tiny hand. I meet Gerty's eyes and she shrugs.

"Uh, sure." I hand Troy my phone.

"Mom, you be in it too, like Winnie's getting a hug."

We squeeze together and Troy pokes on my phone several times before he's finally satisfied enough to hand it back to me. I scroll through a bunch of awful photos, but I find one decent one. I favorite it and text it to Gerty, too.

The rest of the night goes well, but I don't bring up James, my real name, or her partial share in SITB again. I certainly don't invite her to Luke's wedding.

But for the first time in my life, I have someone I wish I could take. For now, I guess that's enough.

14

TRUDY

After working all day on Friday, my energy is zapped. I know that I've got to somehow make myself look fresh and ethereal so I can spend the evening being polite and friendly at Mary's rehearsal dinner. It doesn't help that we have essentially no family, so most of the guests will be people I don't know. I want to make a good impression for Mary's sake, but I'd rather pretend I'm sick and stay home to watch *Gilmore Girls*.

I love my son every second of every day, but I'm a little too cranky with Troy's buzzing exuberance tonight. I answer question after question with as much patience as I can muster, but the second his grandparents pick him up, I breathe a sigh of relief.

And then I feel guilty about it.

Which doesn't stop me from collapsing on my bed and closing my eyes for one second to recover. I almost pass out and sleep through the entire rehearsal dinner, but my phone buzzes before I can drift off completely.

The corners of my mouth turn up. Jack. MISS YOU.

I don't waste any time replying. MISS YOU MORE.

MISS YOU THE MOST.

I'm beaming as I curl my hair and touch up my makeup. Then I put on the green dress I picked. It's so high waisted that it bells out right under my chest. Since I have a generous chest, it makes me look fat.

Really fat.

I went shopping Wednesday night for a dress for Mary's rehearsal dinner, but it wasn't exactly a relaxing experience. Troy didn't want to sit still and kept darting in between my legs and under the dressing room door. I gave up looking after trying on only three dresses. This green one looked the least terrible of the three I tried, and the color is vibrant. I'm pleasantly surprised when it doesn't have dirty handprints anywhere on it.

At least it's not as ghastly as the maid of honor dress I'll be wearing on Saturday. I groan and flop down on my bed, because it's not like I have a choice for either dress. My clothing shopping budget has been non-existent for the last few years, so this green monstrosity is the only fancy thing I own.

A knock at my door alerts me that Paisley has arrived. I force myself to get up and go open it. "Hey Pais." Her silver sheath dress is covered in sparkly embroidery. "You look like a shooting star!" I squash down a tiny pang of jealousy.

"Thanks. Are you excited?" Her grin deflates slightly as she takes in my dress. "Why do you look pregnant?"

I close my eyes.

"Oh my gosh, you didn't relapse with Chris or anything, right?"

"What's wrong with you?" I ask. "I'm not pregnant. I just didn't pick a great dress, okay? Troy was with me, and I was a little distracted."

"Please tell me you didn't already pull the tags off."

I nod my head. "Not that it matters. It's not like I have time to find something else."

"Girl. You should not shop alone. You know this about yourself."

"I wasn't alone," I say. "That was the problem."

Paisley frowns. "This is not good. Maybe we can put you in something else. Literally any dress with an actual waistline would look better."

Paisley starts pulling things out of my closet and tossing them on the bathroom floor.

"Whoa there," I say, "maybe we don't have to make such a big mess that I'll have to spend all day Sunday cleaning it up."

"None of this will work." Paisley puts her hands on her hips.

I plop down on the bed. "I get it. This dress isn't cute, but who cares what I'm wearing? It's a wedding for my sister, not for me."

"You're meeting Paul tonight," she says. "*The* Paul. The person on whom your sister and soon-to-be brother-in-law have pinned all their hopes for your future happiness."

I try not to roll my eyes and fail. "You sound like an A&E miniseries. I don't care about stupid Paul."

"Those are some strong words," Paisley says. "Why not?"

"Because I'm already madly in love with someone else." As I say the words, I realize that they aren't exactly true, but they aren't the outrageous joke I intended either. I do like Jack. More than I should, given how long I've known him. Way, way too much, in light of my list.

Paisley pins me with a glare. "Who, exactly?"

"Cole."

She splutters. "Are you serious right now?"

"What if I am?"

"I am so calling him." She whips out her phone. "He thought you liked your stupid boss so he didn't pursue you, but he thought you were really cute and smart and daring. He'd probably come back out." Paisley taps at the screen.

Why can't anyone ever tell when I'm kidding? I grab her hand. "I'm joking. I just don't want to be set up with anyone right now."

Paisley stares at me as if she's trying to run my words through a lie detector. She stuffs her phone back into her purse with a frown. "What's wrong with Cole?"

I look up at the ceiling and sigh. "Nothing! I am not supposed to like anyone. I just got divorced, remember?"

Paisley searches my face. "Except you do. You already like someone. That part wasn't a joke."

It's like she was trained to ferret out secrets or something. "Yes, I do."

"Who?"

"My boss, okay? Your brother was right. I kind of have a thing for my boss, and I think he might like me, too. Which is a whole mess, I know. I don't need a lecture."

"Your boss is probably awesome, but tonight you finally meet Paul! I've heard he's amazing. Mary says he's also smart ,and to be honest, I was interested as soon as I heard there was a mini-Luke. But if you're sure you have zero interest, that's fine with me. All you have to do to convince me you really have zero interest is wear that maternity dress tonight. And if you do that, then I call dibs on fine, perfect, rich, smart Paul. With you in that green potato sack, his attention will most definitely all be fixed on me."

I stomp my foot. "It's not a maternity dress, and it's definitely not a potato sack."

I don't even know what that means, really. Potato sacks are made of clear plastic, right? But when I look in the mirror, suddenly I see it. I'm wearing a potato sack. All I need is a twist tie for the top. My boobs look like lumpy potatoes, and my neck is where the twist tie would go. My hair is the bunch bag at the top.

I want to scream and throw a tantrum, but we don't even have time for that. If we don't leave immediately, we'll be late.

During my distracted self examination, Paisley went back to rummaging in my closet. She steps out with a box in her hand. It has been sitting on the top shelf in the corner since I moved in, and I have no idea what's in there. A graduation cap and gown? Old photos of Mary and Foster?

"What about this?" Paisley pulls a sky blue chiffon dress out of the box. When she shakes it out, flowers flutter from where they dot the entire the skirt.

"Mary left that. Maybe my drunk drunk dad thought Mary needed it for a Quinceñera," I joke.

"You should at least try it on," Paisley insists. "It's the exact color of your eyes, and it can't look worse than that." She points at my fluffy green mistake.

"It's blue chiffon. Why are we even talking about this? I'm at least fifteen years too old to wear chiffon."

Paisley shakes it at me. "Stop arguing with me and just try it on."

It's easier to do what Pais wants than to argue with her. I shuck my brand new dress off and unzip the blue chiffon. It slides on easily, but when Paisley zips it up, it's snug. It falls gracefully to my ankles and the skirt bells out softly from below a drop waist. The flowers flutter when I move, but it scoops low enough in the front that it doesn't look as juvenile as I expected. It looks... feminine. Soft, even.

"You can thank me now," Paisley says. "Because that dress is amazing. So, so much better than before. It's like Mary Poppins meets Catherine Zeta Jones."

I have no idea what that means, but it's definitely a step above the last one.

"You have to put your hair up," she says. "To complete the whole look."

"The only way I know how to put my hair up is in a ponytail."

"Good thing I'm here."

Twenty minutes later, my hair's half up in a fluffy knot, and curly tendrils spill down my back.

Paisley claps. "Oh my gosh, I know what it is now. You look like Cinderella in that remake movie, right before she loses her slipper and her carriage turns into a pumpkin. You're finally ready to meet your nearly-a-billionaire, LED-light-innovation prince. Unless you're still insisting you aren't interested?"

I scowl at her. "Thanks for your help, but I'm serious. Hard pass."

Thanks to my extreme makeover, we're going to be nearly thirty minutes late. I text Mary. I'M SO SORRY. PAISLEY AND I ARE ON OUR WAY. BE THERE IN TWENTY MINUTES.

NO PROBLEM. WE'RE ALL FINE. WAITING TIL YOU ARRIVE TO START.

How embarrassing. NO! DON'T WAIT. START NOW. PLEASE.

ARE YOU SURE?

YES, YES! I AM ENTIRELY CERTAIN. I really don't want all of Luke's family and friends talking about how rude I am. And I doubt I can eat the french onion soup in this dress anyway. More than a handful of bites and I'll split the zipper.

When we reach the Swan House at the Atlanta History Center, I stare dumbstruck at the beautiful old building. Until I realize we have nine gazillion steps to climb. But while my thighs burn, the huge old plantation home looks so gorgeous that I almost feel like Cinderella running up the stairs to the ball.

I wish I'd had the gumption to ask Jack to come with me. The only thing that would've made this better would have been holding his hand. Which is stupid, because I may have the job I want, but I haven't graduated yet, and I'm nowhere near paying off Mary's loan. I may have set my goals aside for a few exciting dates, but I'm not getting serious with anyone until I've accomplished them.

No matter how cute Jack's smile is. Or how good his biceps look in a t-shirt while he's lying on a picnic blanket. Next to his adorable and well-trained dog. Or playing sweetly with my son. Or kissing me until I forget my own name.

I focus on the last few steps so I don't fall flat on my face and have to march inside, late, and with a bloody nose.

"We're here for the Wiggin-Manning wedding dinner," Paisley tells the attendant at the door. He's wearing a sharp red and black uniform with gold buttons.

He verifies our names and checks us off on a list before saying, "Right this way." He opens the huge doors and shows us into a large room with one tremendously long table.

Everyone stands up when we walk in, and I really do feel like a fairy tale princess. Luke grins warmly and Mary beams and waves at the two empty seats next to her. Trig and Geo are seated just beyond our seats. I walk as calmly as I can toward all the waiting people.

Once I've found my seat, I sit down along with everyone else and look across the table for the first time.

At a very handsome and very puzzled Jack.

Um. What? I turn toward Mary with what I'm sure is an

idiotic expression on my face and whisper, "Why is Jack here?"

She shrugs. "Luke knows a lot of people. We ended up inviting a lot more people than I intended, but I had Geo seat the ones I don't know very well way down at the end. Remind me. Who's Jack again?"

"Hi," Jack says loudly from across the table. "I'm Luke's little brother, Paul."

I frown at him. "Excuse me?"

"I'm Paul Manning," he says, speaking loudly and enunciating carefully. "You must be Mary's sister Trudy. And your last name probably isn't Wiggin, because you were married before and had a son. I wouldn't have any idea what your new last name was, but you probably kept your ex's last name so you and your son would have the same name, even after the divorce. Which I obviously didn't think about until this very moment."

Luke drops his fork on the table. "What is wrong with you Paul? You sound completely insane."

"I'm fine," Paul says. "I'm just catching all of us up." He widens his eyes at me.

I huff. "I'm Gertrude Jenkins, just as it says on my ID. I had to provide my identification as well as my résumé prior to starting my new job. And then I submitted to a thorough background check. So obviously I never tried to hide who I am. Ever. What does your ID say, *Paul?*"

"It says Paul Jack Manning," he says with a grin. "And you may be interested to learn that my mother's maiden was Campbell."

"I'm so sorry Trudy's acting so weird." Mary places a hand on my arm. "Calm down, sweetie. You've seen a photo of Paul, remember? I showed it to you when Luke and I first started dating."

I think about that photo, dredging up my quite fuzzy

memories of it. He was nerdy hot, that I remembered. His hair was combed severely, and he wore thick glasses. "Paul wore dark black frames and looked dorky." Adorably dorky, but I don't mention that part.

Paul drops his fork this time and it clatters against the plate. By now, almost the entire table is staring at us. He turns to glare at Luke. "You sent Mary a photo from Halloween?"

Luke looks from me to his brother with a quizzical expression. "Of course I did. You would have done the exact same thing if you were me. Mary wasn't too keen on dating me yet, and I wasn't about to send her a photo of my much better looking younger brother unless I was sure I looked better than he did."

I close my eyes. Paul was wearing a costume in the photo, which is why he didn't look like he normally would. Which explains why it never occurred to me that Jack might actually be Paul. The lying and subterfuge that included a fake name and a second company threw me too, but the glasses didn't help.

What the heck is going on?

Mary slits her eyes. "It feels like you two know each other, like from more than just a bad photo and the things we've told you."

"I have never met Paul Manning in my life." I say loudly. "I imagine there's a joke here somewhere, but I'm not in on it." I stand up and shove my chair back. "I think I better take a little break. Sorry for being late, and then stepping out abruptly."

Paisley stands up too, but Paul flies to his feet even faster and practically runs around the table. "I can explain."

I stomp out the doors I just entered, Paul on my heels. Once we're outside, I spin around to face him. "My life isn't some kind of game, *Paul*."

He shakes his head. "I'm as surprised as you are. I wanted to invite you to be my date last night, but then I'd have had to explain that I'm actually Paul, not Jack Campbell, and that felt like more than a casual second date conversation. Plus Troy was there and I guess I chickened out."

I nod. "And how did that decision go for you?"

"Clearly it was the wrong one." He runs his hand through his hair. I wish I didn't already know how soft it is.

"Well," I huff. "I'm actually the same person I've always been. Trudy."

"You go by Gerty at SITB," he says. "In my defense. And Luke never showed me a photo, Halloween or otherwise."

"The only reason I go by Gerty, which I hate by the way, is because Nancy had a favorite aunt who went by that. She asked if I had the same nickname and I told her sure. I'd have agreed to being called Prissy Andrews if it would have gotten me that job. I need that job, Jack." I choke. "I mean, Paul." Tears well up in my eyes. I still need the job, but I don't think I can keep working for someone who lied to me for two weeks. "Why would you lie about your name? Is this some kind of office joke? Or are you really the bad guy here? Did you steal all of that tech from that James guy? What's really going on?"

He inhales deeply and then exhales slowly. "Look, you may not understand this, and I get that it was a stupid decision, okay? But my brother Luke, you've met him. He's my older brother and I love him, but I've never done anything on my own. I started college and then he started the next year. He and I started a company together, and we've done really well. Together. Always together, for my entire life."

"Why not just tell him you wanted to try something on your own? I'm sure he'd get it. I've been playing that song on repeat since my divorce. Mary and Luke both offered me jobs." It hits me then that, had things gone another way, I might have been working for Paul at LitUp. Had I not been so adamant about refusing any help from anyone else, he might still be my boss.

"Because I was a coward," Paul says softly. "I didn't want Luke to know I was branching off on my own until I'd already succeeded."

"Luke told me you ran the company for years without much help from him after his wife died. So hadn't you already succeeded alone?"

"He was always there, though. Looking over things, making suggestions. In fact, he came up with both of the huge ideas that took off during that timeframe. He quit coming into the office and started moving when Beth died, but he didn't stop pulling his weight."

Of course he didn't. He's Luke. He and Mary are perfect for each other.

"I've been waiting for the right moment to come clean with Luke since our hearing. I had it all planned out. I was going to show him my prototype, and then explain how I developed it."

He looks like Troy when he's piled an especially tall tower of blocks, desperate for my approval.

"I guess this isn't exactly how you imagined he'd find out," I say. "But what I don't understand is, why didn't you tell your own employees?"

"As you know, my first project was stolen. I wanted to make sure no one involved in the last startup could find me. I used entirely different employees and a new office. Besides, I couldn't risk word of anything getting back to Luke or out in the market. If I trade on the name Luke and I made, I'm still not doing it alone."

That part I understand. Using a reference from Mary seemed like cheating.

I know it's not the same as what Chris did. Paul didn't make me any vows first, and he didn't lie to avoid telling me things he selfishly wanted to cover up, but it feels similar. And he's been lying to his brother, the person who matters most to him, for months and months. That isn't confidence inspiring. I wanted to do things on my own, but I told Mary that to her face.

"Well, you've done it haven't you?" I ask. "Entirely on your own. I hope that feels really, really good. I hope it was worth it." I turn on my heel and head back inside.

Jack, er, Paul, follows just behind me, but he doesn't grab me or try to say anything else. I stop near Mary and lean over to whisper in her ear. I've already made far too big a scene at her dinner. "I love you to the moon and back, and then some, but I'd prefer to sit down at the end of the table tonight. Is that alright?"

Mary opens her mouth to object I think, but Luke squeezes her hand and she nods instead. "Sure. Of course you can sit wherever you'd like."

I pick up my purse and carry it to the end of the table where an attendant's already placing a new chair. I force a smile. "Hi everyone. I'm Trudy, Mary's little sister. I'm so sorry for being late and causing such a disturbance. I promise I'll be perfectly behaved the rest of the wedding."

The man sitting next to me looks amazing in his tux. His features are sharp, birdlike even. His nose is prominent, his dark hair combed neatly, his eyes attentive and quick. His smile reveals huge dimples and perfectly straight, white teeth. "I'm Jim."

He holds out his hand and I shake it. Jim's tuxedo looks nice, like the more-expensive-than-a-car kind of nice. His face is a little severe, but it's handsome too, in a unique and compelling way.

"I'm assuming you're friends with the groom," I say.

He nods. "You probably know all the bride's friends and family already."

I bob my head up and down. "All five of us."

"Luke and I go way back."

"I wish I'd known Luke ten or fifteen years ago," I say. "I can't seem to imagine him any younger than he is. It's like my brain thinks he was born as competent and assured as he is today."

Jim clears his throat. "Luke's one of the world's best people, which is probably why there are so many of his friends here. I met him his first year of college, and he was already pretty competent and assured."

Mary deserves someone like him. And I probably deserve the brother who hides his business ventures because he feels threatened by Mr. Perfect.

"So you went to school together?" I ask.

"We did. Luke helped me in almost every subject. He's got a mind as sharp as a steel trap."

I doubt this guy needed much help. "Clearly you can barely string two words together. How did Luke manage to put up with such an oaf? Or might I sense a tiny bit of false Ivy League modesty?"

Jim's loud laugh surprises me. "You're a little fireball, aren't you?"

He and I make small talk for a few minutes, and by the time they bring dessert, I've calmed down a lot, thanks in large part to Jim's dry humor. Luke and Paul's great aunt on my other side is really nice, but her hearing aids clearly need adjustment. My attempts to carry on a conversation with her resulted in a lot of loud "Whats?" and "Excuse mes?"

"I couldn't help but notice that you knew Paul," Jim says as they place a slice of cheesecake in front of me.

"You could say that."

"Were you upset with him?"

"Let's just say that I knew Paul without realizing I knew Paul."

Jim's brow furrows. "How is that possible?"

I take a bite and let it melt on my tongue. "He's my boss, which is awkward enough, but it's worse actually. We went on a few dates, and he still hadn't told me his real name. Some thing with him and his brother, I don't know." I probably shouldn't be telling him any of this, but it's not my stupid secret, and by the look of things, Paul's coming clean to Luke at that end of the table right now. I've noticed a lot of hands thrown up in the air and pointed glares.

"Be careful there," Jim says.

"Careful?" I ask. "Why do you say that, other than the obvious advice not to date my boss?"

"It's not really my business," Jim says. "Never mind."

"If you know Luke, I'm guessing you know Paul too."

Jim nods. "Met them the same year."

"Are you saying you think he's a bad guy?"

"Not a bad guy, no. I've just seen a lot of disappointed ladies in the wake of Hurricane Paul, that's all. And you seem too smart for that."

I think about poor Cynthia. Whom I shouldn't really pity, since she was essentially a spy. But still, she seemed to genuinely like him, inasmuch as she was able. But then I think about Jack playing with Troy. And throwing the ball for his dog. Plus, he is Luke's brother. How bad could he really be?

Which makes me wonder why Jim's undermining him to me.

"Where did you say you're from?" I ask.

"I didn't say, but I'm from New York. I've lived in the city most of my life."

He's not a big fan of Paul, but he knew him in college. I think about the research I did this past week, about all the shell companies. All the US based ones were registered in New York. Which might not mean anything, or then again it might. "Your name doesn't happen to be James Fullton the Fourth, does it Jim?"

His eyes widen. "It is, yes. How did you know that?"

I shrug. "Let's call it a hunch."

"Impressive hunch. You work for Paul, you said?" A smile creeps onto James Fullton's sharply angled face.

"I do. And last week I found a key logger and helped him follow it to its owner. And then we tracked that back to a shell company, owned by one James Fullton the Fourth."

Jim leans back in his chair and stares at me intently.

"Where did you find Cynthia? That seems like a lucky find, a woman who's willing to spy on Paul. She seemed to genuinely like him."

He sighs. "She does like him. She jumped at the chance to get information from me on how to snag 'Jack's' attention. My advice worked too, because I really do understand what makes him tick. After she took my advice to grab his attention, she couldn't risk backing out on our deal."

"Because you'd tell him she was spying on him."

James nods. "People never think things all the way through."

"Why do any of it?" I ask. "Why steal Paul's ideas and then sell them for what amounts to pennies?"

"Paul got me kicked out of Harvard. Did he mention that to you?"

Nope, he sure did not.

"I had the answers to a history test. A TA from the class sold them to me. I didn't think I'd need them, but I had them on me just in case. I didn't even pull them out, but I mentioned to Paul I had them when I saw him cramming at two a.m. the night before the exam. I offered to make him a copy as a favor."

I didn't peg Paul for a goodie two-shoes, what with his spy operations and fake names, but maybe he's changed a lot in the intervening years.

"You like Luke at least," I say flatly.

James nods. "I never had a chance to pay good old Paul back without hurting his brother, but I kept tabs on him. When I saw the opportunity, I took it."

No regret, no apology, no embarrassment. James is a calculating guy, but he refused to move against Luke, so he has some kind of moral code. "Are you done tormenting him yet?" I ask. "Has he paid enough?"

"Getting kicked out of Harvard caused a rough couple of years for me. My parents weren't pleased, and they cut me off."

"And that wasn't in any way your fault," I say. "For cheating. It's all on Paul?"

James shrugs. "It probably helped me in the long run. But even a well justified beating hurts."

"So you're not done punishing him?"

"I haven't decided yet," Jim says. "But just as he couldn't get me kicked out if I hadn't been cheating, I couldn't have stolen his tech if he hadn't been dumb enough to date Cynthia, and strike out on his own, selfishly."

That's fair.

Jim sips his drink. "You're mad at him, but you seem to genuinely like him too. I'll tell you this about Paul, and I'm not trying to punish him with this. He's not Luke, and he values different things than his brother. And, unlike Luke, when things get hard, Paul bails."

"Duly noted."

"Speaking of bailing, you're in a weird situation now. You're working for Paul, and you know who he really is, and you know your job may be short lived if he sells his prototype."

"That's true."

"If I offered you a job at one of my banks here in town, would you take it?" Jim's eyes look utterly steady. All signs point to his offer being serious.

"You don't even know what I do. I could be the office manicurist."

He looks at my chipped nails and wisely makes no comment. "You found my key logger. You helped Paul identify Cynthia. And you tracked me down and connected the dots from that research to this table. That's good enough for me," Jim says.

"I'm an IT manager."

"I can definitely find you an appropriate position, and I'll offer you a ten percent raise over whatever Paul's paying you." Jim smirks. "I'm not trying to twist your arm, and I don't care whether you date Paul. I'm a very successful businessman because I am always hunting for and rewarding talent. You wouldn't be working for me, not directly at all. I own the majority of Fullmer Bank, but I don't oversee the day-to-day operations. I'm offering you a job as a final dig at Paul, yes, but I'm also offering you one because you're bright and capable. Say the word and I'll make a call to one of our local branches."

"I should trust the guy who sends spies and steals ideas?"

He shrugs. "Is that really worse than the guy who makes

up fake names and dates spies? Other than my inability to forgive when I've been wronged, I'm not so bad."

I don't know how I feel about Jack. Or Paul. Or whoever he is. I never felt comfortable dating my boss. But whether I ought to leave so I can date him, or whether I ought to stay and not date him is all very confusing. Which is one of the reasons I made that list in the first place, so I wouldn't be in this situation.

Even so.

"Thanks for the offer, but I think I'll pass."

Jim shrugs. "I'm going to pretend you didn't answer me yet. I'll be here all weekend, so you have plenty of time to change your mind."

"I'll be sure to let you know if I do."

When he grins, he looks just like a falcon I saw once at the zoo. Right after they released its dinner and it dove down and snapped a rabbit's neck. In spite of his attitude, or maybe because of it, I actually like Jim a lot more than I'd have expected to like the person who spied on Paul. He gives me a card and half bows before walking away. The strangely regency gesture from a clearly modern day man makes me grin.

Paisley grabs my elbow the minute he's gone. "Ready to go home yet? Because I have so many questions for you, it isn't even funny."

"Weren't you sitting by Paul and Mary?" I ask. "I imagine you know most everything by now. It looked like he was fessing up."

Paisley's eyes widen. "He's been hiding a secret company! It's wild. Luke's pretty upset."

Paul approaches us, his hands in his pockets. His eyes meet mine and a spark zooms down my spine. I shiver and rub my hands over my arms. I wish his jaw wasn't so square. I wish he wasn't so tall and fit. But mostly, I wish I didn't want him to kiss me so badly. It's making it hard to hold on to my anger. And I am angry.

"Can we talk?" he asks.

"What about?" I force a frown to cover the tremor in my voice. "Because I don't really see the point."

"I want to explain," Paul says. "Please?"

"When I moved down to this end of the table, someone said, 'it looks like you already know Paul.'" I scowl at Paul. "You know what I realized? I thought I knew Jack, but tonight I found out I don't know him or you. Not at all."

"That's a little overwrought, don't you think?" Paul asks.

Overwrought? Like I need smelling salts or I'll pass out? Or is he worried that I'll make a scene?

I'm not the one being unreasonable. I'm not the one who lied to my entire family to fill some need to strike out on my own. I'm beginning to think Paul's a coward. Well, I've dated one coward and it didn't go well for me. Chris yanked me along for months and months, hiding his girlfriend the entire time. He didn't even bother telling me that he'd checked out of our marriage of four years.

I have no patience for cowards.

"How's this for melodrama?" I widen my eyes at him. "I met one of your old Harvard buddies tonight, a guy named Jim. Once I puzzled out that his full name was James Fullton the Fourth, he offered me a job."

"I saw him down there, but you told him you already had a job." A muscle in Paul's face twitches. "Right?"

"He knows I work at SITB. He may be the only other person here who knows what that means for my future employment prospects, especially now that you're confessing everything to your brother. He offered me better pay and a drama free work environment. Now that you've seen how *overwrought* I become in difficult situations, I think you'll agree that's a promising offer. He also showed me his license so I could verify his real name."

Paul frowns. "No he didn't."

I shake my head. "No, he didn't."

"What did you tell him?" Paul's voice is satisfactorily rough, and his eyes suitably concerned.

"I told him I'd come check it out," I lie. "But as my boss, you should know I'm leaning toward taking it."

I storm out of the room, and when I glance back, Jim's grin looks identical to that falcon's as he tore chunks out of that rabbit.

Mary's standing near the exit to the dining room, telling people goodbye. She hugs me one last time. "I'm sorry about Paul's poor behavior. Luke isn't very happy with him."

Mary makes it sound like Paul stepped on my shoe, or spilled a drink on my dress. "He lied to me and he's been lying to you and Luke. For over a year."

"Family stuff gets complicated," Mary says, "as I'm sure you, of all people, can understand. I'm going to let Luke handle all that, but I'm sorry you got wrapped up in it. For what it's worth, I think Paul really is a pretty good guy. He got a little confused about how to handle his business goals, but he didn't mean to hurt anyone. Especially not you."

"So you'll let Luke handle how he feels about Paul, but you'll tell me how to feel about all of it?"

Mary shakes her head slowly, ruefully. "I'm not trying to manage you, Trudy. I'm sorry it felt that way. I really hope this won't ruin our entire weekend."

My sister's sad eyes bring me back to myself and I realize that I'm acting like a spoiled brat. Mary's getting married tomorrow. I've already thrown a fit in the middle of her rehearsal dinner and screamed publicly at her soon-to-be brother-in-law. "I won't ruin anything else, I promise. I'm sorry for freaking out."

"If you had to draw a lot of attention to yourself, at least you looked good doing it." Mary touches the edge of my dress where it covers my shoulder. "You look amazing in that. I can't believe it fits you so well."

"Where did you get this anyway?" I ask. "I'd never seen it before. Paisley found it stuffed in a box at the very back corner of your closet."

Mary purses her lips and looks at me for a moment before answering. "It was Mom's wedding dress."

"You're kidding."

Mary shakes her head. "Nope."

"It's blue."

Mary shrugs. "Mom wasn't ever very traditional, so I guess that was fitting. I thought it was sort of symbolic actually. We came from terrible parents so that's definitely part of our story, but we can do things right instead of all wrong. I liked seeing you wear it the night before I get married."

Her words sink deep as I walk with Paisley down the hall, around the corner and toward the exit. Am I doing things right? I refused to let Paul explain his reasons for doing something that really had nothing to do with me. And then I threatened to quit my job to work for his enemy, a man I barely know. I want to turn around and run back to Paul, but I need to get home before I turn into a pumpkin. It's late, and I'm obviously not thinking straight.

Which makes it a really awful time for me to open the doors to the outside and see someone I haven't seen in at least a decade. She looks far, far better than she should, given her age.

"What are you doing here?"

FINDING SPRING

"Mary." My mom's sky blue eyes fill with tears. "You're wearing my dress? Oh, you look like an angel!"

My laugh rings far too high, and far too shrill. I try to stop laughing, but I can't seem to do it.

Paisley puts an arm around me. "This is Trudy, not Mary. And who are you?"

"Oh, Trudy, of course." Mom's eyebrows draw together. "Sorry for my mistake. And I'm her mother, and Mary's. Who are you?"

Paisley's glare would fry the paint off of a brand new car. "What are you doing here? You certainly weren't invited."

My absent, uncaring, selfish mother glances from me to Paisley and back again. "Who in the world is this, Trudy?"

"She's our best friend," I say. "And she's right that you weren't invited. Why are you here?"

"I want to see my daughter get married," Mom says. "I'd think that was obvious. Can you believe I found out about the wedding from a listing in the paper? One of my friends pointed out the announcement. It said the wedding was at a private residence, but when I called the paper, they mentioned that Mary's wealthy fiancé booked the Atlanta History Center for the rehearsal dinner."

"Mary and Luke aren't going to give you any money Mom, so you may as well go away."

She presses her hand to her chest. "I can't believe you'd even suggest that's why I'm here. I've never asked you for money."

"You've never been around to ask for anything, and your first words when you show up are that Luke's wealthy."

Mom's nostrils flare. "I don't need money. I only wanted to see my daughters."

Paisley holds out her phone. "I'll save your number. If Mary has any interest in you coming to the ceremony tomorrow, one of us will text you the location."

Mom rattles off some numbers and finally leaves. I pointedly ignore her sniffs and wounded eyes. There's no room left in my life for additional melodrama tonight.

I practically run down the steps to my car once she's gone. After the night I've had, I won't be the least bit surprised if my car has turned into an actual pumpkin. Or if a few wicked stepsisters turn up on my front porch, ready to tear my dress into pieces.

Luckily nothing else happens, and when I shimmy out of Mom's bad juju dress and climb into bed, I try to go to sleep without thinking about Jack. Or Paul. Or whoever he is.

I don't succeed, but I try really hard.

15

PAUL

Mary gives Trudy a hug and she heads out the door. I wish Luke wanted to give me a hug. Heck, I'd be happy with a smile, or anything other than a scowl.

"Now that most of my guests are gone, I think you have some explaining to do, Jack Campbell."

"It's Mom's maiden name—"

"And your middle name. I got it. I'm actually fairly smart," Luke says. "And yet, I'm still struggling with this. You ran LitUp almost entirely alone for four years. And I come back to find out you've started a side project under a fake name? Because you felt like I was too involved for you to do what you wanted? I'm scratching my head here, Paul."

"You won't ever get it, because you're the older brother."

"I can't change when I was born," Luke says. "Do you resent that I own half of LitUp? Because I'll sign it over to you right now. I admit I haven't done nearly as much as you have in the past few years. I'm sorry if that seemed unfair."

"It's not about the money," I say. "Not at all. This was about me, not you."

Luke stares at me while my stupid, cliché breakup line hangs in the air between us. He sits down and puts his head in his hands. "So you want to dissolve our company?"

I yank a chair out and sit down next to him. "No, nothing like that. I love our company. I'm excited for our new launch."

"Then what is really going on?"

"I know we're in business together, but you've always been the boss. At the end of the day, even when you're not around, people look to you for final decision on everything."

"Fine, so I'll assign five percent to you. Then you're in control." Luke leans toward me. "I would have done that ten years ago. I don't care, Paul. If you recall, you're the one who insisted that I have fifty-one percent to begin with."

I run my hands through my hair in frustration. "I know I did. It's not about the percentages. We started the company with your idea. I shouldn't have even gotten forty-nine percent. I hid this from you because I wanted to do something myself, create something of value on my own. And I was afraid of looking like an idiot if I failed miserably without you."

"I'd never think you were stupid," Luke says. "Even if you started something and it flopped. Businesses fail all the time. We got incredibly lucky with LitUp. I thought it was everything we ever wanted, but I guess not."

"I love doing things with you, but I wanted to prove I could do something without you too. I'm sick of being your business plus one. Can't you try to understand that?"

"Um, even before Mary came along, I never felt like that about you," Luke says.

"Hilarious. Yes, make a joke about the real feelings I'm sharing here."

Luke leans back in his seat. "I'm sorry. I am trying to get what you're saying, but it's hard. You're my brilliant, accomplished little brother. You have always been the smart one, the one everyone wanted, the scholar. I've never had any desire to do anything without you. I like working with you every single day. Even when Beth died and I couldn't stand to go into the office and sit down at my desk like I had when she was alive." Luke presses his fist against his chest. "It hurt me physically to not be working with you. I missed you. It just hurt more thinking about how Beth was never coming back."

"I haven't been through that kind of heartache," I say. "So I can't relate to that, but you've never been the tag-a-long little brother. You didn't grow up with parents who constantly said, 'Luke this, and Lucas that.' It was like I wasn't even there sometimes. I'd show them my painting or my paper from school and they'd be like, 'oh that's cute mate, but look at Luke's marble sculpture he whittled from a hunk of rock with his pocket knife on his lunch break.'"

Luke opens his mouth and closes it again. "Uh, you never painted and I certainly never carved anything out of stone."

I want to pull all my hair out. "You're missing the point. No matter what I did, you'd already done something better. And it was easier for you, and you did it with better hair."

"Okay, let's say that's true. You're the one who got into Harvard, not me."

I stand up. "You didn't even apply to college. You went straight into trade school."

"Mom and Dad couldn't pay the bills, Paul. I didn't have a choice."

"I know you didn't," I yell. "And you let me have a

choice, and then you gave up everything to come out here with me, and you didn't pretend not to be Australian just so you could fit in. You didn't bite down on your tongue so you wouldn't scream every time the people around you had life so much easier than we ever did. You didn't resent them and hate them for their entitlement and their wealth. And you were so awe inspiring that a Professor moved heaven and earth to get you into college *six years late*. That's how wide a shadow you cast. Can't you even see that?"

Luke doesn't say anything. He stares at me, his face practically devoid of emotion. I hate Luke's infamous poker face.

"Well, I've had about enough of that." Luke and I both startle when our Dad shuffles across the empty dining room. "You two are acting like a bunch of whiny, snot nosed brats."

"Sorry Dad," I say. "I thought you were already headed—"

"Back to that nursing facility? They can wait. I needed to talk to my sons, who apparently can't handle things like men yet, even though they're plenty old enough."

"I didn't hit him for lying to me," Luke says. "And he's telling me how he feels as clearly as any pre-teen girl would."

"Men don't whinge about their feelings," my dad says. "Just punch him already."

"Excuse me?" Luke asks.

Mary practically jogs toward us. "I've really tried to stay out of this, but I'm going to interject really quick. Please, please don't punch Luke. We've got wedding photos tomorrow."

"I don't want to hit him," I say. "I just want to say I'm sorry. I made a mistake because I wanted to do something to make you proud, not of us, but of me, Dad."

"I was proud of you. Before I found out you'd been sneaking around and hiding things from your family," my dad says. "Now I'm not proud. I'm annoyed."

"I've got three great offers on the table," I say. "I'll just sell my product and close up shop, okay? Trig told me which offer's the highest, so—"

"I'm sorry." Luke leaps to his feet. "Are you telling me that Trig knew?"

I close my eyes. "I needed help figuring out which option was the best and—"

Luke stands up and puts his arm around Mary. "I'm done talking about this. You figure out what you need, and maybe we can talk about it after I get back from my honeymoon. I'm not dealing with any more of this today." Luke moves away from Mary and toward me. He stops less than a foot away. "But if you can't keep the peace around Trudy tomorrow." Luke shakes his head. "If she seems distressed by any of this, or if you badger her in any way, so help me, you'll get kicked out of your own house and you'll miss my wedding. How's that for casting a shadow?"

Luke takes Mary's hand and they walk out.

I sink into a chair and lower my forehead to the table. I've been so selfish, doing my own thing while LitUp should've had my full attention. Luke's come up with idea after idea and split the proceeds with me. Now that I have one or two of my own, I start my own company, unwilling to share.

I'm a selfish, narcissistic baby.

I should be worried about how mad I just made Luke, but I'm not. He's mad now, but he always cools down fast. I bet he'll have forgiven me by tomorrow. He didn't even punch me, which tells me he's mostly just stressed about the wedding and leaving his kids for a week with Beth's parents.

No, Luke doesn't worry me, but Trudy does. She's the smartest woman I've met in years. She shone like a diamond tonight, a blue-eyed diamond, and when she walked inside, I felt like my deepest dreams were coming true. Somehow, she came to the wedding to be my date. When she realized I was Paul, and I realized she was Trudy, I wanted to punch my fist into a wall. Why didn't I tell her last night? I was so close to doing the right thing and I fell short. Again.

I'm such a jerk.

And now she's going to go work for friggin' James Fullton the Fourth. They'll probably get married and have three more kids just as cute as Troy. It'll be all my fault if she does.

My dad slaps me on the back. "You finished crying like a little girl yet?"

I forgot he was here. Again.

"Dad, can you please not right now? It's been a really long week."

"Your brother isn't really mad," Dad says. "He just doesn't understand you sometimes."

And my dad does? "Yeah, I know."

"Your Uncle Edward is a doctor," Dad says.

"Uh, that's nice." Dad does this sometimes. He gets confused and says a lot of things that make no sense.

"I drove delivery trucks, and Edward had not one, but two degrees. And he always made a lot more money than me, and had a way bigger house."

Or maybe he is making sense after all.

"I understand," Dad says. "You did what you had to do. But now that you've done it, does it feel good?"

I shake my head and fight back tears. I'd rather Luke break my nose than break down and sob like a baby in front of my Dad.

"Because that work and money crap doesn't matter. Your Uncle Edward was an alcoholic, and his wife left him. He was a mess. He never had any kids. I never made quite enough money, and your mother had to work as a bookkeeper so we didn't get kicked out of our apartment into the street. We might have been fine if we hadn't had kids. But we had one, and we loved him so much we had another."

My Dad grabs me with his knobby hands and looks me in the eye. "I have never regretted having two kids. I have never regretted driving delivery trucks, or missing out on time with me mates. Your mum never regretted it either. You were the joy in my life, in our life. I'd do it all over again tomorrow."

A tear slides down my cheek.

"You're worrying about the wrong thing, son. Your business and your inventions don't matter. That young lady who stormed out of here, the one you spent all night staring at, she's what matters. She's the only thing that matters. You can invent a hundred more doodads, and you'll feel just like you do now. Incomplete. Alone. Overshadowed. Do you hear me?"

I do hear him, and what's more, my crazy old lovesick dad is right. Luke will get over it or he won't. James Fullmer may steal my ideas, or he may let it go. And none of that matters as much as Trudy, who I lied to, just like her ex lied to her. I'm as bad as idiotic Chris. Having someone to trust, having someone to love, that's what matters.

Luckily, I know just where Trudy's going to be tomorrow morning, and I'm going to be there too. And unlike her moronic ex, I've figured out what I did wrong and I'm ready to make it right.

16

TRUDY

Paisley grills me on the way home about Paul. "So you were totally making out with him all along, and at the same time telling Mary and Luke you wanted nothing to do with him?" Her grin cannot be contained.

"Yep, that about sums it up."

"How could he not realize you were Mary's sister?"

I shrug. "His office manager hired me, so she's the one who reviewed the paperwork. My name means nothing to her. And thanks to her dear aunt, I went by Gerty or Gertrude at work. Well, her aunt and your dumb suggestion that I change my resume to Gertrude. And I really don't have the same last name as Mary. I doubt he'd given Mary's sister Trudy much thought, honestly."

"Still, for a smart guy."

I know. I've thought about it already.

"Hey, so. Not to sidetrack you or anything, but you got to move down to the end of the table by the Hawk Guy. What's his deal? Is he as loaded as all Luke's other friends and family?"

The who?

"Oh come on, don't pretend you don't know who I'm talking about. He was practically eating you up with his eyes. But you can't have every single guy on Earth."

James? "Do you mean the guy in the tux next to me with the dark hair?"

Paisley clucks. "The Hawk Guy. How could I be clearer? Yes, duh, dark brown hair, to die for tux, cheekbones for miles, and the smolder." She glances my way with an incredulous look on her face. "Oh my gosh, you've stopped checking other guys out. You really do like Paul."

I swat her. "Knock it off. I'm tired, that's all. And I would avoid the hawk guy if I were you. He's loaded, but if we're going with this analogy, he's a bad egg."

Paisley narrows her eyes. "What does that mean?"

"He's not a very good guy. He holds grudges and does morally indefensible things."

"So you're saying he's complicated?" Paisley looks like a cat batting at a bug. "I like tortured souls."

Oh my goodness. "Trust me Pais, this guy is not someone you should pity, or anyone you can fix. He's bad news."

"Because Liar Liar Pants on Fire Paul doesn't like him?"

She has a point.

"I'll take your silence as agreement, and I'm officially calling dibs."

"He's all yours. May you fly high and fast together."

Once I'm finally home and my teeth are brushed, I get a text from Paisley with my mom's phone number. I stare at it for a moment hoping it'll go away. There's a whole story about this. Some chicken spends all its time picking wheat and prepping it and then grinding the wheat into flour. It makes bread slowly, then it bakes the bread, asking for help all the while. Then when it comes time to eat the dumb bread, volunteers come from everywhere.

Mom and Dad didn't do anything they were supposed to do as parents. They didn't feed us and bathe us and clothe us. They didn't teach us to read, or make us lunches for school. They didn't attend school functions or show any support. As if complete neglect wasn't already enough, my mom up and left while I was still in diapers.

She's missed my entire life.

Then she wants a slice of bread. At least my dad was sick. What's my mom's excuse? I'm trying not to be angry that she didn't even bother to show up at my wedding. Only for Mary, her perfect child, her child who's marrying the billionaire. And now she's angry that I question her motives?

I don't even want to know her real reason for coming. I shouldn't even mention any of it to Mary. I won't. Not now, the night before her wedding.

Except I had a mom.

For all intents and purposes, Mary was my mom. She potty trained me, and made my lunch. She walked me to school. She wasn't even quite four years older than me, and she should have been tucked in by someone at night herself. But instead, she did everything from teaching me to read, to braiding my hair every morning. She's been there for every single thing in my life, including the time I married a guy she couldn't stand.

She even paid for that stupid wedding.

But she hasn't had anyone to be her mother, not since Mom left. What if Mary wants our sorry excuse for a mom at her wedding and I deprive her of that because I'm jealous? I pick up the phone to text her. Then I throw it to the bottom of my bed, unwilling to give Mom the power to ruin Mary's day.

I don't know what to do.

I hate my mother for putting me in this situation. I

hate her for being such a greedy, lazy, unworthy mess who only shows up for a slice of bread once all the hard work is done. Well, she can't have any bread. She can rot for all I care. But this isn't about me. It's about Mary. So I retrieve my phone and I text her as calmly as I possibly can.

YOU'LL NEVER GUESS WHO SHOWED UP TONIGHT AFTER YOUR DINNER.

Mary texts me back immediately. YOUR BOSS WHO HAPPENS TO BE MY STUPID BROTHER-IN-LAW?

HA, HIM TOO, BUT I'M TALKING ABOUT SOMEONE ELSE, SOMEONE WHO SHOWED UP UNINVITED.

WHO? She asks.

HOW ARE YOU FEELING ABOUT DAD COMING TOMORROW? I test the waters.

INDIFFERENT. I DOUBT I'LL NOTICE WHETHER HE'S THERE OR NOT.

I don't believe that for a second, but I hope it's true. YOU AREN'T ANGRY ABOUT IT, THOUGH?

NOPE. IF HE WANTS TO COME, GREAT. BUT I'M NOT BETTING ON IT.

It's pathetic that we have to prepare ourselves as adults that our sorry parents may say they'll make it to our wedding when they're probably going to flake.

I SAW MOM. SHE FOUND YOUR VENUE FOR THE REHEARSAL DINNER FROM THE PAPER.

Mary sends me an angry emoji. THAT'S EXACTLY WHY I TOLD GEO NOT TO INCLUDE ANY DETAILS.

DON'T WORRY, I SENT HER PACKING. OR TECHNICALLY, PAISLEY DID.

WHAT DID SHE WANT?

SHE WANTS TO COME TOMORROW. MAYBE WE CAN PARENT TRAP HER AND DAD.

Crying laughing emojis. That's promising.

SHOULD WE PLAY BEASTIE BOYS BRASS MONKEY, OR SNOOP DOG'S GIN AND JUICE TO RECREATE THAT AUTHENTIC RELATIONSHIP FEEL FOR THEM?

No laugh emojis this time. WHAT DID YOU TELL HER?

THAT SHE COULDN'T CALL OR TEXT YOU. THAT SHE WOULD GET A TEXT WITH AN ADDRESS IF YOU DECIDED SHE COULD COME. OTHERWISE, SHE'D GET NOTHING. WHICH IS EXACTLY WHAT WE GOT, AND EXACTLY WHAT YOU OWE HER. PERSONALLY I VOTE TO BLOCK HER AND NEVER LOOK BACK.

No reply.

I'm nearly asleep when I finally hear a buzz. I almost ignore it, but what if Mary wants me to text Mom? I check the message.

It's not from Mary.

My phone says it's a message from Jack. My phone's as confused as I was. There is no Jack Campbell.

I'M REALLY REALLY SORRY I DIDN'T TELL YOU YESTERDAY. I WANTED TO, BUT WITH TROY THERE, WELL.

Dots.

I CHICKENED OUT. I'M SORRY.

My heart wrenches. I think about last night at our picnic. With his dog. We couldn't go to his house because he had people there setting up for the wedding, I'm sure. Except he didn't tell me any of that. He didn't let me in, because he was living a fake life as someone else. Chris lived two lives, too. One life with me and another with his girlfriend. He didn't pick me, and then he didn't even have the decency to tell me he was bailing for months.

He got away with that because I'm an idiot. Fool me once...

This time, I shut my phone off and go to sleep.

When I wake up, it's not because of my alarm. It's because Troy's tiny face is inches from mine and he's waving his Spiderman Easter basket around. "It's time for the egg hunt!"

Mary and Luke decided to do a huge Easter egg hunt at Paul's house in the front yard two hours before the wedding. Because there wasn't already enough going on today. It's an adorable idea, I'm just glad I'm not in charge of logistics. It's Easter weekend, and there are a lot of kids coming, what with several of Amy and Chase's friends, some of Mary's friends from work who have kids, and Addy and her twins, and of course, Troy.

I don't want to wear my bridesmaid's dress a moment longer than necessary, so after I shower, I curl my hair and put on an eggshell sundress with pale flowers printed all over it. I pair it with an ecru sweater. Troy's impatient to go, so he doesn't even put up a fuss when I dress him in a little blue suit with an Easter green tie and shiny white shoes. I do have to admit, he looks precious. Mary chose Easter-y colors: pale blue, green and purple. Her other bridesmaids, Paisley, Addy, and one of her work friends, Robin, are wearing pale green with bright blue hydrangea bouquets. But for me, her maid of honor, Mary wanted something special.

Which is how I ended up with a three thousand dollar, lilac, gosh awful monstrosity.

I wad up the dress that could have paid for my last semester in college twice over and stuff it into the trunk of my car. At least my bouquet is gorgeous, a scaled down version of Mary's. Huge white roses, breathtaking blue orchids, and purple hydrangeas with a few perfect, punctuating spots of bright greenery. The florist sent us a photo this morning.

"Ready, ready, ready Mom?" Troy asks.

I load up his bag of stuff and usher him into the back. I buckle him in, and we're on our way.

To Paul's house.

I'm at a red light when Mary texts me. TELL MOM SHE CAN COME AND SIT IN THE BACK.

Of course. Because Saint Mary always does the elegant thing. Why'd she get all the grace while I got all the spite? I shoot off a quick text to our egg donor. YOU SIT IN THE BACK. YOU DON'T EMBRACE US OR GUSH OR MAKE A TOAST. YOU SIT. YOU WATCH. YOU LEAVE. GOT IT?

She replies. YES.

Fine. I send her the address and put my phone down so I can drive the rest of the way safely. When I pull up in the circular drive in front of Paul's house, Troy says what I'm thinking. "Does the President live here?"

The house isn't white, but Troy's too young to know the President lives in a white house. It is absolutely enormous, a traditional red brick facade, but with small white stone accents that seem to emphasize the grandeur. "No, honey, this is Uncle Luke's brother's house."

His mouth forms into a large O. "Uncle Luke's brother must be really, really rich."

"I think you're right."

A valet greets us, and I'm glad we don't need to coordinate parking at this private residence. Geo is really good at her job. I pass my keys off gratefully and help Troy out of his seat in the back. I sling his bag and mine over my shoulders and then open the trunk to retrieve my dress.

"Here let me," Paul offers. I didn't even see where he came from. He's just suddenly here, offering his help.

"It's your friend who's a boy," Troy says. "Hi!"

Paul takes a bag from my shoulder before I can stop him, and then snags my garment bag. He squats down near Troy and says, "You can call me Paul if you want."

"Paul." Troy studies Paul's face, from his short beard to his bright hazel eyes. "I think that's a good name for you."

"Better than Jack?" I ask.

Troy scrunches his nose. "I know someone named Jack at church. He poops his pants sometimes."

I bark a laugh before I can help it. "The Jack I know makes a big stink on occasion as well."

Paul's mouth curves into a smile. "I'm going to stick with Paul then. How does that sound?"

Troy nods. "Good idea."

We follow Paul up the inclined walkway toward his front door, Troy's basket clutched tightly in his tiny hands. When we reach the steps, Troy takes Paul's hand in his free one. My heart skips a beat and I stop walking to watch. Troy's usually so clingy that he'll refuse help from anyone but me. Sometimes he'll allow Mary to substitute, but just as often he refuses even her.

"Mom?" Troy turns around at the top of the steps. "Aren't you coming? We've got to see this cool house. I bet there's a great train table inside."

"Oh no." Paul smacks his forehead. "I don't have a train table yet. I guess I should get one soon."

"Wait, this isn't your house. It's Uncle Luke's brother's house. Mom told me." Troy looks from me to Paul.

"Your mom is right." Paul crouches down again. "In addition to being your mom's friend, I also happen to be your Uncle Luke's brother."

Troy's tiny eyebrow rises and his nose scrunches. "Why didn't you tell me that before?"

"I didn't know," Paul says.

Troy lifts both eyebrows this time. "You didn't know Uncle Luke was your brother?"

Paul laughs. "I didn't realize he was your Uncle. I hadn't figured out who your mother was yet. She worked with me, but we hadn't realized we had another connection."

"That's weird." Troy walks through the front door and Winnie nearly knocks him over.

Paul yanks Winnie back by the collar, but Troy doesn't seem to mind the canine exuberance.

"I agree," I say to Troy. "This whole situation is weird." I follow him through the doorway and into a huge entry hall. Vaulted doesn't begin to cover the arched cathedral ceilings, entirely done in beautiful red brick.

"Why don't you have a train table?" Troy spins around in a circle. "With such a big house, you have room for four train tables."

Paul laughs. "I didn't have the vision for it, I suppose."

"This brick is stunning," I say. "I love it."

Paul beams at me. "It's sort of the theme in the house. It's in the kitchen as a wall accent, the family room in the ceiling again, and on various accent walls throughout the home."

I shake my head. "I have toilets at my place, and they flush." I don't point out that my house doesn't even belong to me.

Paul laughs. "Come on. Easter egg hunt won't start for twenty minutes. I can give you a tour if you want."

Troy claps. "I want one."

Oh good grief. We follow him through all seven bedrooms and all eleven bathrooms. "My favorite room is the library," I tell him once we've returned to the entry. "All those books, and all that dark wood."

"You like to read?" he asks.

"It was the best thing about being a stay at home mom,"

I say. "I used to read as many books as I could carry home from the library. I haven't read a page since going back to school, though. Which is a bummer."

"I never have time lately either. I hope that will change soon."

"Can we go look for eggs yet?"

Chase runs through the doorway and I notice that one of his sneakers is untied, and his hair's poking up in the back in several directions.

"Troy!" he yells.

Everything is yelled when you're less than eight years old, so Troy replies in kind, "Chase!"

Troy follows Chase out the backdoor without another word spoken.

"I'm guessing that Chase knows his way around and can help Troy navigate?"

Paul nods. "He's spent a lot of time here, yes."

"Even so, I better make sure Troy isn't getting into anything he shouldn't."

"There's nothing they can hurt."

I glance around the room pointedly. "I don't see much here that they couldn't damage."

"Let me rephrase. There's nothing I'd be upset about them destroying."

"Even so." I start for the back door out of which Troy just shot.

Paul grabs my arm, and then lets go like I burned him. "Trudy, wait, please."

"What?"

Paul steps toward me hesitantly. "You didn't text me back, so I'm guessing you're still mad. Which is totally fine, but I really wanted to apologize in person. I am so sorry that I hurt you with my deception. I thought I needed to do something alone, without my brother. I thought I needed to prove something."

"And? Did you do it? Do you feel better?"

"I did what I meant to do," he says, "but it didn't prove anything. Or, at least, I realized I was worrying about something that didn't matter."

"That's between you and Luke."

He steps closer, his body heat radiating toward me, closing the inches between us. I sway toward him involuntarily. "Does that mean you aren't mad anymore?"

I look away so I can think. "No, I'm not mad."

Paul shifts so he can see my face. "So we're okay?"

"There's no 'we', Paul. We hung out once, that's it."

"Twice at least, and what if I want there to be a we?"

My heart lurches and my hands shake. "Do you?"

"Of course I do. I thought I'd been pretty clear. My feelings haven't changed. In fact, knowing Mary's your sister just confirms that you are the good person I thought you were."

I look around his house. Two acres on the Chattahoochee River? Ten thousand square feet? A five-car garage? This is a two million dollar home, easy. Probably way more. Harvard grad, business owner, and inventor. Paul's more than I deserve. More than most anyone deserves.

I couldn't even keep Chris' interest. I lost myself when we were married. I disappeared into what I thought Chris wanted. I like Paul. I'd be an idiot not to like him. I'm just not sure that the Trudy who's emerging, someone I like, will be able to survive Hurricane Paul.

"Trudy?"

I open my mouth, but I have no idea what to say. I breathe a sigh of relief when Mary opens the door to the front yard and interrupts us. "Easter egg hunt time!"

Troy runs inside with a smile on his face. Then his eyes widen in alarm. "Mom, my basket!"

I look around helplessly. I don't see it. "Where did you put it?"

"Mom, it's starting! I'm going to miss it!"

Which wouldn't be that bad, honestly. Because Troy needs a huge basket of candy like I need to give Chris a second chance. "Well, sweetheart, you should have left it with me."

Paul snaps his fingers. "I think you left it in the bathtub upstairs. In that white and black bathroom." He sprints up his spiral staircase, and returns a moment later with a Spiderman basket in his hands. Bless him.

Troy darts out the door a split second later.

"Thanks," I say.

Paul walks alongside me and reaches for my hand, but I can't. I pull away and walk faster until we're standing at the edge of the hunt, brightly colored eggs covering the front lawn. Three dozen kids have lined up along the driveway.

"Uncle Paul gets to tell us when to go," Amy says. "Cuz it's his house and that means he's the boss."

"Okay," Paul says, "I'll count down from five."

The kids dart out the second he reaches one, scooping up eggs as fast as they can. Except Troy's one of the younger kids and he's not getting many. His crestfallen look slays me. Paul notices it, too. He jogs over and guides Troy toward the edge of the lawn, where dozens of eggs are hidden in the bushes.

I sprint after him. "Not so many," I whisper. "He's diabetic, remember?"

Paul nods. "It's fine. I know he is, so I changed out the candy for cash."

Seconds later, a kid near the edge of the yard squeals. "There's five dollars in mine."

Kids start cracking their eggs immediately, all of them screeching. "I got a twenty!"

I meet Paul's eye. "Seriously?"

He shrugs. "I had to use what I had on hand and what I could get from the ATM and the corner store at ten p.m."

An image of Paul replacing hundreds of eggs last night once it hit him my son would be hunting here today flashes through my mind. Then I consider the cost. I close my eyes. He puts an arm around me. "I'm sorry. Was that the wrong thing to do?"

It was so right. Too right. More than he should have done.

"No," I say. "Not at all. It was very thoughtful. I'm just sorry you went to so much trouble for us."

"It wasn't a big deal," he says. "Honestly."

I lean my head against his shoulder and watch as Troy cracks his eggs and exclaims over quarters, dollars, twenties and a hundred-dollar bill. I turn sharply toward Paul when I see that.

"I only put in one of those. I knew it was in the bushes when I rushed him over," he admits sheepishly.

I can't even guess what he just spent. I suppose it's not as big of a deal to him, but money is still money.

"You know, there is one really sad thing about you throwing all that money away," I say.

"What?" he asks.

"How will you ever afford to buy four train tables for your entry hall now?"

He laughs. "I may have to settle for just one."

"A real tragedy. Well, at least you have room to put it right in the center of the entry."

"You think it should go smack in the middle, huh?" he asks.

"I mean, I think you need it there so everyone who comes over can marvel at its magnificence."

"Great idea," Paul says. "Vision, like I said earlier."

"Brunch is ready in the back pavilion," Geo announces. "And once you've all had something to eat, I'm going to send Mary to get changed for the wedding."

"Speaking of," I say to Paul. "Any idea where my dress went?"

"I hung it up in the blue guest room for you. You can change in there whenever you want."

"Thanks," I say. "I appreciate it."

Paul walks me and Troy out back and pulls out a few measuring cups to fix Troy a plate.

I put a hand on his shoulder. "What are you doing?"

"I figured since it's my house, we can use my stuff. That way you don't need to take dirty things home. Is that okay?"

I nod. "Sure, that's thoughtful."

He scoops up a half cup of scrambled eggs and dumps them on the plate, grabs a slice of bacon, and even measures the jam with a tablespoon before smearing it on the whole wheat toast.

"Grape is my favorite," Troy tells him. "Because it's purple and I really like purple."

"It's a solid color," Paul says. "Plus, grape jelly is smooth. I don't love seeds in things."

Paul helps me calculate the sugar levels for the insulin.

"You are one brave kid," Paul tells him while I inject it. "I would have cried so much at your age. I did, every time I needed a shot. I may have to call you the Troyminator."

"What does that mean?" Troy asks.

"It means you're invincible, and you're strong, stronger than any other four-year-old I know."

Troy flexes his arms, which look exactly the same as

when he's not flexing, but some tendons stand out in his neck.

"Very impressive. If I need to lift something today, do you mind if I call out to you so you can come help me?"

Troy nods very seriously. "I can do it."

"I bet you can," Paul says. "And I'll be counting on you. But if you're going to be strong enough to help me out, you probably should eat all your food."

I've never seen Troy gobble his eggs down so fast. Ever.

"I'll stay with him," Paul says. "Why don't you go grab some food?"

I do, and it's nice to do it alone, without worrying about Troy finishing.

Paisley shows up as I'm taking my last bite. She's already wearing her fluffy skirted green dress. It looks good on her, like everything does on someone who's thin as a toothpick.

"Morning Paul, Trudy. I'll take over with Troy," she says. "You two need to go get your sister and brother ready for this thing."

I realize Mary and Luke are both gone, probably getting dressed. I jump up. "Are you sure?"

Paisley nods. "That's why I came dressed already. Mary loves me, but she needs her sister in there right now."

I hug Pais and run into the house to grab my dress.

Paul's right behind me. "I put everything for Mary in the guest house. It's right by the pool."

A guest house. Of course he has a guest house. "Oh, right. I'll grab my dress and head over there."

"I should have thought about putting your dress in there. Sorry."

Poor Paul. He didn't invent a new name to trick me. He has his own baggage, but he's not a bad guy. I owe him some kind of acknowledgment. "Paul."

He turns toward me, his face painfully hopeful.

"I overreacted yesterday."

He beams.

"I'm not mad at you, okay?"

"Okay."

"You've been amazing today. You're a really good person. And I like you a lot."

He takes my hands in his and pulls me toward him. His head lowers toward mine, and I don't have the resolve to stop him from kissing me. His lips meet mine and I want to fall into him forever. When he finally breaks off our kiss and stands up straight, my knees are weak and my head feels stuffed with wool.

"Can we pause that, but not stop?" he asks. "Because after this wedding, I think we could use a little more practice."

I nod and he releases me. I can still remember exactly how his lips feel against mine when I reach the door to the guest house.

"Trudy!" Mary says. "I'm so glad you're here. Can you help?"

I help her zip up the back of her dress and walk around to look at her. She chose a full skirted, drop waisted, sleeveless gown. The skirt has a thousand layers of fluffy tulle that spring outward like a cupcake, but the bodice. . .

Hundreds of delicate crystals float across the bodice, heavy along the bust, and spreading out toward where the top joins the skirt. They must have just finished doing her hair, her shining blonde hair. It's pinned in a loose bun near the top of her head with tiny crystal stick pins interspersed all over, all glinting in the lights. I grab her veil and tuck it under the bun.

"You look. . ." I sigh. "I don't even have words. Like a princess, like a model, like an angel."

When she smiles at me, she looks even more radiant.

My eyes fill with tears. "You made my wedding as perfect as it could have been, and I will always love you for that. But Mary, you're marrying a real prince today and you deserve it. He loves his kids, and now he loves you just as much. They all do."

"I'm scared," Mary says.

I shake my head. "Why? What could you be afraid of? You're already such a great mom."

"Because Amy and Chase really are little angels. They're so easy right now, but what about when they aren't? I won't have any idea what to do."

"What about Luke? Does he scare you too?"

Mary closes her eyes and a peaceful look crosses her face. "Never."

"Then have faith in him. When you don't know what to do, you have someone to ask who you trust."

"Yes, thank goodness for that." Her smile lights up her entire face. "You're right. I'm marrying Luke, not just adopting two cute kids. The two of us can handle anything together."

Mary rests her forehead against mine and squeezes my hands. "I'm so glad you're here. You always know what to say."

Click.

I spin around to see a tall woman with a white shirt and black pants, just like the valets. "Oh, don't mind me, I'm the photographer."

Uh huh. Just carry on like normal while I point this camera at you and click away.

Mary shrugs. "Luke wanted it all documented and Geo said a lot of times brides say the day's kind of a blur. Try to pretend they aren't here."

I laugh. "Sure, why not. We're just sitting in the guest

home of a local palace, pretending photographers aren't following us around to document a casual moment spent in designer gowns. Nothing out of the ordinary for me."

"It does seem a little surreal," Mary says. "Doesn't it?"

I bob my head. "Like something from a movie."

"Let's hope there's a happy ending," she says.

"I'm about to stand next to you during that part," I say.

I put my wreck of a dress on next, and luckily Mary doesn't notice how fat I look when I'm dressed up as a grape cupcake. We all have high-waisted versions of her gown, which was a cute idea in theory, but since I'm bustier than all the other svelte bridesmaids. . . Well, it's not a good look.

But today isn't about me.

Mary doesn't have a train, so no one needs to carry that for her. But I'm going to give her away. So when Geo pops her adorable head through the door to tell us it's time, Mary and I walk out together. I hear the notes of the bridal march through the open doorway.

"Are you ready?" I ask. "Because they will totally wait if you need another moment."

Mary shakes her head. "I'm ready. I don't want to go any longer without being married to Luke."

"Oh good," Amy says. "Because I'm really ready, too." She bounces on the tips of her toes. "Geo said I can go as soon as you're ready." She's swinging a wicker basket full of flower petals. "So I can go now, right?"

Mary nods and Amy shoots up the path, chucking full handfuls of petals like she'd lob softballs.

I'm laughing when I hold out my arm for Mary. When she takes it, I walk with my perfect sister in her perfect dress down the winding path toward the pavilion. Pitchers full of blue orchids line our walk, and bowers full of hydrangeas, more orchids, and white roses cover the raised platform. I walk Mary to the front where Luke's standing in a black tux with a brilliant tie, striped in all three of her colors. The blue orchid in his pocket is bright, maybe a touch too bright.

But nothing can compete for attention with the look of absolute giddiness on Luke's handsome face. His eyes sparkle, the skin around them crinkling. He's staring at Mary like she's Christmas morning, a Super Bowl win for his favorite team, and a shiny new invention all rolled in one. To him, I think she really is all those things and more.

Paul stands next to Luke, but Chase and Troy come to stand right in front of him. Trig stands to his left. On our side, I'm next to Mary, with Paisley, Addy and then Robin stretching out. Amy comes to stand in front of me, taking my hand every now and then.

The ceremony isn't long, but it's beautiful. I wipe my tears away several times and I'm not the only one. Mom sits at the very back on the left side. Dad's on the last row on the right. It's like they coordinated it. I don't think Mary even notices.

Which is probably for the best, honestly.

When the pastor tells Luke he can kiss the bride, Luke doesn't press his lips against hers. He grabs her around the waist, spins her around and dips her, knocking over a vase of flowers in the process. The laughter seems fitting for the love they share. Equal parts romance and humor.

After he finally lets Mary back up, Amy cheers loudly. "Woohoo! Nice one, Dad! No one even noticed the flowers, I swear."

The entire audience bursts into applause.

17
TRUDY

Most wedding receptions start late and go far into the night, but Mary and Luke didn't want to make the kids miserable. They eliminated the photo shoot block, opting for exclusively candid photos instead, and set their reception to begin right after the ceremony.

Which is why it's only two o'clock when I watch Mary smash cake on Luke's face.

Paul walks up behind me, his hands in his pockets. "That went well."

"They're a great couple," I say.

"I probably shouldn't say this, because I really loved Beth, but Mary's even better for Luke than she was. I've never seen him this happy, and he's generally a joyful person at a baseline. When Beth died, I thought it might have broken him forever. He slid into a hole. It's nice to see him not only out but thriving, and that's all thanks to Mary."

"That's good to hear."

"She really worked a miracle."

"She does that pretty regularly," I say. "She should have gone into the clergy."

Paul touches my arm. "Can I get you something? A drink? Some cake?"

Geo's wedding team has started cutting cake and passing it out on sparkly plates.

I shake my head. "No, but thanks. I'm good."

"That's quite a dress," Paul says.

I don't need to look at his face to know he's teasing.

"Mary probably spent more on this stupid dress than you did on that egg hunt. What a waste."

"You pull it off."

"Angelina Jolie couldn't pull this off." I wish I could go change clothes, especially knowing Paul is staring at it, the image of my enormously fluffy form probably burned into his retinas. "But this isn't about me."

"You're really good with that."

I turn to face him. "With what?"

"With not making things into a bigger deal than they need to be."

"You're saying this after being present last night?" I practically ruined the rehearsal dinner.

"Even then, you stormed out and dealt with me outside, and then you calmly moved to the end of the table. It felt big to you, because you never make scenes, but it wasn't. Most people have no idea what was going on. For all they knew, there was a spill on your seat."

Mary and I learned not to take up too much space at an early age. Maybe it's become a habit for me.

All conversation stops when Luke leads Mary out on the dance floor for their first dance. I sigh, watching how Luke gracefully spins her around, her skirt twirling, her eyes twinkling. Everything about Mary threatened her last boyfriend, Foster. She was too much for him, but Luke loves her for her intelligence, her leadership skills, her giving nature, her competence, her spirit, her dazzling energy and her verve.

"Care to dance with me?" Paul asks softly after the first dance ends and couples begin to join them on the dance floor.

I can't think of a reason to say no. "I guess."

Paul's strong hand takes mine and leads me out, his other hand resting at my waist.

"I don't really know how to dance," I say.

"I'm supposed to do the heavy lifting. Let's see if I remember how." Paul's hand guides me and I'm impressed. He really knows what he's doing. And as much as I hate this dress, at least the skirt twirls beautifully.

I'm acutely conscious of his hand at my waist, and his eyes on my lips. When the song ends, he pulls me closer. "Another?"

Before I can reply, James interjects. "Oh come on, Paul. You can't hog her all night. Surely you can spare one dance for me, Trudy."

Paul's hand stiffens at my waist and his eyes harden. "Buzz off, James. You've done enough."

"It's okay," I say. "I don't mind."

Paul doesn't argue, but his eyes are wounded when he passes me to his hawk-faced nemesis.

"One dance," I say to James. "No more than that. I'm not interested in causing a brawl at Mary's celebration."

"I wouldn't dream of anything so pedestrian," James says. "Not my style."

"You're not hot tempered, huh?"

"Oh, I've had my moments. But I prefer a long slow burn to a flash in the pan. In any case, even if I were inclined to make a scene, I wouldn't do that here. Luke deserves all the happiness he can find."

"He does."

James leads almost as well as Paul, which is good since my dancing career began and ended with the Macarena.

"You two seem to have made up," James says.

I roll my eyes. "I told you. We've been on like two dates. We aren't together or anything, but I realized he wasn't trying to trick me."

"No, not you. Only his brother."

True enough. I glance at Paul out of the corner of my eye. He's talking to several other guests and gesturing animatedly. He's completely at ease as the center of attention, and everyone laughs and beams at him. I think about the kind of boss he is at the office: competent, organized, powerful, inspiring and commanding.

"You are smitten though," James says.

"Maybe," I admit. "But I've only been divorced a few months. I'm not jumping into anything."

"Does he know that?" James asks. "Because he's been scowling at me even more than usual. I think he's ready to base jump into something."

"We haven't had a big talk or anything," I say, "but I'll explain it."

"Oh good," James says. "I'm sure once you explain that you want something casual, he'll be fine with that."

Except the next time I meet Paul's eyes, I know that he won't. He's my sister's brother-in-law, which means I'll be seeing him pretty often. He's not fling material. And on top of that, he's used to getting whatever he wants. He steamrolls anything that gets in his way. Beyond all of that, I'll be seeing him every single day at work.

That thought hits me like an anvil in the head.

My list wasn't childish. It wasn't stupid. It wasn't an arbitrary set of goals. They were things I could finally do now that I'm not beholden to anyone else. Those three goals are things I need to do for me, for Troy, and for our future. I was finally free, and graduation, a job I can grow into, and repayment of my debts are my next steps. Important steps I need to accomplish.

I completely lost myself with Chris. I was subsumed into what he wanted, into who he was, into his goals and his life. I became what he needed, not what I wanted. And Chris is a dinghy compared to Paul's yacht.

I can't date Paul. I will disappear.

"Oh my gosh." I glance at Paul one more time, where he's charmed half a dozen guests. "He won't be fine with anything casual, will he?"

"No," James says quietly. "Paul likes you, more than I've ever seen him like anyone. I was wrong last night. I hadn't seen how he looked at you. He's got real feelings for you, and he's sick of dating around. He's glanced over here no less than fifty times during this one dance."

My heart soars and then crashes immediately after, but I know which one matters most. Paul is too dangerous. Like trying to tame a mountain lion when I haven't learned to handle a house cat. Which means I need a new job, because I can't work with him and see him every day. My resolve will falter. I know it will. It's just a matter of time.

"Are you still willing to line up an interview for me?" I ask.

James grins and I realize Paisley's right. He looks just like a hawk, a beautiful, sharp eyed, hungry hawk. "Absolutely."

"And I wouldn't be working with you, right? You live and work in New York."

He nods. "You wouldn't see me at all."

"Then I would really appreciate it."

When the song ends, Paul's waiting to offer me his hand. James hands me off to him with a half-smile, but he doesn't say a word. He doesn't pick a fight. He whispers, "I'll have Luke pass along my contact information."

Paul and I dance again and I let myself enjoy it. No sense in picking a fight at the beginning of my sister's party. Luke claims a dance with me, and tells me their plans for the honeymoon. After that, Trig asks for a dance. He's not as good looking as his fiancé Geo, but honestly, no one is. He is charming and kind, and he spends most of our dance trying to speak coherently while watching his fiancé with an almost pitiful look of complete adoration.

I want that kind of adoration aimed at me, but I need to be worthy of it first.

Troy dances in one corner of the room with Addy's twins, Amy, Chase, and a handful of other kids. His moves are almost as bad as mine, but he has no idea. Ignorance really is bliss.

Before I can blink, Geo's team is passing out bags of flower petals for us to throw at the departing couple. My eyes well with tears as I watch my sister climb into Luke's Raptor to head for the airport, where they'll take a late flight to Italy.

Mary has always wanted to see Italy.

"Eat gelato every day," I yell.

She blows me a kiss and they're gone. Amy hugs my leg.

I squat down so we're on eye level. "You can still come stay with me, you know."

She shakes her head. "It's okay. If I go with you, who will take care of Andy?"

Luke's cousins are staying with Chase and Amy for the next week in their new house, with Mary's big fluffy dog.

I tap Amy on the nose. "You finally get to live your dream."

Amy smiles and her one dimple pops out. "A house

without wheels. A perfect dog, and a new mom who's prettier than a Barbie."

"Exactly," I say.

"When are you getting a dog?"

"I don't know," I say. "I'd need to find exactly the right one first."

"Uncle Paul has a great dog." Amy glances behind me to where Paul's patting someone on the shoulder. "And he has a pretty cool house, with a huge pool!"

"What's wrong with my house?" I ask.

Amy shrugs. "Nothing. But it doesn't even have a yard really, much less a pool. At least it doesn't have wheels, though, so you can have pets and plants and stuff. And you have room to play good games."

She's right about that. And she's right about Paul, too. It would be so easy to slide right into a fabulous life with him. His dog, his house, his everything. Except, I don't want to slide into someone else's life. I want to create my own life, and pick my own dog. I want to buy my own house.

"I'll keep that in mind," I say. "But I think I might want a little yappy dog, not a big lick-y one."

Amy considers that. "Little dogs probably make little poop."

Spoken like someone who has been helping with dog chores. "Sage words, young Amy. I'll keep them in mind."

She darts off to play with the twins and I call Troy over. "We better get ready to go, buddy. Paul needs us all out of his hair so he can get his house cleaned up."

Paul steps toward me at the sound of his name. "Not at all. In fact, Geo has the clean up handled already. Besides, nothing's happening inside. I'd love it if you guys wanted to stick around. There's so much food left over I could feed you both for weeks." Paul leans closer to Troy and drops his voice. "I told Luke he could have his wedding here if I got to keep all the leftover food."

"I really want to throw the ball for Winnie." Troy turns pleading eyes on Paul. "Amy didn't believe that I could do it good."

Paul ducks inside to grab a ball and leads the kids away from the party area, into a small side yard near the garage. "Winnie," Paul shouts.

A streak of gold flies our direction immediately. Paul hands the ball to Troy. "Knock yourself out kid, but throw it that way." He points away from the party.

I walk a few feet away from Troy and Winnie, and Paul follows me.

"I appreciate the invite," I say, "but we can't stay."

"Can't?" he asks. "Or don't want to?"

This is going to suck, especially because I don't want to do it at all.

"Here's the thing. I've been thinking about this a lot, and I don't think I can keep working for you at SITB. What does that stand for, anyway?"

He answers absently. "Second is the Best. It's a joke between me and Luke, and it's stupid, but let's get back to what you said first. Why can't you work with me anymore?"

I shake my head. "I can't work for you."

"Why not?" He looks at me like I kicked a baby duck. "What did I do?"

I shake my head. "It's nothing you did. It's who you are."

"I don't understand."

"You know I only recently divorced," I say.

He nods.

"I got married young, way too young, and I put my life on hold for Chris. We did what he wanted, lived where he wanted, and ate what he wanted. I thought making him happy would make me happy, and it did for a while, but you can't live like that forever. Eventually, nothing I did made him happy. The more I tried, the more he couldn't stand me at all."

Paul throws his hands up in the air. "I'm nothing like that guy."

I take his hand in mine. "I know you aren't. Nothing like him."

"Then I don't get what you're saying."

"I know you don't, and you may never really understand this, but it really isn't about you. This is about me. I made this list after the divorce, things I needed to do before I could date. I couldn't even think about dating until I'd paid my sister back, graduated from college, and found a great job."

"You have a great job."

"I know I do. I really do love working for you. But I can't see you every day and not want to date you." I shake my head. "I know I can't, and as great as you are, that's bad for me right now. I need to carve out a space for Troy and me. I need time to do that, so I can learn to stand on my own. Can you understand?"

I expect him to argue. I expect him to persuade and wheedle. He scratches his beard and lifts both eyebrows. "You're asking me whether I get that you need to do something for yourself, by yourself?"

I laugh. "I guess you might understand after all."

He closes his eyes and exhales dramatically. "Please tell me you aren't going to work for James."

I shrug. "I don't know, but I've agreed to an interview at least. It's not like I'd ever see him."

"You can get a job anywhere. Name the place, and I'll call them," Paul offers.

"Ah, ah, ah, that's exactly what I mean."

"Right, right," he says. "Sorry, I forgot for a second."

I call out to Troy. "Sweetie, it's time to go." I ask the valet for my car, and when they swing it around, I buckle Troy into his seat.

Paul catches my hand before I climb in myself. "I understand your reasons, but that doesn't mean I'm throwing in the towel."

My heart does a little somersault.

"I'll give you your space and I'm not in a rush, but I'm not going to sit in the corner with my hands folded, either." He leans down slowly and brushes his lips over mine. My heart quakes in my chest. "I'll be patient, and I'll wait, but every time you see me, every time you hear my voice, every time I smile at you, I want you to know that you're missing this. We're missing this because you need space, not because I'm not all in." He kisses me again, even slower this time. And then he steps back and stands up straight, his eyes still locked on mine. "I'm ready when you are Trudy."

Breaking off eye contact and driving away is the hardest thing I've ever done. Luckily, Troy doesn't notice the tears streaming down my face the whole way home.

18

PAUL

Once everyone's gone and I finally pick up my phone, I notice an email in my inbox.

Harvard for Trudy. We're even. JF.

I should be mad. I realized today how much I actually like Trudy. More than anyone I've ever dated, and she dumped me before we were even officially dating. And then she quit her job so she wouldn't need to be around me.

I should want to throw my phone across the room. And if James really had anything to do with it, he deserves a punch in his smug, condescending, grudge-holding face.

But I don't think he can take credit for this one. I think Trudy made this decision for herself, and she didn't even seem mad about me lying anymore. Which means it has to do with her, just like she said. She's only been officially divorced a little while, and her loser ex only left them a few months before that. She's got a son with a lot of medical needs, so I get it. She needs to stand up on her own feet, and know that she can do it. Isn't that what SITB was all about for me?

The thing is, I wasn't just interested in her if everything

was easy. And I'm not bailing because she isn't ready today, or tomorrow. To play a long game, I need to think smart and make sure she doesn't forget about me, or meet someone else while she's getting her head straight. I'm not going to sit on the bench and hope she calls me in a few months when she feels better.

Pining is for losers. Pathetic, lovesick idiots throw in the towel. I'm going to give her space, but I'm going to be around to lend a hand whenever she needs it. Accessible without badgering her. Available all the time.

My phone buzzes and I check the screen. Luke's texting me on his wedding night. Sheesh.

I SAW YOU TALKING TO TRUDY. WIGGIN WOMEN AREN'T EASY TO WIN OVER, BUT THEY'RE WORTH THE EFFORT.

How do I make an effort when she's cut me out of her life? That's the real question. There's a fine line between tenacious and stalker. I need to make sure I don't cross that, but I also need to see her. Regularly. Non-threateningly. I think about following her to the grocery store, but that's probably over the line.

She did mention church, and tomorrow's Easter Sunday.

I text Luke back. WHERE DOES SHE ATTEND CHURCH? I'VE BEEN FEELING A LITTLE MORALLY BANKRUPT. I PROBABLY OUGHT TO SEE TO THE WELLNESS OF MY IMMORTAL SOUL.

CORNER OF BLEEKER AND DUNLOW.

I pull up google maps and jot down the info on the church. From there, it's easy to pull up their service schedule. I know where I'll be at ten a.m. tomorrow. Or maybe nine-thirty. I'm not following her if I get there first. I can imagine it now. "What? Me? I always come here. What are *you* doing here?"

Ha.

Luke texts me again. MARY SAID SHE USUALLY KICKBOXES MWF AT LIFETIME. 7:30 AM.

It's nice to have people pulling for me. I can see her four times a week, as long as I don't completely freak her out. It's not every day, all day, like it would have been at work, but I can do something with this. I'm not out of the game yet.

The next morning, I'm dressed in a suit on the very last pew at nine-fifteen. I might be a little nervous. I text Trig.

I NEVER SHOULD HAVE MADE FUN OF YOU AT MACARONI GRILL. I'M AN IDIOT.

He texts back immediately. THAT'S TRUE ENOUGH. BUT WHAT BROUGHT ABOUT THIS SUDDEN AND UNCHARACTERISTIC INSIGHT?

NOTHING. I'M JUST VERY SELF AWARE. AND EVOLVED.

Trig sends me a rude emoji. Creatively rude. I'm almost impressed, except it feels inappropriate to be impressed in a church.

Before I can put my phone away, he texts again. WHO ARE YOU STALKING EXACTLY?

I put my phone in my pocket and ignore the buzzing. I'm not stalking anyone, not at all. It's rude of him to suggest that.

Two buzzes later I pull it out again and check his messages.

TELL ME.

IT'S MARY'S SISTER. RIGHT?

Trig is obnoxious. I never should have texted him. I wish Luke hadn't just left the country. Except he deserves a honeymoon, but still.

YES.

GEO KNEW IT. SHE'S SMART.

DON'T TELL HER ANY OF THIS! I text him immediately. THE WOMEN ALL TALK.

SHE ZIPPED HER LIPS. THAT MEANS SHE'LL KEEP QUIET.

Yeah right. I'M NOT STALKING HER.

THAT'S WHAT EVERY STALKER SAYS UNTIL A COURT RULES DIFFERENTLY.

I scowl until it occurs to me that he can't even see me. SHADDUP.

BUT SERIOUSLY. GOOD LUCK. Thumbs up emoji. Geo has practically turned Trig into a teenage girl with all these emojis.

I might need to see a chiropractor tomorrow with the number of times I crane my neck around whenever someone new walks in. Every kid sounds like Troy.

The service starts, and there's still no sign of Trudy or her curly haired son. Also, no one sent me the memo that people don't dress nicely for church anymore. I guess that's on me for not coming much, but I'm the only person here in a suit. The guy in front of me looks like he's wearing swim trunks. Have some respect, dude.

It occurs to me that Luke and Mary might have punked me. Luke does have reason to give me a hard time, and now I'm stuck here for the entire service.

"Excuse me, can we sneak past you?"

I turn to look at the latecomer and stare right into Trudy's startled, cerulean eyes.

"Oh," she whispers. "What are you doing here?"

"I was about to ask you that question," I say.

"Excuse me, I always come here."

"Are you implying I don't?" I grunt and shift back against the pew so she can slide past me. "I love God. Even more than I love French fries, and that's saying something."

She rolls her eyes, but Troy claps when he sees me. "Uncle Paul!"

Uncle? Yuck. "Uh, maybe call me Mr. Paul," I whisper.

Troy nods. "Mr. Paul." He climbs up on my lap. Trudy looks a little flabbergasted, but she sits next to me without arguing.

The next hour passes too quickly. Trudy has a bag full of toys for Troy, and he's clearly accustomed to sitting still and quiet. She pulls out a big book with different activities on each page, all silent. A Tower of Babel made of felt. A fabric mock-up of a dress shoe that Troy can lace up and practice tying. A basket to weave out of ribbons for baby Moses.

"Where did you get this?" I whisper.

"I made it," she says.

"How?" I ask.

"Be reverent," she hisses.

I pretend to be chastened, but really, I'm too busy admiring how her eyes flash when she's scolding me. When the service ends, I high five Troy. "Nice to see you, buddy."

He looks up at his mom. "Can Mr. Paul come over for dinner? He will love your chicken and dumplings, I know it."

Trudy blushes. "No sweetie, he can't. He's busy."

I want to protest. I have all day free, and I'd love to come! But that's not what I'm doing here. I'm not pressuring or wheedling my way into her life, or at least, not in an obvious way. I stand up and brush the goldfish crumbs off my pants. "I can't come today, but you're a very polite gentleman to offer." I wink at Trudy. "Maybe some other time when it's your mom's idea to have me over."

Troy kicks the pew. "Alright."

"Don't be disrespectful in God's house, sir."

Troy frowns. "It's not a very good house. There isn't

even a bedroom. I checked that time you thought I was lost."

I suppress a chuckle at Trudy's choking sound.

"We better go," she says.

Troy turns back around to face me when they're ten or fifteen feet away. "Can I sit by you next week Mr. Paul?"

I bob my head. "Fine with me, but that's up to your mom."

"Pretty please, Mom?"

Trudy sighs. "We'll see."

"You always say 'we'll see.' But I don't ever see anything. I think that really means no."

I wonder how often she had to say that about whether he was going to do something with his dad. I bet Chris didn't do what he said he'd do very often. My parents didn't have a lot of money, but they were there for everything we ever did.

I'm on my way out when a lady in a grey dress with very curly hair stops me. She smiles and points to the left. "Sunday School?"

Uh. I can't exactly say I'm here to follow someone, and they've left, so I'm headed home too. I regretfully mumble, "Sure."

After all, I seem to have some catching up to do with religious stuff.

The next morning, I expect to groan when my alarm goes off earlier than usual, but I pop up out of bed energized. Turns out, unrequited love is motivational, at least for me it is. I put on a pair of nylon pants and a t-shirt. Then I second-guess it. What should I be wearing to kickboxing? I've boxed off and on at boxing gyms since I was a kid. How different can it be?

The meathead standing by the door at Lifestyles holds

up a hand when I try to walk past him. "Membership pass, sir."

"Uh, I'm not a member yet."

"You can't just come in," he says in a voice so deep that he's got to be faking it.

"But I did just walk in. Like, literally two seconds ago."

"You can't go inside, sir, not without a pass."

"You guys suck at recruiting," I say. "You need to work on that. How about you offer to let me try a class and if I like it, I can fill out all your forms."

He frowns.

"Which word didn't make sense? Let me guess. Recruiting?"

He scowls.

I step a little closer and drop my voice. "Look Popeye, there's a girl I need to see today, okay? She shut me down, but I'm not ready to give up yet. I need to get into that kickboxing class." I point at the back wall where there's a sign that says "Group Fitness."

"We're not supposed to do that," he says. "You can look into the class, but you can't take it until you're a member. There's legal forms."

"Okay, I know. I'll arm wrestle you for it." Four or five people are listening in now, and the guy's eyes are shifting around, which tells me he knows and cares. "If I can beat you, you let me run into that class before it starts and fill out the forms after."

Popeye sizes me up. I don't look so big, especially compared to him. He thinks there's no way I can take a guy with pythons like him. After all, he's done sixteen million and one arm curls. Today. But he hasn't really arm-wrestled anyone, except as some kind of party trick.

He has no idea I paid for my books every semester decimating a bunch of frat boys who spent a lot of time on free weights, too. It's easy when you know the physics behind it.

"Fine."

I point at a table covered with a stack of little rolled up towels and he nods. Less than a minute later, we're set up. Even in such a short time, a crowd of onlookers has gathered.

I'm a righty, so I bring my right foot forward, hugging my right hip against the table. That ensures my arm won't be the only thing doing the work. When he reaches out, I make sure to grip high up on his hand, lifting my wrist higher than his. And when he yells, "Now," I curl my wrist over immediately.

My hook flattens his wrist, and I push for where I imagine Popeye's shirt pocket would be, if he had pockets on his stupid tank top. Pushing for the nearest corner saps his strength and relieves the pressure on my upper arm. Five seconds later, I've shoved the back of his hand into the table. I ignore the hoots and hollers and stand up.

"So it's this way?" I point at the big room in the back and check out the clock. Four minutes until class. I better get in there.

I'm lucky Trudy didn't walk in during my stunt, but I hope she shows at some point, or I wasted a lot of time and pissed off Popeye for no reason. I walk to the back and look around.

I'm the only guy in the room.

Can that be right? It's martial arts, right? I also see no bags hanging from the ceiling. Not a single one, which leaves me wondering what exactly we're supposed to be kicking or boxing. I don't see mannequins, either. Am I really supposed to spar with one of these hundred pound chicks?

The music kicks on and every female in the room starts

bouncing around, punching. . . the air. Not what I expected, but I roll with it. After some initial stretching and bouncing knee strikes, we settle into a lot of uppercuts, jabs and hooks. This I can do.

I notice the second Trudy walks in, five minutes after class started. I'm sensing a pattern.

She puts her hands on her hips. "You've got to be kidding me."

"You go here?" I ask. "What are the odds?"

She lifts one eyebrow, but before she can say a word, we switch to doing some kind of jumping lunge. To say it's not something I'm comfortable with might be generous.

By the time we finish that set, Trudy's laughing so hard that tears are streaming down her face. "You look like a marionette piloted by a lunatic."

I ignore her and practice the elbow strikes the instructor is doing. The lady next to me in tiny black shorts and a crop top says, "Don't listen to her. You're doing great. We all sucked our first class, and we're happy to have a hot guy in here for once." She frowns. "Which probably means you're gay. Please don't be gay."

I shake my head. "Not gay."

She grins and looks me up and down. "I'm Alice. Welcome to class."

I consider turning on the charm like I usually would. I could probably have half a dozen phone numbers by the end of class, even if I look like a puppet with cut strings. But ...although jealousy might work with some girls, I don't think it would help my case with Trudy. She needs to see me often, but watching me act like a flirt might set off warning bells. I doubt her ex cared much about making her feel special.

"Thanks," I say. "But I'm sort of not-so-secretly pining

over the woman who thinks I look like an asphyxiating fish."

Alice widens her eyes. "Good luck."

"I need it," I say.

After class ends, Trudy doesn't even talk to me. She races out of the room and toward the childcare area to pick up Troy. I head over to the membership desk to sign up. I can't have Popeye's head exploding every time I arrive.

After the gym, I head into SITB to come clean. I call everyone to the conference room and explain my real name, my reasons for using my middle name and mother's maiden name, and tell them we've received several offers to purchase the tech we've been working on.

"What's going to happen to our jobs?" Andrew from digital programming asks.

"I'm still deciding which offer to take. But no matter which one it is, the buyer will want a skeleton crew at a bare minimum to go with the product and help get it ready for a launch. Some of you will certainly be on that team, and I'll make sure I negotiate raises for you. Whoever isn't included will be welcome to come work with me at LitUp, the company I own with my brother Luke. I've already cleared that with him. That company will buy the other ideas we've been working on, and job offers will be extended to each of you. No one is going to be fired or laid off."

A collective sigh of relief brings a smile to my face. "I'm sorry about all the secrecy. My decision to do this had nothing to do with any of you. You've all been phenomenal to work with, and you'll continue to be amazing, I'm sure."

I'm just relieved I was able to purloin an IT guy from LitUp so I won't need to search for a new one myself. I could really use a new assistant, but when I call Nancy, she assures me she'll be back in the office soon.

"This baby's sleeping like a dream. I can actually start doing several hours from home each day this week, and I think I'll be back to full time well before six weeks."

"I had a friend analyze our offer and I'm making a counter offer today. Hoping to get this laid to rest by the end of this week, so we may be at LitUp by the time you're back."

"Does that mean the employees with a share in the company will get paid soon?" Nancy tries to sound casual about it and fails miserably.

I laugh. "Soon enough. It won't all be distributed until we dissolve the corporation, and first we need to complete this transaction. Assume at least a month, probably more. Due diligence, paperwork, patent amendments, etc."

"Still exciting," Nancy says.

"Yes, it's still very exciting."

The rest of the week of Luke's honeymoon flies by. I negotiate forty percent more and sign with 3M. I kickbox two more times. Badly. Worse than my lack of natural talent at cardio kickboxing is that Trudy pretends I'm not there at all. It's a little disheartening.

I head home Friday night, beat, ready to watch TV and eat Chinese food. I've just changed into flannel pajama pants when my phone rings. It's Trig.

"How do you feel about game nights?" he asks.

"Are you kidding me? Like Monopoly?"

"Given our respective business backgrounds, Geo thinks Monopoly isn't a good call. She's suggested charades or maybe Pictionary."

"Geo must really like games," I guess.

"I think it was Paisley's idea, but yeah. I just bought Geo a house and she wants to throw a party. I know it's last minute, but we thought you might need to get out of your house."

I think about the night I have planned. Chinese food. Pajamas. Jack Ryan. It sounds so good to me that I know I ought to get out.

"Fine," I say. "I'll come. Text me the address."

When I arrive and Trudy answers the door, my jaw drops.

"What are you doing here?" she asks.

"You'll have to take that up with Trig," I say. "He didn't actually mention to me that you'd be here."

Trudy sighs. "If we're going to be thrown together, and it seems we are now that you've found God and a love for air sparring, we may as well reach some kind of truce. Otherwise, I may never talk to any of my friends again."

I walk through the door and close it behind me. I lean back against it. "I agree. What did you have in mind?"

"I'm, unsurprisingly, still in the same place I was seven days ago. I am not ready to date. Not you or anyone else."

I nod.

"But that doesn't mean I'm opposed to having a friend who is a guy. Now that you can't order me around, I think we could be pals, as long as you don't press for more. You have to promise me."

I cross my heart with my fingers. "I swear."

And I'm off the bench.

19
TRUDY

Last year's Trudy never would have believed my situation right now. Last year's Trudy had a husband who never came home, a bank account with twelve dollars in it, and no way to earn more, other than making crafty signs and quiet books for toddlers on Etsy.

Last year's Trudy spent an hour tidying up the crappy apartment, ensuring her makeup was perfect, and trying to cook something halfway decent from whatever food her husband had bought when he went by the store in their one car.

Now I wake up in the morning and help my darling son prepare for the day. After we've eaten, I go to the gym to work out. There's always a stupidly handsome, goofy guy there. He pretends I've knocked him out and falls on the floor. He pretends to hit himself in the chin. He dances like a disco king to the music. He acts like he can't recall the names of any of the women in the class other than me.

The same guy comes to church every Sunday and helps me with Troy. Actually if I'm honest, Troy might prefer him to me during church. He's got a completely silent motorcycle game on his watch, he bounces him on his knees, and he's taken to bringing snacks. Cheese sticks, roasted chickpeas, and beef jerky, all things a diabetic kid can eat without too much drama.

And I usually see him on one of the weekend nights, either at Mary's, Paisley's, or Geo's. He almost never flirts, but he tells me my eyes are prettier than tanzanite. He admires how well I refocus Troy when he spins out. Sincere, heartfelt comments regarding things he appreciates about me. Last weekend, neither of us even bothered asking anyone else to be our partner at the game night Luke set up. When we played team spades, he slid me two cards instead of one, and I didn't miss a beat before sliding two back. We destroyed Mary and Luke, who would never even consider cheating. Paul told everyone it was because I'm such a talented player, but really it's that he gets me.

Basically, he treats me like a queen.

I work at a bank James Fullton's family owns, where I manage three branches worth of computers. I spent the first few weeks frantically scrambling and occasionally calling one of my professors in a panicked state, but I haven't had to call anyone in more than ten days. I'm settling in, and my paycheck is more than I expected to make for several years. I'm paying rent, utilities, and even after my normal expenses, I'm paying Mary a monthly chunk down on the loan she gave me for Troy's medical.

Plus, I have health insurance, the good kind. The kind with a copay that costs less than you'd pay for dinner at Denny's. I know how much that costs, because sometimes I take my son out for dinner now.

I took the day off work today so I could take my finals, my last round of tests ever. I graduate in two days, on Saturday, assuming I pass. I didn't sleep much the last few nights, reviewing my notes and worksheets to prepare. Luckily the exams are a snap. I finish them in half the time I thought it would take, so I pick Troy up early and take him to Chick-fil-A for lunch.

I stop at the mailbox on the way inside the house, since our mailman usually comes early, and grab a stack of letters. One of them is a huge manila envelope addressed very clearly to Ms. Gertrude Jenkins. The return label is a law office. I inhale quickly and my hands shake a bit. What could a law firm want with me? I filed my taxes on time. I don't owe anyone money, or I don't think I do. Could Chris be suing for custody? He hasn't seen Troy in months.

Surely not.

I usher Troy inside and pull out the boxes of blocks he's been asking for, stacking them absently. Once he's happily playing, I walk into the kitchen. I shove the ominous letter to the back and open the rest of the mail. Bills, mostly, and a birthday card from an old neighbor. She's a week early, but it's still a really sweet gesture.

I stare at the envelope again. I've been waiting for weeks now, or months really. Waiting for something terrible to happen. My life never stays this good for very long, so I knew the other shoe would drop eventually. I was hoping for a few more weeks. A few more days. I set the envelope down. Maybe I can wait to open it for a day or two.

"Mom!" Troy yells, and I look up, startled.

He's opened the door and he's outside. I race out, my heart in my throat. Did he fall? Cut his hand? "Troy?"

I almost run over him. He's standing on the front porch holding the watering can. He looks up at me with wide eyes full of wonder. "Look!"

His zombie plant isn't dead. Five bright green leaves have spread out from the center of the pot, and a tiny shoot pokes up in the middle, clearly the stalk of a small bloom.

"I told you it wasn't dead," Troy says. "It was just winter."

My small son is wiser than he knows. Sometimes we think things have died that aren't dead at all. We give up on them. We throw in the towel, sure that investing in them would be a waste of time. But maybe we should be patiently waiting on the spring thaw.

I pick him up and hug him close. "I love your faith, buddy. It warms my heart."

"Take a picture, Mom. Send it to Aunt Mary. Tell her I kept her plant alive."

I snap the photo and text it to her with this caption: SPRING IS HERE.

She sends me a row of hearts back.

My brave, trusting, faithful son gives me the strength I need to open the envelope. After all, if he can withstand losing his admittedly lousy dad, moving to a new place, going to stay with a friend every day while I work, and being stuck with needles multiple times each day, I can open an ominous envelope, no matter who it's from.

Dear Gertrude Jenkins:

Enclosed please find a check for your pro rata share of your ownership interest in S.I.T.B. Pursuant to the Articles of Incorporation, the LLC has been dissolved. A copy of the fair market valuation performed by Sailer and Parsons is attached. You have thirty days to contest this valuation should you choose, but 3M recently purchased the sum total assets, so the valuation is fairly straightforward.

As you will see on the attached check, your share was the same as all other standard employees who met the qualifying conditions, 1/8 of one percent. Nancy Jones owned 1/4 of one percent due to the leadership override. The total sales price of the

S.I.T.B. assets came to one hundred and fourteen million. Less costs, liabilities and expenses, the net amount was one hundred and ten million, and five hundred thousand. Your fractional share comes to $276,250. This check is valid for ninety days. You will need to consult with a tax professional of your choosing to determine the proper way to report this income, but it was not held for more than a year and will not qualify for long term capital gains.

Should you have any other questions or concerns, do not hesitate to contact us.

Yours truly,

Annabel Shepard, Esq.

I fumble through the rest of the papers, holding the check with trembling fingers. This can't be real. How could I be a qualifying employee? Is this a joke?

I call Luke.

"Hey Trudy. You ready for graduation?"

"I need to talk to you."

"Uh, okay," Luke says. "Well you're in luck. Because you are talking to me."

I sound like a bumbling idiot. Get it together, Trudy. "I got a weird letter in the mail today. I'm kind of freaking out."

"Okay, breathe in and out. It'll be fine. Whatever it is, Mary and I are here, and we'll help you take care of it. What does Chris want?"

So Luke has no idea what's going on either. "It's not from Chris. It's from Paul."

Luke swears under his breath. "Send me a screenshot."

I hang up and send him a photo of the letter.

Two minutes later he calls me back. "Trudy, that's not even from Paul."

"It's from his company. Same thing."

"No, this is a corporate formality. He probably doesn't

even know the amount of your check. Honestly. It's not just you. It's all the employees who met the requirements."

"What requirements?" I ask. "I was there two weeks."

"Paul told me what you did, and what you risked, and he decided to cut you in long before he had any idea who you were. You were simply doing your job as best you could, and you saved him. He appreciated it. You earned that money. Since without your help, Paul would have lost everything, you could argue he's dramatically underpaid you."

"Come on, Luke. Be serious."

"I'm dead serious," he says. "You earned every dime of that money. Your sister will tell you the same."

After he finally convinces me not to shred the check, I hang up.

Two hundred and seventy-six thousand dollars. I can't even comprehend.

My phone buzzes. It's a text from Mary. YOU NEED TO SET ASIDE A BIG CHUNK OF THAT FOR TAXES. IT'S GOING TO BUMP YOUR BRACKET, FOR ONE. ASSUME THE GOVERNMENT WILL KEEP AT LEAST A HUNDRED K OF IT.

Trust Mary to jump straight to the depressing part. I wish she were here so I could hug her. After Mary, the first person I want to call is Paul. Which is stupid. He's just a friend. It's not like I need to call him and tell him I'm loaded now. And it's not like this is a lot of money to him. It's one eighth of one percent and he got the rest. A hundred million or more, easy. Plus he was loaded before this.

I wait an hour, and my fingers are still itching to text him. YOU'LL NEVER GUESS WHAT I JUST GOT IN THE MAIL.

Paul replies right away. TELL ME IT'S FROM VICTORIA SECRET.

Eye roll emoji. YOU PROMISED.

I'M STILL MALE.

I'm not sure whether it's because Paul's flirting, or because of the check, but my fingers and toes are all tingly. I want to jump around and... I don't know, shout and sing, or kiss something.

Or someone.

HELLO?

I'M HERE, I text.

BUT WHAT DID YOU GET IN THE MAIL? OH I KNOW. CHICKENS.

WHO GETS CHICKENS IN THE MAIL? I ask.

IT'S A THING, he insists.

IT ABSOLUTELY IS NOT.

THEN A MAIL ORDER HUSBAND.

ALSO NOT A THING, I text.

FINE. YOU STARTED THIS. SO SPILL ALREADY. I'M OUT OF GOOD IDEAS.

YOU'RE NEVER OUT OF GOOD IDEAS. Why am I flirting?

THAT'S TRUE. OKAY, IT'S A PACKAGE OF TWENTY RAZOR BLADES FOR $5. NOW YOU WANT ME TO TAKE YOU DANCING SO YOU CAN SHOW OFF YOUR RECENTLY SHAVED LEGS.

HA. ALSO WRONG. IT'S A CHECK FOR ALMOST 300K.

I THOUGHT PUBLISHER'S CLEARINGHOUSE FOLDED, Paul texts.

I roll my eyes. YOU KNOW WHO IT'S FROM.

IT'S YOUR SHARE. IT'S NOT A BIG DEAL.

LUKE SAID THAT TOO, I admit.

LUKE'S A SMART MAN. NOT AS SMART AS ME, BUT HE TRIES.

SO YOU'RE SAYING THIS ISN'T SOME GRAND GESTURE.

Dots.

I hate waiting on dots.

Then the dots disappear and that's worse.

I hate texting. Why don't people call anymore? When my ring tone jangles noisily, I nearly drop the phone. I fumble it around in time to see that it's Paul calling, as though he could read my mind. My heart tries to beat out of my chest. I have to answer. He knows I'm home, because I got my mail. And I've been texting him. Dang it.

I swipe to answer. "Hello?"

"Trudy."

"Paul."

"Believe me, if I were to make a grand gesture, you'd know it, and it wouldn't come through a lawyer. Besides, I made you a promise. A Victoria Secret joke may slip though my filter now and again, but in my wildest dreams, I would never try to buy someone's affection with a partial share in a business transaction. Besides, I made the determination to cut you in long ago."

It sounds utterly absurd when he says it like that. And I sound arrogant, so arrogant. How do I climb out of this hole? Or maybe I just stay here and bury myself. At this point, I need to say anything, even something stupid. Say something, Trudy. Now.

"Trudy? You still there?"

"Yep, I'm here. Sorry, Troy was ..." What could Troy have been doing? "Washing his underwear in the sink."

"No I'm not, Mom. Gross. Why would I do that?" Troy yells. "Who are you talking to?"

I hold my hand over the phone and shake my head at him.

"I'm not Mom. My underwear is on my body. I'm not even in the bathroom."

I wonder what the chances are that Paul didn't hear my son yelling at the top of his lungs about what a liar I am. If I had to choose between this conversation and a root canal, I'd drive to the dentist right now.

"I better go," I say.

"See you tomorrow," Paul says.

What? Oh, at Lifetime. "Yep. I guess so."

I spend twenty minutes getting ready for kickboxing on Friday morning. Which is idiotic, since I know I'm going to shower after and wash all that makeup off. Even so, I look pretty good.

I'm annoyed when Paul doesn't show up.

It bothers me more than I want to admit, but I don't mention it to anyone. Not that I could if I wanted to. I haven't told anyone else that Paul comes to church with me. Or kick boxes with me. It doesn't seem like it's any of their business. And I don't care whether he comes or not. He's a friend, nothing more.

I'm in a funk all day at work. My boss asks whether I'm okay, and so does my friend Carol. When I get a call at three p.m., I'm downright cranky.

"This is Trudy," I answer.

"Trudy," a familiar voice says. "I've been hearing good things about you."

"James," I say. "My boss said you're like her boss' boss' boss' boss. She said no one she even knows reports to you."

He chuckles. "Nice to hear from you, too."

"You called me."

"Indeed I did." I hear the sound of shuffling papers and then some mutters in the background.

"Is this a bad time?" I ask. "You could call me back

another time. I'd offer to call you, but I don't feel comfortable calling the owner of the entire company."

"I finished a meeting and there were some people who hadn't cleared out yet, that's all. Look, I'm calling because I have an offer for you. I know your life is in Atlanta, but I could use someone resourceful who I can trust who also speaks computer. Someone young who can stay on top of all the newest trends."

"You're offering me another job?"

"Would that interest you? The pay would be much, much more than you're making now."

"How much of this is about tormenting your poor friend Paul?" I ask.

"Are you even still talking to him?" James asks.

"Does it matter?"

"Not to me," James says. "You and Paul can get married and move out to New York with your seventeen kids for all I care. I'll even throw in a relocation package for your boyfriend, fiancé or husband, should you have one."

"I don't understand then," I say.

"How's this for an explanation? You're excellent at your job. Your branches have had one-third the downtime of any of our other branches nationally. And you've only been there for seven weeks. Think what you could do once you've had a little more time under your belt. The reason I'm your boss' boss' boss' whatever is that I have a knack for spotting talent, and I always reward it. Incentives drive the free economy, you know."

I should be chomping at the bit here. This is my window. My opportunity. Except zero percent of me even contemplates his offer. My family is here. My life is here. I like this new job I have only because it allows me to provide for Troy. I enjoy using my mind and being independent, but none of it matters if I'm not spending my life with the people I love.

"It is a very tempting offer," I lie. "But I'm afraid I'm not interested in anything that takes me away from my family."

"I thought you'd say that," James says. "I wanted to at least try. But since you turned that down, maybe you'd be okay taking some contract work from me on the side now and again. Interpreting things for me, analyzing some stuff. Sometimes I need someone to explain things so that I can look like the rock star I am."

"I'd be, like, your computer tutor?" I giggle. "Your cheat sheet, as it were?"

"Exactly."

"I think I could do that," I say. "Extra money is always nice."

"I'll send a standard contractor agreement over. You can have your lawyer take a look and assuming it looks fine, get it executed so it's in place when I need work. It would be outside the scope of what you're doing at the branches."

"Understood."

After a long day at work, I'm looking forward to dinner at Mary's. Maybe a little more than I should. I don't touch up my makeup or put on anything fancy because twice in one day would be pathetic. Besides, Paul probably won't be there anyway. Just because he has been at Mary's every single other weekend I've been invited since the wedding doesn't mean he'll be there today.

Troy waters the Gerbera daisy, and I realize the color of the flower is already visible, even through the back of the petals. When the bloom opens all the way, it will be hot pink, as if to say, "Look at me, Trudy. You doubted my existence, but I'm here and I'm fabulous."

When we arrive at Mary's, Amy and Andy meet us at the

door, both of them bouncing, both of them exuberant. I wave Troy back to the playroom and look around the house, scanning. Living room, empty. Dining room, empty. Office, empty. Luke and Mary are standing in the kitchen chatting. Mary's stirring something, and Luke's holding a glass of water.

No one else is here.

"Hey guys," I say. "Thanks for inviting us over. I was too tired to cook."

"I thought you were buying us all dinner tonight," Mary says. "Now that you're loaded."

I pull a personal check out of my purse with a smile and slide it across the counter. "This is the balance of what I owe you."

Mary shakes her head. "I've told you a dozen times. It was a gift."

"No," I insist. "It was a loan, and it saved me. Paying you back doesn't lessen that. It just means I'm growing. As my Smom, you have to let me."

"Your 'Smom'?" Mary arches one eyebrow.

"It's my sister-mom. You know, you fill both roles. You're fun and understanding and supportive as a sister, but also you're helpful and sacrificing and you teach me, like a mom."

Mary drops her spoon and pulls me into a hug. "I'm proud of you."

Tears stream down my face, and I'm not even sure when they started. But I think it's because I believe her. And I believe her because I'm proud of me, too.

Luke clears his throat. "I'm going to check on the kiddos. Last time they were this quiet, they covered the walls and their clothes in acrylic paint."

I pull back from Mary and glance at her pan. "Spaghetti?"

"I made the sauce myself. The key is to simmer it all day."

"I'm definitely intrigued," I say. "Since all I ever simmer at my place is Prego."

"Luke loves to cook and I think it's contagious," Mary says.

"I like it."

Mary has always commanded a room. She's always been a rock, but she hasn't always looked so happy doing it. She shines now, like, well, like a bright bluish LED."

Hey, guess what?" I ask.

"Yeah?"

"That photo I sent of the daisy? That's Troy's zombie daisy. It's alive, and it's about to bloom. Probably tomorrow."

"You're kidding! That's great." She reaches for a pot, probably to boil water for the noodles.

I take it from her and fill it up myself. "Chalk one up to the faith of a child, I suppose." I shut off the water and then have an idea. "How many noodles are we making? I mean, is it just us?"

Mary wipes her hands on a towel. "Who else did you think might come?" Her eyes dance.

I refuse to ask. "I don't know. Trig or Geo, maybe? Paisley? Carol or Addie?"

Mary shakes her head. "Nope, none of them are coming."

"Okay."

"Just ask," she says.

"Ask what?" I refuse to give her the satisfaction.

"You want to know whether Paul's coming."

I turn away from her and haul the pot across to the stovetop. "What if I do?"

"I'd say the daisy isn't the only thing that survived a long winter."

My heart swells and I realize maybe she's right. Maybe Chris did something to me, torched my ability to love. I thought my heart was dead. I thought I'd never trust anyone again. But with regular watering, my heart may have revived like those blackened daisies to sprout new growth. Because I sure feel like spring inside, warm and tingly and full of promise.

"Where is he?"

"He's not coming," Mary says. "He had plans tonight."

"Did he say with whom?" I ask, trying to sound casual, not meeting Mary's eye.

"He didn't specify."

But he wasn't at kickboxing, and now he's not here. What if he got tired of waiting? What if he never liked me that much anyway, and he's met someone else? Someone who was already blooming? It's probably for the best if he did. I mean, even if my heart is sprouting, I still have a lot of baggage Paul doesn't deserve to have to unpack.

I don't mention his name again. Mary's spaghetti tastes great, although Troy manages to splatter it all over his yellow polo shirt. I finally drag him home and put him to bed. I should be elated right now. I should be calling Paisley and asking her to come celebrate, or even calling my ex-in-laws so I can go out dancing.

Instead I just want to call Paul. Which is too pathetic. I pick up my phone and dial.

"Trudy? Is it really you?" My mom actually answered on the first ring. Did I call to invite her to my graduation?

"Uh, yeah. Hi."

"You didn't even speak to me at the wedding." That's true. And I don't want her there tomorrow, either. Then why did I call her? "Are you still there?"

"Uh, yeah, I'm here," I say.

"Why are you calling?"

It's pathetic she has to ask why I'm calling my own mother. But seeing as this is the first time I've actually known her phone number in ten years, it's probably not a strange question. It's not like I'd call her to catch up, and I'd certainly never ask for a favor.

"I wanted to ask you something."

"Okay," she says.

"Why did you marry Dad?"

Now she's responsible for the awkward silence.

"Hello? Mom? Did you hear me?"

"Are you sure you want the answer?" she asks.

No. But I need to hear it. "Yes."

"I never loved your father. I liked someone else, someone smarter and better looking. Someone more exciting. I thought your father would help make this other guy jealous, and I used him. Unfortunately, in the process, I got pregnant."

"You didn't think about terminating the pregnancy?" I ask.

"Of course I did. It wasn't easy to do back then."

Which means if it had been... Super.

"Look, you asked me and I'm being honest. After I had Mary, I thought about leaving, but I was too depressed to do it. And then I got pregnant with you."

"Which is why you split the second you could after I was born."

"Not the second I could. I really tried. No one ever gives me credit for this, but I stayed for more than three years."

I think about Troy. He's four, and getting him to this point was hard. It's still hard now, but it's beautiful too. He counts on me, and even when I'm a mess, he loves me.

When I cry and pout and yell, he forgives me. I can't imagine Mary and me were way worse than Troy, and she walked away from us. Knowing my father was, well, what he was. She didn't care enough about her children to even take us with her.

"I gave what I could to you two, and there wasn't anything left." My mom exhales. "I was drowning. I felt like I'd rather die than stay in that house another second. I had to get away and do something I wanted to do, anything but what I was doing."

"You became a trucker, Mom."

"Don't act superior," she says. "I saw the world. I paid my own bills. I never stayed in the same place, and I met a lot of interesting people."

I don't even ask what she's doing now. I don't care, because I've realized something important in talking to her. She may have given birth to us, but I have no idea where we really came from. Neither Mary nor me are anything like her at all.

"Thanks, Mom, this has been eye opening."

"Sure."

I hang up.

When I finally go to bed, I don't worry about my heart anymore. No matter how bad things got with my life, I've always loved Troy more than anything in the world. I've always loved Mary. I would do anything for them, anything at all, including walking into a burning building, or cutting off my leg. I also do the hardest thing, which is giving my all every single day, in and out, rain or shine. I never walk away, and I never call in sick. I am nothing like my mother, and nothing like my father. I fight when it matters. I do the hard things to enjoy the beautiful ones, and my life is full of immeasurable beauty as a result.

Which means my crappy parents couldn't break me,

and Chris couldn't burn me down. I'm an IT manager. I'm a sister. I'm a friend. I'm debt free. I'm a mother. And tomorrow, I'll be a college grad.

I am beautiful, just like that spunky little hot pink daisy that refused to die. And I'm going to surround myself with people who water me, who fertilize me, who shine on me, and who lift me up. I'm done with anyone who burns me, suffocates me or tears me down.

I take the red list out of my nightstand and tear it in half, and then tear it in half again and again. I'm done with my list, which means it's finally spring, and I'm ready to bloom.

20

PAUL

The auditorium at Georgia Tech is so cold that I'm shivering, and I'm wearing a suit. Luke's already given his jacket to Mary. Chase is sitting on her lap, and Amy's perched on her dad's knee.

Troy taps my leg. "Can I sit on your lap, Mr. Paul? I'm freezing."

I nod and he climbs up.

"I'm glad you came today. I think my mom will smile."

"You think?" I ask.

Troy nods. "She was really crabby when you weren't at Aunt Mary's last night."

I can't help grinning like a moron. "Is that true?" I look over at Mary.

"It's true," Mary agrees. "For someone who repaid her debts and had a graduation coming, she was borderline hostile."

"I am so sorry I'm late," Paisley squeezes past the people at the end of the row, her pink peacoat unbuttoned, her floral scarf waving in the frenzied air conditioning. "Why is it so cold in here?"

She sits down next to me and opens her arms to Troy. "Come see Aunt Paisley."

Troy shakes his head. "I like Mr. Paul. He lets me play with his watch."

"Play with his watch?" Paisley huffs. "I changed your diapers, you little punk. I've cleaned up your puke. Now come warm my lap."

Troy rolls his eyes at me, but lets me hand him off.

Before I can say anything to Paisley, the ceremony starts. The sea of golden robed graduates stretches across the stage, and I can't quite spot Trudy at first. But when I do, I can't look away. She's listening carefully without any idea where we're sitting, so I can study her as brazenly as I want.

It's a rare treat.

I don't usually allow myself to stare, since I'm supposed to be keeping it casual. I'm supposed to be present without flirting, around often without pressuring. It's been hard. Actually, it has downright sucked. I want to hold her hand. I want to stroke her face. I want to tuck her hair behind her ears, and kiss the tip of her nose.

If I'm being honest I want to kiss her, well, her everything.

I think she's getting closer. She was crabby when I wasn't there yesterday. I hold the thought against my chest like a warm blanket. When they read her name off, I stand up and cheer as loudly as I can. Louder even than manic Paisley.

Finally, after an hour of formality and inspirational speeches, after what feels like years of names and walking and diplomas, they toss their caps into the air, and Trudy walks down the aisle to where she's noticed her sister and Paisley. It helps that Paisley has clawed her way across the row and is standing in the aisle jumping up and down and screaming, a frantic ball of hot pink shimmer and flowers.

When Trudy finally turns my way and sees me, her face lights up. She strides toward me then, her eyes soft, her lips slightly parted. "Hey."

"Hey," I say back.

"You came."

"I'll always be here for the big stuff," I promise.

Her hand darts up and wraps around my neck and she kisses me, full on the mouth. I catch up quickly, my hands reaching through her robes to circle her tiny waist. She drops her cap to the ground and reaches up to pull me even closer with her other hand.

I'd never have stopped kissing her, but Troy taps my hip. "Mr. Paul?"

Trudy and I jump apart and look down at him. "Are you going to come live with us now?"

My mouth drops open.

"No, honey, Mr. Paul already has a house."

"It's a better house than ours. Are we going to live there?"

"No," Trudy splutters. "No one is moving anywhere."

"So Mr. Paul isn't going to be my dad?" Troy's lower lip trembles.

Trudy drops to her knees. "Honey, Mr. Paul can't be your dad. You *have* a dad."

His tiny face falls and he looks down. He kicks the chair in front of him, which is thankfully unoccupied. "Not a very good one."

My heart breaks and I crouch down next to him. "I will be around to do whatever you want to do," I say. "We can play fetch with Winnie. We can go get ice—er, salty pretzels?" I look up at Trudy and she smiles.

"Why can't you just *be* my dad?" he asks. "Amy and

Chase got Aunt Mary for their mom even if they didn't grow in her tummy."

"Sometimes things are more complicated than that," Trudy says. "But I think we might be seeing more of Mr. Paul in the future."

"You better believe it." I pick Troy up and toss him in the air like a graduation cap. "You won't be able to get rid of me."

"We can build some train tracks?" he asks.

I nod. "In fact, I have a surprise for you."

"You do?" he asks.

I stand up and face Trudy. "I may have violated the rules a little bit and prepared a little party. For you."

Her eyes widen. "For what?"

"A graduation party, you idiot," Paisley says. "I've been helping him."

"I thought you had a surprise for me," Troy says.

I ruffle his hair. "I have something for you too. You can see it if you convince your mom to come over to my house for her party."

Trudy grins. "Sure, I'll come."

Troy claps. "I hope it's a tiger."

A tiger? Uh. I meet Trudy's eye and she laughs. "Troy dreams big."

"Nothing wrong with that," I say.

We walk out of the auditorium together, Troy swinging between Trudy and me. I swipe his booster seat from Luke and Mary, who gave Trudy and Troy a ride, and they load up in my Range Rover.

"I like this car," Troy says. "It's got a lot more room in it than our car. Can we get one, Mom?"

Trudy rolls her eyes. "Sure. When I win the lottery."

I feel like I've already won when she looks at me and smiles. Then she reaches over and takes my hand. I'm glad my car's an automatic, because I don't let go of her cold fingers the entire drive to my place.

I usually park in the garage, but that would ruin the effect. I pull up into the circular drive and cut the engine. "Alright Troy, are you ready?"

He's unbuckled and out of the car before I can even circle around.

"Child safety locks," Trudy says. "They're a miracle."

"I'll look into them," I say.

I unlock the front door of my house and wave Troy through.

"Whoa!" He rushes over to the huge, knee-height table I had custom made for my enormous entry hall. It's covered with every Thomas the Train piece I could find for sale. It took me four hours to set it all up.

"Sorry it's not four tables," I say.

"But it's the best one table in the world!" Troy immediately pushes the button to turn on a green train. Percy, maybe?

"What do you think?" I turn toward Trudy, and notice she's crying.

I pull her into my chest. "I'm so sorry. What did I do?"

She shakes her head against my chest. "Nothing, it's perfect."

"Oh, you cry when you're happy."

She shrugs. "When I'm happy, when I'm sad."

"You're a confusing woman."

She pops up on her tiptoes and kisses me. When she pulls away, she says, "You're a bright guy. If you stick around, you'll figure it out."

"I'm not going anywhere."

* * *

I leave the house early, but I'm still worried traffic might make me late. I call Luke. "I'm on my way."

"We just left."

"See you there." I hang up.

When I reach Withrow Jewelers, my heart is pounding. The last time I planned a party, it went so well. Trudy beamed the entire time, and stole kisses from me whenever no one was looking. And sometimes even when they were.

I really want this party to go at least as well as that one did.

Luke and Amy are already there when I walk in, which I know because his bright red Raptor is parked outside.

"So what kind of birthday present are we looking for exactly?" Luke asks.

"A very special one," I tell him. "One that would go here." I point at the ring finger on my left hand.

Luke's eyes widen. "Is that a good idea? You've only been dating two months."

"I'm sorry," I say. "What was that? You proposed like six weeks after you met Mary. I've known Trudy for almost six."

Luke sighs. "Five. And the point isn't how long you've known each other. It's whether you think she'll say yes."

Amy cocks her hip. "You were super duper scared Mommy was going to turn you down. You told me if she did, I was supposed to let you watch MacGyver and bring you ice cream all night."

"How do you even remember that?" Luke asks.

"Because I'm a genius like my parents." Amy taps on the glass. "Get this one."

I bend over to look at the ring she likes. It's a sapphire heart. It costs a hundred and ninety-nine dollars.

I frown. "It's on sale."

Amy beams. "Aunt Trudy loves to find things for cheap. She will like it more once you tell her that."

I exhale. Maybe asking for their help was a bad idea.

"What about this one?" Luke points.

I walk over to see what he's suggesting. Mary does seem to love her ring, so maybe Luke's got a good feel for this stuff. He's pointing at a huge, round diamond on a platinum band. It's nice, but kind of boring. Trudy isn't boring. She's zesty and unique.

The jeweler has been standing quietly and letting us confer, but when I wave at him, he zips over. "Yes sir. How can I help?"

"I want something classic, beautiful, but also different. Personal. Maybe a pear shaped diamond, the biggest you have, with sky blue accent stones. Or something a little different, but in a classic setting. I just don't want to cross over into cheesy, or gimmicky."

The jeweler smiles. "What's your price range?"

I shrug. "More than rock star, less than Arabian prince."

He beams. "Come to the back with me."

Luke nods and shoots me two thumbs up.

"If I'm not back out here in fifteen minutes," I joke, "call the cops."

"Oh, if you aren't back out," the jeweler says, "I'll already have called them."

Luke laughs, and I hear Amy squawking about our joke as I follow the short man with dark glasses into the back.

"I travel to Belgium twice a year," he says. "I just came back last week. While I was there, I saw a diamond so beautiful, it took my breath away. I had no idea if I'd ever be able to sell it. I don't have much in the way of rock star clientele." He stops and turns around.

I nearly barrel into him. "Okay."

"It's bigger than I usually buy or sell, and it's unique. It's one of a kind. It's a fancy green-blue diamond. Some might call it a sky blue, or azure diamond."

He spins back around and clicks a light on. Then he

removes a stone from a case and sets it on a pillow. "This is a five point six carat green-blue heart. Boron and nitrogen got together to make it this stunning color."

I step toward the case and I know, just like I knew that day at the park. Just like I know every time I see Trudy and don't want her to leave. She's a unique mix of all the elements I need to bring me joy, to make me whole.

"I want it as a solitaire. How soon can you have it ready?"

The jeweler names a time and a price. I always negotiate, because haggling is an art form I've mastered. But not for this. I simply nod. Trudy's worth any price, and this is perfect for her.

Luke and Amy insist on seeing the diamond. Amy grumbles as she follows us out the door. "I still think she'd have liked that other one better. It looked way less expensive, too."

I chuckle. I may not know much about women yet, but I feel good about taking my own path this time. The jeweler has the ring ready exactly as promised. I pick it up and drive back home in time to meet the caterers.

Geo's there, fine tuning last minute details. "Are you sure you want this many people here?" she asks.

"If I'm wrong about this, she's going to turn me down, and it's going to suck that so many people will see it."

"That's kind of my point," Geo says.

"But I don't think I'm wrong."

Geo clucks. "I admire your guts."

She doesn't say she hopes I'm right. She doesn't have to.

I make plans to take Trudy out to dinner that night while Paisley watches Troy. Except we're almost to the restaurant when. . . "Aww crap," I say. "I forgot my wallet."

Trudy pats my arm. "I'll pay."

"Absolutely not," I say. "You aren't paying for your

birthday dinner. I'll call them and ask them to bump the reservation."

"I'm pretty hungry," she says. "You can pay me back."

I knew she'd say that. She's always difficult. "Fine. You brought your wallet?"

She looks down at her tiny purse, the one she always uses when she's wearing her silver heels. She swears, which is ridiculously cute. It's like watching a unicorn fart.

"I'll call the restaurant." Except I call Luke instead. "Yes, this is Paul Manning. I'm hoping you can bump my dinner reservation." I pause. "Uh-huh. Well, we hit a little snag, but we're still coming." Pause. "Right. Sure, forty-five minutes should be fine."

We drive toward my house in silence.

A few blocks from my house, Trudy says, "You make my life better, Paul. I'm glad we met. I'm really glad you didn't give up."

I pull up in the circular driveway and turn to face her. "You make my life better too. And I couldn't have given up, not from the moment you bent over my desk and found that key logger."

She rolls her eyes. "I mean it. I love you, and I don't say that lightly. You're part of my life, like Mary and Luke. Like Paisley. Like Troy."

The ring is burning a hole in my pocket, but I stick to the plan. "We're here. I should go get my wallet."

"Okay," she says.

I get out and head inside the house. I wonder how long she'll give me before she comes inside. Everyone is here, and they're restless. Paisley and Addy and several of her new friends from work. Pam and her son Benson. Amy and Chase, Luke and Mary. And Nancy Jones brought her two kids as well. Geo and Trig came too, and I realize they're holding tiny cymbals.

"I got something noisy for everyone," Trig says, gesturing around.

He's always been super weird.

"I have a blower thing," Troy says. "See?" He blows on his kazoo and I cover my ears.

"Shhh," I remind him. "Not until she comes inside."

"When is that going to be?" Mary asks.

I text Trudy. WINNIE MADE A MESS. GONNA BE A MINUTE. WANT TO WAIT INSIDE?

The front door opens twenty seconds later, and everyone cheers.

Trudy's jaw drops, and she searches the faces for mine. When she finds it, she tilts her head and I know she's happy. She crosses the room until she's standing in front of me.

"No dinner, then?" She puts one hand on her hip. "Because I wasn't kidding about being starving."

I kiss her then and everyone cheers. "I know you get crabby when you're hungry, so there's definitely food. But first I need to ask you something."

I drop down on one knee and pull the ring box out of my pants pocket. I hold it up but don't open it. Not yet.

Winnie rushes over to try and lick my face and Trudy laughs at me. I shove Winnie away. "Not now, dog."

I wave around the room with my free hand. "When we met, you thought your value came from your job, or your education, your appearance, or even your net worth. But I figured it out pretty quickly. Your worth is in the love and support you give to everyone around you. Your friends, your sister, your co-workers, and your son can all attest to the same thing. You're a giver, and you're not ever stingy with your love or your service. You are the best sister, friend, and mother I've ever met."

Trudy tries to pull me to my feet, but I shake my head.

"I'm not quite done. You have a degree now, and your debts are repaid. You've got a fancy job, and your son has health insurance. But none of those things matter to me. I know people usually do this in private, but I wanted to recognize the most central part of who you are and involve your family in this moment. Gertrude Madeline Wiggin Jenkins, you dazzle me. You astound me. You complete me." I open the ring box. "Will you marry me, too?"

Trudy claps her hand over her mouth and starts to cry, which is how I know her answer is yes. I stand up and swing her in a circle. Then I slide the ring on her finger.

"Oh good," Mary says. "She's crying. That's a yes."

Geo waves her arms and a half dozen different people walk in with vases full of brightly colored daisies and set them all over the room. On the counters. On the floors. On shelves and niches. Trudy looks around at all the Gerbera daisies and cries even harder.

When she can finally talk again, she whispers in my ear. "I'm so glad you were willing to wait for spring." Then she kisses me and time stands still. Spring, summer, fall, winter. They all flash before my eyes. We're going to be together for all of them.

Like always, Troy taps my hip. "Now can you be my dad?"

Trudy beams at me. "Yes sweetheart, now he can."

I pick Troy up. When Trudy and I hug him between us, my world finally feels entirely complete.

THE END

If you enjoyed the third book in the Almost a Billionaire series and want more, don't worry! The fourth book,

Finding Liberty (Brekka and Rob's story) is out now! Check it out here, or read on to check out a sample chapter.

If you want a FREE full length book, sign up for my newsletter at: www.BridgetEBakerwrites.com! Already Gone is a full length YA romantic suspense.

Finally, if you enjoyed reading *Finding Spring,* please, please, please leave me a review on Amazon!!!! It makes a tremendous difference when you do. Thanks in advance!

21

BONUS CHAPTER: FINDING LIBERTY

Every single one of my friends in high school hated something about their bodies. Matilda hated her abs. Sydney couldn't even look at her thighs. Abby wore long sleeves year round to hide these tiny little white bumps she always picked at on her arms. Angie complained daily about the girth of her calves.

Not me.

I loved every last thing about my body. My long, lean legs shifted infinitesimally in whichever way I needed, effortlessly holding up the weight of my torso as I carved the snow, one beautiful slope at a time. My hands gripped the poles perfectly, not that I needed them often. My abs and core muscles held everything else together on the slopes and looked pretty great in a bikini in the summer, too. My lungs never failed me, no matter how high the altitude or how frosty the air. My sharp eyes spotted every indentation in the snow, every stick and branch, every patch of ice.

Unlike all my friends, I was one with my body from

birth, and it performed like my dad's Shelby Cobra 427. Perfectly, with precision, and without complaint.

Until it didn't.

I stare at the useless lumps the doctor persists in calling my legs. There should be a different name for legs when they betray you. You should get a new name for every body part that quits working, for everything that malfunctions and fails you when you need it. When a stallion's man parts are snipped off, they call him a gelding. My legs should be called flegs. Failed legs.

The doc picks up my chart, her eyes squinting to make out the tiny print. I know exactly what it says. Incomplete T_{10} fracture. Stabilized. Partial function.

That's the biggest joke of all. Partial function. It's like saying a Shelby Cobra has partial function because the interior lights still turn on. The car won't run. It can't do anything that made it useful in any real way, but you could still sit inside of it and, I don't know, read a book or drink a milkshake. It's more like a sofa than a car, but somehow that would be partial function. Similarly, my thighs are more like pant holders than actual legs.

"Miss Thornton," the beefy doctor says, her cheeks ruddy, "I'm not sure why you're here."

"You're the one who sent me to try the aqua treadmill. You still claim I have partial function. I've been doing physical therapy twice a day, or sometimes three times—"

She frowns at me, her crows feet becoming even more pronounced. "You're only supposed to do it once a day."

"I'm an overachiever, so sue me." I wheel toward her a few inches. "I haven't had any improvement from anything. Not a single bit. I still can't support myself with arm braces for more than a step or two. I've been flying out weekly for those treatments in Michigan you suggested. That underwater treadmill, the newest best hope. Still no improvement."

Dr. Captain purses her lips. "Miss Thornton, I told you there were no guarantees. We never know how much progress a patient can make until you've tried as many things and pushed as hard as you can. The fact that you can ambulate from your chair to the toilet and into a shower chair using only hand rails, and without any other assistance is tremendous progress."

"Yes." Tears threaten and I focus on my anger instead. Better to rail at her than to break down and sob. "I should be giddy I can go pee without a chaperone."

Dr. Captain drags a chair over next to me, sits and looks me in the eyes. "I understand you're frustrated and disappointed, angry even. You aren't going to want to hear this, but I don't have anything else to offer you. The Hydroworx is what we use for professional athletes and celebrities. It's the gold standard. You're one of a handful of non-professional athletes who has even used one. I'm not trying to preach or anything, but you're very lucky to have the means to try this sort of treatment. If it didn't work. . ."

I can't stop them this time. Tears stream down my face unchecked. As frustrated as I was that everything kept failing, knowing we've reached the end of the line, the last trick in her bag, well. That's even more depressing. "You're saying this is as good as it gets for me, and I should be grateful it's this good."

She nods.

I can't bring myself to meet her eyes. I've been dealing with this for years, and even so, every time I try a new therapy, my hopes soar. Barometric chambers, neuro-stimulation, acupuncture, ChABC injections, and now underwater treadmills. I've tried every single non-surgical option available. There's nothing left to try.

Which means it's time to abandon all hope of ever being normal again.

"You have a good quality of life," she says. "Full mobility in your upper limbs, partial mobility in your legs. Sensation through your pelvis. Intermittent sensation in your legs and feet. You have every reason to expect a long and healthy life, and these disabilities are workable."

"Yeah, thanks." I check out for the rest of the appointment, responding with nods and grunts. I won't be scheduling another appointment here.

What's the point?

When Dr. Captain's nurse tries to push me out of the exam room, I snap at her. "If I wanted to move without making the conscious decision to move, I'd have bought a power chair."

I wheel myself through the door. If there's something my body can still do, I do it. I've grown enough muscle through my shoulders and back and enough calluses on my hands that I don't even notice long treks. My older brother Trig kept trying to convince me to buy something with an electric option at least, but they're so heavy and difficult to transport. Besides, I won't rely on a machine to do anything I can still do myself.

A magazine catches my eye as I wheel past the waiting area. It's not a new issue, but it's one I haven't seen before. Which means Trig worked overtime to make sure I didn't. As my hand reaches for it, the air around me thickens into jelly. Time collapses to nothing and my fingers shake. I press past it all and force my hand to close around the glossy pages of the Outside Magazine.

Winter Olympic Issue.

My fingers trace the face of my former best friend where it smiles at me from the cover. It's not Annelise Mayberry's fault we aren't close friends anymore.

The blame for our withered friendship falls squarely on me. Five years ago, we were both bound for the Olympics, the best two downhill skiers in America. Annelise trailed me by a hair on downhill, and by a wide margin on slalom. I was going to medal in both the downhill and the Super G at the Olympics. Everyone knew it. Even the Swedes cringed when they heard my name.

Until the accident.

Without me on the team, Annelise still snagged a bronze, and at the time she told every news network who would listen she wouldn't have won it if she hadn't trained with me. She was a loyal friend, but I didn't care. I couldn't talk to her, or even congratulate her. It only reminded me of what I lost.

I can't stop my fingers from flipping to the spread on her from the most recent Olympics. Even though it's been more than four years now, I couldn't bring myself to watch any of it. Sometimes I pretend the Olympics died. No one cares about them anymore, and they disappeared. But of course, wishes aren't horses, and other people can still ride.

Annelise's huge, shiny teeth gleam at me from the centerfold. Her cheeks are rosy, her eyes sparkly, and my lungs almost fail me as I read the blurb. "Three time Olympic Gold Medalist Annelise Mayberry has it all: speed, accuracy, and control. That's how she conquered the Combined, the Downhill and the Slalom in this year's Olympics, the first sweep by any woman from the United States of America."

My hand crumples the glossy pages involuntarily, and when I force my fingers to uncurl, it slides to the ground. I wheel out of the office without meeting anyone's eyes and beeline toward my Range Rover without thinking. I open the door and then wheel back in close to the seat. I hit the position two button so the chair leans back, and then I lock the wheelchair in place. I shift my feet out of the footrests on my chair and toward the car, and then I lean forward, and using my arms, I boost myself out of my chair and into the driver's seat. I reposition my legs. Then I pull my seat cushion off and tuck it behind the seat of the car. Next, I pop off the huge back wheels one by one and stow them, too. Finally, I lift the middle section, collapsing the body of the chair and swing it into the passenger seat.

I've done it so many times that I can switch into robot mode as I do it. Somehow the familiar routine calms me down a bit. I drive home a little too quickly, my heart still racing a bit, but I'm not stupid enough to pick up the phone when Trig calls, even if I'd like to hear his reassuring voice. I never use my cell when driving. Not to text, not to call, and certainly not to check any social media. Not since that day.

I call my brother back once I'm at the office, in front of my desk, with the file on our newest acquisition open on my computer screen. "Sorry I didn't answer. I was driving before."

"No problem," he says. "It wasn't a big deal." Except his words are clipped, his tone clearly agitated. He actually sounds about like I feel.

"It wasn't?"

"Nope."

I wait silently, because something clearly was a big deal to him. Eventually he'll spit it out, whatever made him upset. I've learned that when I press him for details, he doubles down like a tick that a vet's trying to evict. Can't go popping my own brother's head off.

"Fine, I'll just tell you." He sighs heavily. "So you know Geo's best friend Rob?"

"The marine with huge biceps and perfect hair?"

He grumbles. "They aren't that big. But yes, that's him, and you know yesterday was Memorial Day."

"Yes," I say. "I mean, I've never met the perfect Marine myself, but I did know it was Memorial Day."

"Well, Geo always spends Memorial Day with Rob, or she has ever since her fiancé died anyway. She asked if it bothered me, and of course I said it was fine. But when I told her I'd like to come along, she looked at me like I suggested she dip her French fries in strawberry yogurt."

"Wait, sweet potato fries or regular ones?"

"Brekka!"

"Sorry, I'm just kidding, okay? I'm listening, I swear."

"She didn't want me to hang out with them," he says. "I could tell, so I didn't go."

"Okay." There must be more to it than this, right? I mean, Trig adores Geo, and she is completely bonkers for him. But her fiancé died in a huge explosion with perfect Marine Rob, so I'm not surprised they'd spend Memorial Day together. It's a little awkward since he's a guy, I suppose, but it's not like Rob and Geo ever dated or anything. I'm not sure what question to ask next. I don't really get why he's so upset.

Trig clears his throat. "I never told you this before because you get a little protective sometimes."

"Me?"

Trig snorts.

"Fine, I might look out for you, but you're just as bad. We only have each other. Which is exactly why you can tell me, no matter what it is. I promise I won't judge."

"After I asked Geo out on our first date—"

"When you stalked her to Macaroni Grill, you mean?"

Trig grunts. "When I happened to run into her and Rob at dinner at a local place, yes. Anyway, after Paul and I left that night, Rob told her he loved her."

Wait, what? "Perfect Marine Rob tried to snatch her out from under you?"

"Not exactly snatch her, since they'd known each other for like twenty years. But he did finally profess his love for her, and he told her he considered their dinners to be dates. He had loved her since her fiancé died, or sometime around then, or maybe it happened after. I don't know. The point is, Geo didn't feel at all the same, but he did like her, or he does, so it made me kind of ... nervous to send her over there alone all day."

"Basically, she wanted to spend all day with a super muscular, caring, fairly rich guy who's besotted with her? And she didn't want you to come along."

"I don't know whether I'd call him super muscular, but sure. That's essentially right."

I lean back in my chair. "That sucks. Why didn't you call me on Friday or Saturday or whenever you first heard about all this?"

"I had it under control. Geo loves me and I know that. If she wanted Rob, she'd have picked him, but she didn't. She picked me."

I lean forward again. "Uh, okay. So then what's wrong? This story reminds me of one of Dad's." His stories meander like a third grader playing right field.

"That's rude."

"Then get to the point."

"I let her go, but then I didn't hear from her. She didn't come home last night, and she didn't answer my calls."

I almost drop the phone. "Is she okay? Did creepy Rob like, kidnap her?"

Trig's voice drops. It sounds nearly menacing. "I'd end him."

"Okay, then what?"

"I drove over to his house, obviously."

"Obviously." But wait, at what time? "When did you go over there? Before or after you called the police?"

"Before. I mean, I didn't even call the police, okay?"

"You suck at stories, Trig. What time did you go over there?"

"Three a.m. I went over at three."

"And?"

"I saw Geo, all curled up and adorable, in Rob's lap."

"Uh, wait, are you saying she cheated on you?"

"No," he practically shouts. "But she was asleep. On Rob. On hot Rob's lap."

I think about Geo. She adores my brother. I don't doubt that. In fact, my brain was trying to reject the possibility of her cheating on Trig, even as I asked. But I can see how this Rob guy would make Trig nuts. He and Geo have been friends for a long time, and they hang out all the time. They've been through a lot together.

"How long have they been friends again?"

"At least twenty years," Trig says. "They lived a few doors down from each other growing up. They met playing kickball or something. I guess Rob beat up some kid who told her she couldn't play."

"What a freaking Boy Scout."

"Right?" Trig huffs. "I know nothing happened, but I'm sick of them having their little club that I'm not a part of."

I wonder if he'd care if Rob was a girl, or a really unattractive guy. Probably not. Even so, it's a valid irritation. At the same time, I can't fault Geo, not really. Especially since she doesn't seem to have many friends. I can relate to that deficit, and it makes the thought of cutting off anyone you care about a painful prospect.

"What are you going to do about it?"

"Probably nothing," Trig says. "Seeing her asleep with him, all curled up, with his arm slung around her shoulder, well. It pissed me off, but I just drove back home. She called me the next morning and apologized. She told me she fell asleep on Rob's couch next to him."

"Which is true. At least she wasn't withholding information."

"Whose side are you on?"

"I'm always on yours," I say. "Every minute of every day of every month of every year."

"I know you are. It actually helped just to tell someone. I love Geo, Brekka, and it's hard. It's so hard watching her care about anyone that much. Someone who's not me, I mean. Does that make me a monster?"

No, it makes him human. "Not at all. Maybe tell Geo how you feel, but try to remember she's lost her dad, and her mom too, essentially. That means she has you, and me of course, and her friend Paisley, and Rob. That's pretty much it. So asking her to not be his friend might be... a steep ask."

"Oh, I'm not doing that, not at all. I can handle it. And I don't need her to think I'm coming unhinged." He sighs. "Did you have a chance yet to look over the comparative analysis and EBITDA on Parker Family Holdings?"

I run him through my assessment, and then hop off the phone, ostensibly to finish digging through our leads. Instead I find myself pulling up the purchase order I recently approved to Franklin Graham Honda, Rob's Honda dealership. Sixteen Honda Accords to use for company cars. My eyes stop at the address.

I should not even consider flying out to Atlanta and giving Rob a piece of my mind. Trig doesn't need my help.

Even so.

I pull up the same purchase order twice. Then I google the dealership and work out a plan to get there. I don't have a car in Atlanta, and I have a little control over my lower limbs, but not enough to drive myself without a modified car. I need at least a push pull or I'd be a total hazard on the road.

I mentally shake myself like a wet dog. I need to let this go.

Trig doesn't need me to get involved. I force myself to review the files, but every time I close my eyes, even for so long as a blink, Annelise's face flashes in front of my eyes.

I was better than her. So much better than her, but I didn't win a single solitary gold medal, much less three. I'm a loser stuck in a metal chair. I can't ski. I can't walk. I can't even crawl using my knees. The best I could manage in a pinch would be dragging my body behind me like crazy Ivar the Boneless in that History Channel show, *Vikings*. The only value I add to the world now is in analyzing companies to determine whether they're a good investment.

Which is exactly what I should be doing right now, instead of imagining I might storm Rob's office in Atlanta and let him have a piece of my mind. I evaluate the file and type my recommendation for Trig. I send it through the ether and glance at the photos on my desk. Trig swinging me around at a dance recital when I was twelve. Trig photo bombing at my high school graduation. Trig and I on the slopes, his arm slung around my shoulder.

My mother is a power vampire who hammered Trig and I like a drill sergeant. If anything, she's grown scarier with age. My father hasn't been in the same room as her for more than thirty minutes in years, and we usually have to photo shop us all into the same photo for Christmas cards.

Dad, on the other hand, always purchases lavish gifts, like a jet for my birthday, or a Porsche Cayenne for Christmas. He even gives gifts for things no one else does, like the Fourth of July, but I wouldn't bet on him remembering my middle name, much less listening to me lament about matters of the heart. I'm not sure he even realized how the accident led to the ruination of my hopes and dreams. He hasn't once asked how I'm doing since I lost use of my legs. I'm sure he cares about me, I'm just not sure he thinks about me much.

In the industrial strength vacuum left by my parents' multitudinous shortcomings, my brother Trig stepped up. He came to every dance recital, every swim meet, every spelling bee, and every important ski run of my life. He cheered me on, he buoyed me up, and he stayed up late to commiserate when things didn't go my way. Trig has been there for me from birth until present day, showering me with love and affection for more than twenty-seven years. He bought me my first pair of skis, and paid a fortune for a custom-made titanium wheelchair when I wanted to curl up and die.

The more I think of everything Trig has done, the more worked up I get that Rob would do anything to hurt my brother. I may not be able to compete in the Olympics, but I can sure as heck survive an unplanned trip out to Atlanta.

Robert Graham is going to rue the day he was so inconsiderate of Brekka Caroline Thornton's brother's feelings.

**If you enjoyed this sample chapter, check out the full length book, which clocks in at 376 pages, here!

ACKNOWLEDGMENTS

First and foremost, thank you Whitney. You are my shining light. As I did my final edit pass, you were watching all the kids so I could have a writer's retreat, here, at our home. I kicked you all out so I could have it all to myself. (Me, and nine other writers, anyway!) While you watched the kiddos, you read TWO of my books and told me how great they were. I don't deserve you, but I sure am glad I tricked you into thinking I do.

Thanks to my mom next, as usual. She's always happy to lend a hand, and she tirelessly slaves over edits, or cheerleading on drafts or whatever I need. And you let my kids and hubby come crash at your house, too.

Thanks to my Dad for telling me nice things about my writing in your own weird way. There's no one else quite like you, and I wouldn't and couldn't love any other dad on earth as much as I love you. Your devotion has set a wonderful example to me in writing love stories.

Thanks to Esther for lending a helpful and friendly ear.

Thanks to the Writing Gals for their tireless efforts to bolster the indie community.

Thanks to my friends and ARC group for help and feedback on the blurb! I hate blurbs! Why can't it just say "please please read my pretty book?"

Thanks to my cover artist, Shaela Odd, for her tireless efforts and patience with my tiny changes, my indecision and my general hemming and hawing over covers. You. Are. Amazing. Thanks for bringing Trudy and Paul to life.

And last, but not least, thank you to Tony Jennings, who worked with me on the tech issues so I wouldn't completely embarrass myself. The key logger was his solution and I love it! Thanks so much for your consulting time and efforts!!

ABOUT THE AUTHOR

Bridget loves her husband (every day) and all five of her kids (most days). She's a lawyer, but does as little legal work as possible. She has a yappy dog and backyard chickens. She makes cookies waaaaay too often and believes they should be their own food group. To keep from blowing up like a puffer fish, she kick boxes every day. So if you don't like her books, her kids, or her cookies, maybe don't tell her in person.

ALSO BY BRIDGET E. BAKER

The Almost a Billionaire clean romance series:

Finding Faith (1)

Finding Cupid (2)

Finding Spring (3)

Finding Liberty (4)

Finding Holly (5)

The Birthright Series:

Displaced (1)

unForgiven (2)

Disillusioned (3)

misUnderstood (4) -March 15, 2020

Disavowed (5)- May 15, 2020

unRepentant (6)- coming spring 2020

Destroyed (7) - coming spring 2020

The Sins of Our Ancestors Series:

Marked (1)

Suppressed (2)

Redeemed (3)

A stand alone YA romantic suspense:

Already Gone

Made in the USA
Monee, IL
18 May 2020